Praise for *The Jewel of the North*

"A dazzling display of raucous American history and the seamless blending of perfectly drawn vignettes of some of the most colorful figures of the period into a tale of high adventure and mystery. London is the perfect two-fisted literary hero. King pulls it all together in a tale full of back alleys, bawdy encounters, and violent twists in the style of a turn-of-the-19th-century adventure. May this be the first of many Jack London tales from the masterful Peter King." —Stuart M. Kaminsky

"A jewel of a book. Surely, King has led a previous life among the hard cases and colorful characters of post–Gold Rush San Francisco's Barbary Coast. London himself would heartily approve, and probably not change a word. Cleverly plotted and written with a rare combination of gusto and suspense, this one will keep you reading and guessing to the end." —John Lutz

Praise for Peter King's previous mysteries

"King's novels are filled with cliff-hanger endings and near-death adventures. . . . A fun read." —*Ventura County Star* (CA)

"An appealing detective series. . . . [King] keeps the well-spiced plot bubbling along." —*People* (Beach Book of the Week)

"[An] engaging hero." —*Alfred Hitchcock* magazine

"Fast, fun, delightful characters." —*Library Journal*

THE
JEWEL OF
THE NORTH

A JACK LONDON MYSTERY

BY
PETER KING

Ⓞ
A SIGNET BOOK

SIGNET
Published by New American Library, a division of
Penguin Putnam Inc., 375 Hudson Street,
New York, New York 10014, U.S.A.
Penguin Books Ltd, 27 Wrights Lane,
London W8 5TZ, England
Penguin Books Australia Ltd, Ringwood,
Victoria, Australia
Penguin Books Canada Ltd, 10 Alcorn Avenue,
Toronto, Ontario, Canada M4V 3B2
Penguin Books (N.Z.) Ltd, 182–190 Wairau Road,
Auckland 10, New Zealand

Penguin Books Ltd, Registered Offices:
Harmondsworth, Middlesex, England

First published by Signet, an imprint of New American Library,
a division of Penguin Putnam Inc.

First Printing, August 2001
10 9 8 7 6 5 4 3 2 1

 REGISTERED TRADEMARK—MARCA REGISTRADA

Printed in the United States of America

PUBLISHER'S NOTE
This is a work of fiction. Names, characters, places, and incidents either
are the product of the author's imagination or are used fictitiously,
and any resemblance to actual persons, living or dead, business
establishments, events, or locales is entirely coincidental.

BOOKS ARE AVAILABLE AT QUANTITY DISCOUNTS WHEN USED TO PROMOTE
PRODUCTS OR SERVICES. FOR INFORMATION PLEASE WRITE TO PREMIUM
MARKETING DIVISION, PENGUIN PUTNAM INC., 375 HUDSON STREET, NEW
YORK, NEW YORK 10014.

To my wife, Dorie,
for all her love, help, advice and encouragement.

Chapter 1

The burly seaman with the three-day growth of matted beard had his arms around two pretty Mexican girls and he squeezed them closer. One of the girls evaded his attempt to kiss her, pouted sweetly and said in a wheedling voice, "I want another drink. Gets me in the mood."

The seaman focused his bleary gaze on her glass. He could have sworn it was full but he had no need to order. The waiter girl—evidently some kind of mind reader—was already placing another full glass in front of her.

Clouds of cigarette smoke swept up from a table where half a dozen rough-looking characters were playing faro. The acrid odor of the raw tobacco almost overcame the smell of stale beer and damp sawdust, but all were submerged in the normal atmosphere of the Hell's Kitchen and Dance Saloon.

The hands of the two Mexican señoritas were active now and the seaman needed little urging to stagger to one of the tiny cubicles that surrounded the dance floor. Within minutes, he would pass out either from the drugged drink or—if the girls got impatient—one of them would crack him over the head with a shot-loaded stocking. As soon as they had emptied his pockets, the bouncer would be summoned to throw another drunk out into the alley.

It was a common scene in the Devil's Acre, part of

the Barbary Coast in San Francisco. There, every form
of vice and depravity known to man was to be found.
It was a solid mass of saloons, dance halls, bars and
theaters, most of them featuring bawdy songs, obscene
sketches, nudity and carnal acts with human and animal.

The bagnios, the brothels, the cribs, the parlor
houses and the deadfalls offered uncounted thousands
of girls and women in housing ranging from opulence
to near poverty. Opium dens offered an escape from
the world. Five thousand places of all types sold alco-
holic drinks.

Rubbing shoulders at all hours were murderers,
thieves, burglars, gamblers, pimps, prostitutes and de-
generates of every kind. It was a rare night that was
without at least one murder and a dozen robberies.

In Hell's Kitchen, a tinny piano struck up a jarring
refrain that was lost amid the clink of bottles and
glasses, the loud chatter and the whoops and shouts
from the card tables. The piano player thumped
harder as six girls came onto the stage. They wore
short, frilly lace skirts of crimson and white, white
stockings, and tight lace bodices cut extremely low,
and they carried parasols that they twirled as they
wiggled their bodies suggestively. The din subsided a
little and some heads turned to watch. One of the
heads belonged to a young man standing at the bar
who was watching the girls appreciatively.

He was six feet tall, had broad shoulders and was
strongly built. An unusual feature was the bright blue
eyes that showed an interest in everything. From time
to time, he ran a hand through thick, brown curly hair.

The bartender was spindly and had a bony face and
wispy hair. "Another drink, Jack?" he asked and was
answered with a nod.

"Still scribbling them stories, Jack?" he queried as
he set the foaming mug on the bar.

Jack London smiled. "Still at it, Bernie. Might put

you in the next one," he added. "What would you rather be—a sheriff or a U.S. marshal?"

"Anything but bartending. Say, how about a senator?"

"I'll see if there's an opening," Jack told him. He emptied the beer mug in a few swallows.

"Another one?" asked Bernie.

"No, thanks. Got to be on my rounds."

"Where next? The Best Idea?"

"The Midway Plaisance—they serve free food."

It was a lean time for Jack London. Since returning from the Yukon gold rush, he had worked at a lot of jobs, from dishwashing in cafés to selling vacuum cleaners door-to-door. At times, his faith in his writing faltered but he persevered, and at the moment he had several stories out with magazines. The highlight of his day was always the opening of his mail when that most wonderful of all events might happen—a check might flutter out of an envelope.

Jack's "rounds" took him from music halls to bars to melodeons and fed his insatiable appetite for characters and settings and situations to feed into his stories. The Midway Plaisance had just ended its first show when Jack entered.

It was large and its square design made it seem vast. Colored bunting hung behind the bar and along one wall. Another wall had large framed paintings of unclad girls and the huge stage had a backdrop of a European castle with snow-clad mountains.

This provided the Alpine atmosphere for the musical number that two dozen dancers were performing in extremely abbreviated skirts that revealed a lack of underwear and tightly cinched bodices that strained unsuccessfully to restrain jiggling breasts. A five-man orchestra was just making itself heard above the din but Jack knew that it would have to increase its volume when the number of customers doubled.

At the bar, Jack ate pickled squid, fried shrimp and

salted fish nuggets with his beer. He could eat enough for a meal this way.

Like the Cobweb Palace and the other music halls on the Barbary Coast, the Midway could offer entertainment over a wide range. At one end of the range were raucous skits and sketches that ended with girls losing their clothing as well as any dubious chastity they might still possess. At the other end were recent appearances by Enrico Caruso in *Aida* and Tyrone Power in Ibsen's *Brand*. Somewhere in between came a comedy extravaganza starring Weber and Fields.

The barkeep was a friendly fellow called Andy. He had aspirations of making a fortune in the goldfields that were never likely to be realized and he always had a flow of questions to ask Jack—the man who had been there. Andy kept Jack informed on a variety of subjects, and as business at the bar was still quiet, Andy came over to him.

"Flo's in the back."

That was the name she was called by those who knew her well. The public knew her as "Little Egypt."

She had been a sensation at the World's Fair and her name rang around the world. The "hoochy coochy" dance she had originated at the fair was in feverish demand everywhere, but she was a sensible, level-headed girl and knew how fleeting such fame could be. Despite dozens of tempting offers, she gave up dancing and became a teacher. She was here at the Midway Plaisance to teach the girls how to perform the hoochy coochy and to rehearse them in numbers that included it. Jack had met her and formed an immediate bond. Flo was passionate but controlled—a combination that Jack found rare and exciting. At the same time, it suited his present state of enjoying female companionship without any ties. A few words with Andy sent a waiter girl backstage with a message. Minutes later, she was back with a nod and a brief "Dressing room twelve."

Flo was barely medium height but she had the most exquisite figure Jack had ever seen. She used it to perfection and her grace and lithe sensuousness were all the more appealing as they were so natural. She hardly needed an act. All she had to do was move across the stage with occasional twists and turns to arouse an audience far more than any rehearsed act.

Jack kissed her passionately. Her body was warm and soft. It quivered with scarcely contained desire. "I thought you must have headed back for the icy wastes," she told him with a tempting smile. She had a delicate heart-shaped face, serene and composed. It made an irresistible contrast with the fiery abandon of her voluptuous dance.

"I thought I might catch you in a performance," Jack said.

"I'm too busy right now," Flo said. "I have these classes every day. Teaching the girls how to do the hoochy coochy so we can fit it into this next show, 'Slaves of the Nile.'"

"So you're a schoolma'am," Jack said.

She struck a provocative pose, pulling up her skirt and flicking open the top button of her blouse. She pouted her lips and her eyes glinted. Jack laughed. "I may have to take that back. I never had a teacher that looked like that."

They sat on a basket-woven love seat in the small dressing room, crowded with clothes on racks, shoes in boxes, feathered garments, silk scarves in dazzling colors, beaded belts.

"Do you really enjoy teaching?" Jack asked.

"It's a challenge," Flo admitted.

"Can these girls really learn to do the hoochy coochy? You've told me enough about it to make it sound really difficult—and I know you're a perfectionist. You won't settle for anything but excellence."

"These girls are all willing but that's not always enough."

"Didn't you tell me that it requires the use of muscles that are not normally developed in routine dancing?"

"That's the problem. Being enthusiastic is absolutely necessary, but not every girl is prepared to train new muscles to do things they've never done before. It can be very exhausting—and the girls have to have this training as well as put on five shows a night."

Jack put his arm around Flo. "Speaking of training new muscles . . . tell me something. Why do you have a love seat in your dressing room?"

Flo turned her lustrous dark eyes on him. "Oh, I think that's just a name," she murmured.

"Must be a reason for it," Jack persisted.

"Well, there's one way to—"

Flo paused in what she was saying as a scream split the air. Flo and Jack stared at each other. Another scream came, followed by loud voices crying out in anguish and terror. The sounds seemed to come from nearby. "The girls' dressing room," Flo said with a catch in her voice.

Both rose quickly. Flo was the first out of the door. Two girls, barely dressed, were already in the corridor. Their faces were pale under makeup. One whimpered, unable to speak. The other pointed to a room a few doors away, her hand shaking.

Jack and Flo hurried there. The door was partly open. Two girls were inside already and another was entering, apparently attracted by the noise.

"Who screamed?" Flo wanted to know.

"Mimi did," quavered a buxom, dark-haired girl. She indicated the other girl with her brown curls surrounding a pretty young face whose main feature now was the two brown eyes, bulging with fright.

"What's wrong?" Flo asked her. "Why did you scream?"

Mimi was shivering, unable to control herself. Flo put an arm around her and pulled her close.

"What is it, Mimi? What happened?"

The girl swallowed, made a desperate attempt to pull herself together. Instead, tears came fast, then a torrent. Jack and Flo exchanged puzzled glances. Flo gave her a moment, then picked up a scarf and dabbed her eyes.

Mimi grabbed the wisp of cloth, wiped her face, whimpered, then pointed to a closet door. "In there."

Jack strode to it and pulled the door open. A girl's body came sprawling out onto the floor. Flo gasped and the other two girls cried out.

"It's Jenny Morris!" Jack said, his voice choking.

The two girls were clinging to each other. Voices were loud outside and other girls were trying to push their way in out of curiosity.

"Keep that door closed!" Jack rapped.

He gently eased the body over so that it was supported by the closet door. Horrified gasps burst out again, even Flo unable to contain herself. Jack, no stranger to death, gave an involuntary cry. The face and the upper nude torso were slashed with cuts and blood oozed from all of them.

Jack felt for her pulse but there was none.

"Jenny's dead," he said in a low, bitter tone.

He stood, looking down at her. She was a pitiful sight, smeared and dripping blood coming from a dozen cuts. Her once-pretty face was contorted with pain, her lips drawn back from her white teeth.

"Who would do something like this?" murmured Flo.

One of the girls spoke up for the first time. It was the one who had been with Mimi. "Only last week, it was Lola Randolph," she whispered.

Flo looked at Jack. "That's right. Lola Randolph at the Cobweb Palace. She was murdered last week."

Death was a frequent visitor to the Barbary Coast and life was cheap. But now, confronted with it and seeing the bloodied cuts and the face of terror, the impact was shattering.

"Send someone for the police," Jack said forcefully. "I'll stay here until they come."

Chapter 2

Jack was surprised to see Police Captain Patrick O'Donnell in charge of the investigation. Dance hall girls were among the many unfortunates to meet their end on the violent Barbary Coast, and a sergeant was usually delegated to those cases. Was there something different about this one? Jack wondered.

The night performances went on as scheduled. The girls were tearful and too stunned to protest. Friedrich Danner, known as Fritz, had arrived, summoned from another bar. Fritz was German but he presented himself as either Austrian or Swiss whenever the occasion required. He called himself the owner, but popular gossip said that the real owners were two prominent San Francisco politicians who preferred to conceal the fact of their ownership from the voters. Whatever he was, Fritz acted as the manager and his first decision was to keep the shows going. He professed to want to get everybody's mind off the murder, but Jack did not doubt that his true motive was merely mercenary.

The police turned one dressing room into an interrogation room. Mimi, the girl who had found Jenny Morris's body, was the first to be questioned, then the other girls who had been present. Jack was next. He had encountered Captain O'Donnell on a couple of occasions previously, and the burly captain gave Jack a nod as he sat before him at a makeshift table.

"You used to be with the Fish Patrol," O'Donnell said. "I remember you. What are you doing here?"

"Came for a drink and to see Flo."

"Girlfriend?"

Jack nodded.

"She in the show?"

"Yes," said Jack, rather than explain.

Muted sounds came from the auditorium but they were quieter now. Word had spread and gossip was rife but only a few customers had left, presumably those with guilty consciences who had no intention of being spotted by the police.

O'Donnell's questions were quickly answered. Yes, Jack had known Jenny Morris; he knew a great many of the girls on the Barbary Coast. He had no idea of who might have treated her this way. She was a girl who was well liked. No, he had not seen her recently.

The police captain was about to wrap up the interrogation when Jack asked a question of his own. "Lola Randolph, she was murdered last week. Is there any connection?"

"What do you know about that?"

"Only what I read in the *Examiner*," said Jack.

"Had you seen her recently?"

"No," Jack said. "I didn't really know her. Just saw her in the show at the Cobweb Palace."

O'Donnell nodded. He seemed to be undecided, unsure whether to continue the conversation.

"That's all I know," Jack said, helping him to make up his mind. "If I think of anything else, I'll let you know. Always ready to help the law."

The captain probably heard that a dozen times a day and at least eleven of them would be insincere. But Jack believed that O'Donnell knew he meant it.

"Be around tomorrow. Might be some more you can tell us." The captain's look was unfathomable but Jack nodded and left.

* * *

Jack was hard at work the next morning. His pencil moved rapidly while his mind was scrabbling in the icy gravel of the Yukon, desperately seeking the gold that would save his family from starvation. It was an environment he still remembered vividly and he had no difficulty in conjuring it up and putting the words on paper.

He frowned angrily as he heard an authoritative rat-a-tat on the door of his room. He considered ignoring it—he expected no one and hated to be interrupted—but the knock came again and he went to the door.

A slim, black-haired man in a neat suit stood there. He had lean, intelligent features and Jack looked at him uncertainly, finding his appearance familiar.

"Hello, Jack. Back from the Yukon, I see," greeted the newcomer.

Jack was still striving to put a name to the face. The other said easily, "Don't you remember me? Ted Townrow, your old college mate at the University of California?"

They had not exactly been college mates. Townrow had been in his graduation year when Jack was just a sophomore at Berkeley, where they had run into each other a few times in the literature club.

"Come in," said Jack. The other showed no interest in the small, shabby room and Jack gave him a chair.

"It's been a few years," Jack said.

"It has at that," Townrow agreed. "How's the writing going?"

"Sold one to the *Morning Call*," Jack said, not adding that the sale was three years ago.

Townrow nodded congratulations. "Jack London is getting to be a well-known name on the Barbary Coast."

"I wish it was getting to be well known with editors," Jack said ruefully.

"That sale to the *Call* was a while ago, wasn't it? Yes, it's a hard way to make a living," Townrow said.

"Still, it's because your name is getting to be well known on the Coast that the mayor wants to talk to you."

Jack's head jerked toward him. "Me? The mayor wants to talk to me?"

"Yes," he told him. "Right now."

"You work for the mayor?" It was not surprising. He knew that Townrow had always been interested in politics and had always been ambitious.

Ted Townrow consulted his watch, snapped it shut, motioned to the door. "Yes, I do. He's outside."

His mind in a whirl, Jack followed Townrow outside. They stood on the sidewalk and Jack looked up and down the street, puzzled. A hansom cab came around the corner and pulled to a stop before them. The door opened, and Townrow jumped in and beckoned Jack.

His Honor Hiram T. Nelson, Mayor of San Francisco, eyed Jack as he climbed into the cab with black-shuttered windows. Townrow slammed the door and gave the mayor a quick nod. The driver immediately whipped the horse into a steady trot, for the mayor had no intention of being seen in Oakland. Eugene Schmitz had already proclaimed his determination to become the next mayor, and he was a man who would miss no opportunity of ascribing sinful motives to any doubtful actions.

"Your Honor, this is Jack London."

A practiced smile broke out on His Honor's smooth face, especially effective as it looked spontaneous. He had a firm jaw, a strong brow and even white teeth.

"I'm pleased to meet you, young man. I've heard a lot about you."

Jack nodded, not knowing what to say.

"You were born in Oakland, I understand. You've lived all your life in the Bay Area—that's good. I need someone who loves this city as much as I do, someone who knows the people and wants to help them."

Jack wondered about that last touch. Did the mayor know he was a socialist?

"San Francisco has a problem," the mayor went on, "and it is going to take a man with your abilities to help us—the city government—to solve it."

He smiled that vote-winning smile once more. Then he let it fade, to be replaced by a stern look that presaged his next words. "It's about the murder of these two saloon girls."

Jack gave a slight nod to let the mayor know that he knew about the violent deaths of the two girls. Two! That meant that he already knew about the murder of Jenny Morris last night. Were the two connected in some way after all? It had been the question that Police Captain O'Donnell had declined to answer.

In any case, why should the mayor be concerned about these incidents? Two or three dozen men and women were killed every month in the Devil's Acre. Jack had a caring streak in him that was part of the reason he had inclined toward socialism. Many of those deaths were villains and criminals. He had little sympathy for them but he hated to see people die who did not deserve it—especially these girls, no matter how they earned a living.

He glanced at Ted Townrow, sitting next to the mayor. Both were facing him. He had heard something about Ted's progress in city hall but he had not realized that his erstwhile "college mate" had climbed so close to the most important man in San Francisco. The hack lurched as a wheel bounced over some obstacle in the rough street. As it righted itself, the mayor continued.

"You're probably wondering why I am so concerned with this matter. Well, human life is precious to me, of course. I grieve every time I open a newspaper and read of an unnecessary killing. But we have a police department that does its best. . . ."

Not a very good best, thought Jack, but he kept the thought from showing.

"However, what we have here is a situation that goes beyond what we can expect from Chief of Police William Quinn and his fine body of men. It calls for another approach—an unofficial approach."

The cab lurched again and Mayor Nelson waited for it to regain equilibrium with the same perfect timing he displayed waiting for a hostile crowd to settle down before resuming a political speech.

"The murders of these two unfortunate girls are threatening the future of our fair city. In the coming months, the producers and the impresarios who work so hard to provide us with diversion and entertainment are bringing some famous names here. Lillie Langtry, Sarah Bernhardt, Luisa Tetrazzini—these are just some of them."

The mayor leaned forward to look Jack in the eye. "Already one of them is asking what we are doing to ensure their safety. We understand that the others are similarly anxious. Cancellation of engagements is possible. Something must be done and more than one group has been in my office demanding action."

So it's not really the deaths of these two poor girls you're worried about, thought Jack. It's the pressure of influential groups who helped put you in office and are scared at the possibility of seeing big profits vanish due to half-empty theaters.

He kept that to himself though and said, "Mr. Mayor, people—including saloon girls—get killed in San Francisco far more often than any of us would like. Judging from the efforts of the police to date, nothing they can do is succeeding in changing that. Nor does it seem that anything I—or any other citizen—can do is likely to change that."

Mayor Nelson leaned back in his comfortably padded seat. He looked at the shutter in the hack as if he could see through it. He turned to the man beside him.

"Ted, would you tell—"

Ted Townrow nodded, obviously prepared for this moment. "Jack, this is not just two random killings. When the first girl, Lola Randolph, was killed, the police assumed it was another death from jealousy or drunken anger—the usual reasons for saloon girls being killed. This was despite the fact that no such motives could be found. The death of the second girl changed that. Jenny Morris was killed in exactly the same way and again no motive could be found."

Jack London looked from one man to the other. He was intrigued despite himself. "Motives aren't always obvious," he said. "If the police keep looking, they'll find the reasons." He paused, wondering if he should go on. Well, why not? he concluded; they came to me, not the other way around.

"They won't keep on looking though, will they? The police aren't going to spend much time investigating the deaths of two saloon girls."

Townrow flicked a glance at the mayor, who waved for him to go on. "Jack, there's more to it than that. Both girls were killed in exactly the same way—by a thin-bladed knife in the side of the throat. It's an unusual way of killing, very expertly done and in such a way that no external blood is visible. All the blood-letting is internal. When the bodies were found, no trace of the murder method was evident, and it was only when the second body arrived in the morgue that the medical examiner made a detailed search and found this tiny incision in the neck of each girl."

"But I was there when Jenny Morris was found," said Jack. "She was slashed all over with cuts—they were still bleeding."

Ted Townrow leaned toward him. "Jack, all of those cuts were superficial. None was more than half an inch deep. None of them caused death."

Jack stared at Townrow, wide-eyed.

"Both girls were treated that way. Both were killed

with that thin-bladed knife," Townrow went on. "As a matter of fact, all of those slashes were inflicted after the girl had been killed."

"I didn't know that," Jack admitted.

"Hardly anyone does. We kept it out of the newspapers," said the mayor authoritatively.

"And of course," said Townrow, "it means that both killings were by the same person."

"When I first read about it in the *Examiner*," Jack said, "I thought it was a threat by one of the places— it's happened before, you know: frighten a rival by killing one of their girls. Then when Jenny, the second girl, was murdered, it looked like a vendetta between two rival places—that happens all the time too."

"Murders of that kind are not committed in such an expert way," Townrow said. "Besides, which places? The Thunderbolt, Calico Jim's or the Eureka—that kind, they often have wars among themselves. But, Jack, you must know that these two girls worked in the music hall–type of place, not the bordellos."

Jack nodded reluctantly.

"No, Jack," said Townrow, "there is more to this— much more—and we want you to help us find out what it is."

Townrow's points were valid. Even so . . . "But why me?" Jack asked, looking at the mayor.

"Prince of the Oyster Pirates. Isn't that what they used to call you?"

Jack's boyish grin made him look younger than his twenty-odd years.

"You fellows made pretty good money, didn't you?" The mayor smiled.

"Sure did. Two hundred dollars a night or more."

"Yet you gave it up to take a fifteen-dollar-a-week job with the California Fish and Harbor Patrol, working as a law-enforcement officer."

Jack admitted to himself that here was one public

official who knew how to dig into a person's background and make use of it. Townrow's work, no doubt. He darted a look at his "college mate" but his face gave nothing away.

"I'm wondering why you did that," the mayor mused.

"I wonder why myself sometimes," Jack said grudgingly.

"It's because you have a strong sense of civic duty. You felt easier in your mind upholding the law than breaking it. One thing I have to admit about socialism," said the mayor, who never admitted anything about socialism, "is its adherents care about their fellow humans and are ready to do what they can to help them."

You'll never say that outside this cab, Jack thought, but said nothing.

Townrow moved in with the clincher.

"That's why we're asking for your help now, Jack." He sounded serious and sincere—even for a politician. "You asked, Why you? It's because no other man in this city is better qualified to help us. You are known and liked at all levels. You know saloon keepers, bartenders, dance hall girls, pimps, entertainers, waiters and bouncers as well as police, hoodlums, informers, fences, not to mention newspapermen, seamen and cable car drivers. Your writing is becoming recognized and any investigating you might do could easily pass as research for your stories. If anyone can uncover any information that might lead to the apprehension of this vicious murderer, that man is you, Jack."

Townrow was well-prepared, Jack thought as he looked from one solemn face to the other. The mayor must find him a valuable assistant.

"We have to consider practical matters too," said His Honor. "You'll receive five dollars a day—that's the same as we pay police." He waved a hand at Townrow. "Ted, give Jack a week's pay in advance."

Townrow took out a billfold, extracted notes and sat, the notes in his hand.

Jack nodded. "All right. I'll keep my eyes and ears open. I knew Jenny Morris and I know several of the girls in the same places she and Lola Randolph worked. I may be able to learn something. But I'll be glad to help anyway," he continued, getting a little carried away now that the die was cast. "I hate the idea of these girls being killed—they have a tough life at best."

"Good man!" the mayor said and slapped Jack on the knee. Townrow smiled, partly with relief, Jack thought. He must need to prove his worth at regular intervals.

The mayor rapped his knuckles on the roof and the cab picked up speed. There were a few more minutes of discussion; then they were stopping a discreet distance from Jack's room. Jack jumped out and the cab drove off hastily.

As he went back to his room, his thoughts were on his new job. The five dollars a day that the mayor was paying him would be very welcome.

The money was not his only motivation however. He smiled as he wondered if the mayor had the slightest idea that he would have taken the job for a dollar a day—for that was how he felt. He had a genuine sympathy and affection for the thousands of girls on the Barbary Coast and a burning animosity toward whoever was committing these vicious murders. Not that five dollars a day meant anything to the mayoral budget, but Jack also realized that Ted Townrow did not know Jack as well as he thought he did.

Still, Townrow had provided the mayor with an accurate summary of Jack's early days. Formerly an oyster pirate (the word was really *thief* but *pirate* sounded better), he had been persuaded by a sympathetic but shrewd cop, Bill Grady, to join the Fish and Harbor Patrol. At a single stroke, the astute Grady

removed one pirate from the Bay and increased the
number of law-enforcement officers by one.

Jack's life had always been entangled with the sea.
He had bought his own boat at sixteen, he had served
as an able-bodied seaman on several vessels, and he
had been seal-hunting. Interspersed were periods on-
shore as a coal heaver and as a hobo crossing the
continent from coast to coast. He had worked in a
jute mill amid diseased and crippled children for ten
hours a day at ten cents an hour.

Writing had always been his passion though, and he
saw all his hardships as contributing to that. Hard
study at the University of California had honed his
work, for he knew it had been crude initially. His first
success had been a sale to the *Morning Call* when he
was seventeen. Since coming back from Alaska,
though, he had not been able to sell a single piece—
not even to *Alta* magazine, which he considered to be
at the bottom of his list as they paid only a miserable
ten to fifteen dollars.

His thoughts moved to Ted Townrow. They had not
been that close at the university, but he was surprised
that the other had made so much progress in the field
of local politics. The mayor certainly seemed to rely
on him, and Jack was impressed that he had wanted
to satisfy himself that he was not wasting taxpayers'
money, much as he valued Townrow's opinion.

A more serious thought crept in—that both men
wanted to be sure that Jack was capable of facing
death in the hundred fiendish ways that would
threaten him when he began to ask questions along
the blood-spattered streets and alleys of the Barbary
Coast.

Chapter 3

At eleven o'clock the next morning, Jack London was leaning on another bar in the Devil's Acre. This one was shiny and well polished compared to the dirty, grainy mahogany of the bar in Hell's Kitchen. Even the brass rail glistened, reflecting the meager light of a new but gray day.

Those features were in contrast though to the rest of the Cobweb Palace and Jack surveyed it with an awe that was unabated after many visits. The Palace had opened in 1856 and the first owner, Abe Warner, had operated it for forty years. Abe loved spiders and refused to allow any of his staff to kill one. Once the insects realized that they were immune, they proliferated and made the place their own. No one remembered what the originally intended name had been, for everyone knew it by its new and appropriate name of the Cobweb Palace.

Cobwebs hung everywhere, over all the walls and from every inch of the ceiling. They adorned the light fixtures and even festooned the bottles behind the bar. Sea captains who had been regulars had given Abe Warner parrots, monkeys, parakeets and macaws, and cages full of these stood in rows against the walls, cobwebs draped over them. One parrot, believed to be at least eighty years old, had the freedom of the place and fluttered out of his ever-open cage door at intervals, frightening newcomers. He could swear fluently in four languages and did so whenever he was inebriated, which was frequently.

Whales' teeth, sealskins and walrus tusks added to the museum-like atmosphere, which was augmented by Abe Warner's personal collection of over a thousand drawings of nude women. An unintentional modesty was bestowed on these by the masses of cobwebs, which forced most viewers to peer closely.

Next to Jack stood the present owner of the Cobweb Palace. Hap Harrison was a veteran of the War Between the States and never let anyone forget it, though he was careful to conceal the fact that he had fought on both sides.

He was a loose-limbed, awkward-moving man, tall and with very prominent facial features. The smile that was nearly always on his face had prompted the nickname of Happy, now contracted to Hap, but it was a reckless or badly informed customer who misread that smile. Jack could not see the ten-inch buffalo horn–handled bowie knife that Hap kept under his left armpit but he knew it was always there.

"Don't usually get up this early, Jack," said Hap with a belch and a hiccup. He was wearing a clean white shirt with pearl buttons, and the baggy black trousers that were known as auctioneer's pants were held up with gaudy red suspenders. "But they told me you were here and you're a friend—a good friend. You know that, don't you, Jack?"

Jack knew that Hap stayed in his saloon, personally supervising the activities until the later hours, and he seldom rose before noon. Their friendship was based on an article of Jack's that had appeared in *Overland* magazine. It had as one of its characters an irascible but kindhearted bar owner. A rarity among the Cobweb Palace's patrons—a reader of magazines—had brought it to Hap's attention, suggesting that the character was based on him. Jack was a regular customer at the Palace in those days, when his girlfriend of the moment was one of the Palace's pretty waiter girls.

When Hap had confronted Jack with his word image on paper, Jack had hedged long enough to be sure that Hap was flattered, uneasily aware that if he were not, he might receive a reproving slash across the wrist with that ten-inch bowie knife. Fortunately, Hap had loved seeing himself on paper and Jack admitted using him as his model without mentioning that the character owed much more to Tommy Tree at the Eureka saloon.

Still, Jack reasoned, if Hap wanted to believe it was really him, that was fine with Jack. Being known as a friend of Hap's could be invaluable and was certainly safer than risking him as an enemy. Consequently, Hap considered Jack a firm friend.

A friend? Jack was not sure of the reaction he would get when he revealed the purpose of his morning visit.

The cavernous music hall was empty but for the two of them at the bar and two other figures. One was a Negro who was swabbing the floor with a long-handled mop and a bucket of water. Jack knew that he was a deserter from the Seventeenth Cavalry, one of the black regiments being shipped out to Manila to fight the seemingly endless war against the insurgents in the Philippines. The other was Tippy, the piano player, who was sleeping with his head cradled in his arms, draped across the piano keys. He snored loudly and unmusically.

"Hey!" bellowed Hap. "Less goddamn noise!" Hap was accustomed to making use of his voice to cut through the hubbub of two or three hundred boisterous customers, and as it was a voice that had been likened to the roar of a bull moose in pain, it shivered the rafters of the empty Cobweb Palace.

Tippy raised his head, blinked owlishly and tried to raise his arms. He found them too heavy and collapsed again onto the keyboard with a discordant crash of notes. This blasted him awake. He stared around in bewilderment, then, recognizing his environment, went into an automatic rendition of "Danny Boy."

"Go home and sleep, goddamn it!" shouted Hap.

Tippy paused between bars. "Ain't got a home."

"Then go wherever you usually sleep!"

Tippy's playing was getting slower by the note.

"Usually sleep here."

Further admonition from Hap was not necessary. The playing slowed to a stop and Tippy collapsed into a disorderly sprawl across several teeth-jangling octaves. His snoring resumed, almost as unmusical as his piano playing.

Hap laughed, shaking his head. Jack grinned, glad of the chance to prepare his words. A bartender, unshaven and with unkempt hair, appeared with a crate of bottles. He began stacking them and Hap turned to Jack.

"So what's on your mind this early, son?"

Jack took a breath. "It's about these girls."

Hap squinted at him. He was not cross-eyed but he had a peculiarly unfocused gaze, as if the two eyes operated independently of each other. Some thought that he must have lost his vision in one eye, but opinions differed as to which eye and no one had yet been bold enough to ask. His face tightened at Jack's words and Jack took a deep breath and found himself holding it.

"You mean Lola and that other girl?" Hap banged a fist on the bar. Jack thought it was emphasis of his question but the bartender identified it more correctly. He stopped stacking bottles, took one from the shelf and poured a glass full for Hap.

"Yes," said Jack. "The two girls who were murdered."

"You know something about it?" Hap's voice was a throaty growl.

"No, but I want to find out. I want to find the sons of bitches who killed them." He made his voice as harsh as he could.

Hap sipped his whisky. Jack knew that he always had a partly full glass in front of him but he did not drink that much in the course of a day. While he often appeared drunk, he was always in possession of his faculties. It was a factor that had an unproved connection with a small but indeterminate number of unsolved deaths by bowie knife.

"What business is it of yours?" Eyes that had been sleep-filled a short time ago were now clear and penetrating. The voice was sharp.

"I know a lot of these girls on the Coast," said Jack. He found Harrison's corkscrew gaze unwavering and unnerving but he plunged on, speaking faster and louder, for though he was mindful of his mission for the mayor, he was sincere in his personal feelings. "One way or another," he added, "I'm going to find these sons of bitches who are going about killing these poor girls here—here, where I live. The police aren't doing anything to find them and I'm not sure what I can do but I'm sure going to try."

Hap Harrison did not take his gaze from Jack's face, but he thumped his fist on the bar and motioned to Jack. The bartender repeated his actions and set a full glass in front of Jack, who took a grateful gulp.

"She was a good girl was Lola." Harrison was staring into the mirror behind the bar, where bright labels adorned bottles of scotch that had never known Scotland and Jamaican rum that had been made last week in a bootleg still only a few miles away. The vast room was silent but for the clank of bottles, the sloshing of the Negro's mop and Tippy's snoring. In hours, it would be transformed into a brawling, shouting, rowdy maelstrom of drinking, gambling and whoring, calmed only when the shows came on stage.

"I was at Bull Run, y'know."

Jack nodded. He knew. Every man who drank at the Cobweb Palace knew.

"It was bloody killing—like a slaughterhouse. Guts and gore everywhere," snarled Harrison with sudden vehemence. "It was massacre gone berserk. Boys like me—never been away from home, many of them. Where did they find themselves? Staring at a bayonet sticking out of their own chest, watching their life's blood pour out of them." He shook his head furiously. "But that was war, Jack. It was war, we had to do it!"

Jack wondered whether the "we" meant the North or the South but he knew better than to ask, just as he did not intend to refer to the rumors that said Harrison had been in a jail cell in Chancellorsville, accused of rape, at the time of the Battle of Bull Run.

"Killing these girls is wicked—cruel!" He banged a fist on the bar again and the startled bartender looked in puzzlement at the glass, still nearly full. "You know, Jack, when Lola was killed, I thought it was one of the other places."

Jack knew that he meant one of the other saloons. Once in a while, a small war erupted and killing resulted—the ultimate stage in violence after a place was burned down or blown up with a few sticks of dynamite.

"But there's no ill will right now," Hap went on, "not that kind anyway. We're all getting along. So what's the reason for these murders? It must be some kind of maniac!"

Jack could not tell Harrison what Townrow had confided, that the two murders had been committed in exactly the same way, with a very thin bladed knife wielded by an expert. It could just possibly be a maniac as Harrison suggested, but there had been a knowledgeable air about the conviction of both Ted Townrow and Mayor Nelson that there was some sinister purpose behind the killings. Besides, Jack reasoned, they would not have called him in to help catch

a maniac. Jack had an uneasy feeling that the two of
them knew more than they had told him. They admitted that they had kept some details of the murders
out of the newspapers. They would have no qualms
about withholding information from him.

His pulse had settled down to normal now and he
emptied his glass. It was good Kentucky bourbon, not
the stuff they kept for drunken miners, cowboys and
sailors.

"Well, I wanted to tell you how serious I am about
this, Hap," Jack said. "I'm glad you see it the same
way I do. I'm going to find out who's killing these
girls and why. So if any of your people hear anything,
I hope you'll let me know."

"And good luck to you, lad. What else can I tell
you now?"

He knew little about the girl, Lola, it seemed. She
had been here at the Cobweb Palace for five or six
weeks and was well liked by the other girls. Men
friends? Well, the girls would know more about that,
Hap said, and recommended asking Meg Ballantine,
who had been her closest friend. "Meg will be in any
minute," added Hap. "They're going to rehearse a
new show."

The music halls had to change their shows frequently. The competition for customers was fierce and
the rewards were high. "I have another show
planned," Hap said, and the look of smug satisfaction
on his face surprised Jack. "The man who wants to
put it on should be here right now. You ought to meet
him—he's a writer like you."

"A writer? What's his name?"

Hap smirked, pleased at being able to keep Jack
perplexed. "Oh, you know his name. In fact, it's good
you're here—he's worried about what Lola's murder
might do to attendances. He's put on shows in London
and Paris and he loves big crowds."

Noises came from outside and one of the big doors

swung open to admit a rotund figure that made Jack gasp. He did indeed know his name—he recognized him from innumerable sketches and cartoons in the newspapers and journals.

It was Oscar Wilde.

Three sensational trials and a spell in prison where conditions were harsh had left their mark on the man who had been described as "the wittiest man in the world." Jack shared that opinion while, at the same time, despising his lifestyle, which also contributed to his appearance.

Wilde's teeth were blackened from the mercury he took in an attempt to moderate the ravages of syphilis, his face was purple-veined and his jowls sagged. The eyes remained bright though, and despite the stories that his brain had been affected by his time in Reading Jail, the less prejudiced among his contemporaries in the theater maintained that his satirical wit glittered as brightly as ever.

He greeted Jack politely, declining to comment on Hap's description of Jack as "one of our outstanding men of letters." Jack had no doubt that Wilde had never heard of Jack London, nor was he likely to have read any tales of fishing, sailing or prospecting for gold whether by Jack or any other writer. Everything about the great man implied a life of sophisticated hedonism that seldom strayed outside the drawing room, the theater or the best restaurants in London and Paris.

He apparently had no objection to Jack being included in the discussion with Hap over his projected show. He nodded courteously to him as he turned to address Hap.

"I'm hoping to get Sarah Bernhardt to play the role of Salome," Wilde said. "After all, we were lovers once and she still adores me. I'm not alone in that statement as I am sure you are aware." He addressed Jack as he came to the last words and Jack nodded as if he was aware. "Divine Sarah says she has had over a thousand lovers, including all the crowned heads of Europe and the Pope."

"She'd be a great draw," Hap said eagerly, and Jack recalled hearing it whispered that Hap had grandiose ideas of making the Cobweb Palace a cultural center for great plays and artists. There was some sniggering at his pretensions, and the whispers were probably true that only artists entering the twilight of their careers would condescend to come here—artists like Wilde.

Jack studied him as he talked. The tight mouth was that of a sullen child but the wit still shone. The long brown frockcoat and the old-fashioned waistcoat were probably what he wore in London, and he swung a long cane with a gold knob in a debonair flourish.

"It's a wonderful play," Wilde said, without a hint of bragging about his own work. "Salome is a true harlot, obedient to her passions, savage, hateful, delighting in flaunting her cruel female temperament."

"She'll appeal to our audiences!" Hap said, an ardent fan already. His swiveling gaze did not appear to bother Wilde in the slightest. The offbeat circles that the great man frequented must contain many with much more bizarre habits.

"No other actress can play the role as she can—her delicate yet haughty profile, those eyes that glitter, cold as precious stones—and those costumes! Blazoned with peacock feathers and glowing emeralds!"

She'll need a formidable bodyguard if she wears those here, thought Jack. Robbery was a common crime on the Barbary Coast, and a display of emeralds might be too much of a temptation for some of San Francisco's more covetous citizens.

"I can't wait to see her." Hap was almost slavering and Jack could see dollar signs flashing in his head. Sarah Bernhardt certainly sounded like a crowd-puller, and even after doubling the seat prices she would appeal mightily to an audience. It would not even matter if some of Wilde's best bon mots were over their heads.

"We can improve on the show we put on in Paris," said Wilde.

Jack admired the touch of Irish blarney that Wilde was using to convince Hap of this unparalleled opportunity.

"We must depict Sarah on a cushion with an ebony lyre. She will be heavily painted, curled magnificently and with two—no, four collars of pearls at her milky-white throat."

Wilde turned to Jack in an abrupt change of thought. "So, young man, you're a writer?"

"He's written some good stories," said Hap. "Put me in one of them."

"Really? Tell me, what do you write?"

He listened attentively as Jack briefly described them. Wilde bravely repressed a shudder at the raw violence, the raging storms at sea and the biting pain of an Alaskan winter. "Good," he murmured, "very good. Very—er, primitive."

"You prefer writing plays, I believe," Jack said.

"Yes." Wilde drooped his head sadly. "But I'm not writing anymore. The only ideas that come to me now are in French and can be expressed in two lines. Why, I can't get more than a guinea for two lines. Fortunately"—he raised his head, brightening—"I love putting plays on the stage, not only my own but those of others. Every performance is a fresh one, another challenge, more opportunities for improvement. Now here"—he waved his cane at the stage, its outlines dim on the far side of the vast room—"it will all be yellow, except for, let me see, ah, yes, a deep violet sky—"

He broke off and Jack wondered if the ravages of prison, drugs, drink and debauchery were affecting his brain. But his eyes still moved purposefully, and Jack

wondered what dazzling scenes were being designed
in that brain, damaged maybe but still uniquely active.

"We have to talk about a sad business though, don't
we, Mr. Harrison?" Wilde said suddenly. "I'm referring to the murders of these two young women. Sarah
has heard about them too, and though not a nervous
person by any means, she is understandably worried."

"She need not be, Mr. Wilde," said Hap. "Several
safety measures are being brought in—as a matter of
fact, Jack and I were just talking about that when you
came in."

Wilde looked critically at Jack, as if he doubted that
his youthful appearance concealed any crime-fighting
ability.

"Jack's had a lot of experience in law enforcement."
Hap had put on the fawning tone that he did so well,
but he was shrewd enough to read Wilde's mind on
this point, adding, "He's older than he looks, three
times as tough and knows the city better than anybody. He's going to catch these murderers long before
your first rehearsal. More than that, I can't say. It's
an undercover operation."

Little does he know how right he is, thought Jack.
Wilde was studying him reflectively and Jack did not
think that outlining his role in the California Fish and
Harbor Patrol would go very far in allaying Wilde's
concern. Instead he put on his best countenance of
confidence and determination.

"So you can guarantee Miss Bernhardt that she
doesn't have a thing to worry about," Hap concluded.

Wilde looked reasonably satisfied. He swung his
cane. "Very well. Now, Mr. Harrison, we haven't
talked about money yet. What say you and I discuss
financial matters, eh?"

"By all means." Hap's double-barreled vision
roamed around Wilde's portly figure, doubtless blending images of the Divine Sarah in peacocks' feathers

and emeralds with piles of crackling twenty-dollar bills.

Jack recognized his cue to go. "I have to go and talk to Meg," he said to Hap. "She'll be here by now, won't she?"

"She'll be in back," said Hap.

Jack shook hands with Wilde. "Best of luck with your writing, my boy," said the playwright, "but don't let it interfere with your protecting my Sarah."

Chapter 4

Backstage, the day was beginning to take on life. Girls in various stages of undress were moving around, shouting, arguing, calling each other unladylike names. Each seemed engrossed in locating costumes, all of which seemed to be in the possession of another.

Jack asked for Meg Ballantine and followed the directions further backstage. A skinny, Mexican-looking man with a mustache intercepted Jack, mistaking his motives. He said his name was Arturo and he was the stage manager trying to get a rehearsal started. He demanded Jack's prompt departure, but the use of Hap's name was sufficient. Jack was able to draw Meg Ballantine into a space behind pieces of scenery representing a woodland glade.

Meg was pretty with fair hair, soft eyes and a pleasing figure. With stage makeup and the right scanty costume, Jack could see that she was the type in demand in the Barbary Coast's music halls and saloons. She was also the type that flowed here in large numbers from the Eastern cities, for they could earn many times more money than at home and had a chance to snag a rich husband.

"You were Lola's best friend, weren't you?" Jack asked after explaining his determination to investigate the deaths of both Lola and Jenny Morris. "Can you tell me anything about her that will help?"

She smoothed down the thin cotton dress that she

had not yet removed. Jack's youthful good looks and his frank blue eyes appealed to her and she was willing to tell him all she knew.

"She didn't have any close men friends. I mean, she saw a lot of men, went home with some of them, but no one in particular—not since I've known her."

"How long had she been here in San Francisco?"

"Just a few weeks. This was her first job."

"Where was she before?" asked Jack.

"Kansas City."

A hub of transportation between East and West, Kansas City was a busy and growing town. While not nearly as wild as San Francisco, it had its share of saloons and music halls.

"Did she tell you about her life there?"

"I remember one of the girls asking her. She was from Kansas City too but Lola didn't seem to know anything about the city."

"Other places she worked?"

"No, didn't mention any—oh, she said something about Wichita once."

"Did she get along with the other girls here?" Jack asked.

Meg looked alarmed. "You don't mean you think one of the girls might have killed her! No!"

Jack agreed with her. His strong streak of masculine superiority made it hard for him to believe that the murderer could be female. "I'm just looking at all the possibilities," he said quietly.

Meg shook her head decisively. "No, Lola had squabbles with some of the other girls, we all do. Over silly things like shoes and clothes and—and men," she added archly, but went on to add quickly, "but there was never any serious argument, no reason for anybody to kill her."

"Did Lola know Jenny Morris at the Midway?"

"I don't know."

"The men here. Any of them fancy Lola?"

"She was popular, friendly. Men all liked her."

Jack chatted with her a while longer. After he had asked all the questions he could think of, he talked longer, seeing that she was nervous after the death of her friend. He hoped he had reassured her when he left the Cobweb Palace.

Something from his conversation with Meg Ballantine bothered Jack, but no matter how much he racked his brains, he could not isolate it. He spent a while going over the discussion in his mind, trying to pinpoint what it was but without success.

So he turned to his writing. Most of his work to date had been essays and articles, but in order to achieve any recognition as a writer, he knew he had to write fiction. Everything he had read about writers and writing stated firmly that a beginner should write what he knew. Jack had followed that advice with his nonfiction and intended to do the same with his fiction. He had decided to set his short stories in the harshest climate and in the most dangerous place he knew—the Klondyke.

He made notes of the characters he planned on using, and opposite them he listed the men and women he had known whose appearance, mannerisms, thoughts and actions could contribute to fleshing them out, making them real. As ideas for settings, locations and incidents came to him, he jotted them down too.

He wrote without a stop until he glanced at the big brass alarm clock and saw that it was after six. He was hungry and thirsty, and as he put his notes into piles, he was planning to take care of both problems with his next stage of the investigation.

Luna's was one of the Barbary Coast's most prominent rendezvous. The potted plants, the polished darkwood chairs and tables, the brass fixtures and the paneled walls put it in a very different category from the saloons with sawdust-covered floors. Its location gave it the opportunity of describing itself as in San Francisco rather than in the notorious Devil's Acre, for it was situated right on the line between the two and had the reputation of having no address.

It catered to a very different clientele too. The newspapermen, the journalists and magazine writers used it as their regular watering place and it was equally a favorite with poets and writers of all kinds. The atmosphere was different, as it operated more like a fashionable men's club. Jack had been there only a few times, usually when he had sold an article, for its prices were at levels that kept away itinerants.

At the bar, Jack ordered a small beer, the cheapest drink. A schooner was three times the price. As the barkeep placed the drink in front of him, Jack asked, "Frank Harris in today?"

"Not for a few days. He's either sleeping one off or out of town on an assignment. It's probably the first and his editor thinks it's the second."

"How about Ambrose?"

"He's here somewhere. Ah, there he is."

Ambrose Bierce was just detaching himself from a trio at a table when he caught sight of Jack. "You must have sold a piece. What was it this time? 'How I Panned for Gold in the Yukon—and Came Back Without Any'?"

Bierce was nearly sixty years old—almost three times Jack's age—but he looked well and active. His fair hair and luxuriant mustache and eyebrows made him look younger. The two had had a strange relationship for some time. Bierce was widely known as "the unspeakable Ambrose." He was caustic, sarcastic, biting and often cruel in his words, both written and spoken. He treated Jack as his young protégé, although Jack did not recall ever receiving a word of true encouragement from Bierce. Nevertheless, Jack had learned from him, from his writings, from conversations with him and even his acid criticism.

Bierce's skill as an editor was legendary. He had spent some years in London, where he had made *Fun* magazine into a strong competitor of the prestigious *Punch.* He wanted to stay in London but the fog and the damp weather irritated the asthma that had plagued him all his life. He returned to San Francisco at the same time that a young man called William Randolph Hearst arrived there, having been kicked out of Harvard. Hearst's father owned the *Examiner,* the strongest Democratic paper in the state of California.

Bierce had gone into the *Examiner* to apply for a job as a columnist. A frail young man who looked about seventeen years old appeared and Bierce thought he was an office boy, come to take him to the boss of the paper. "I am William Randolph Hearst," said the "boy," who had been put in charge of the paper by his father. His lack of years and experience were misleading. He recognized Bierce's ability and promptly appointed Bierce editor.

The paper was already powerful, and under Bierce's forceful leadership it greatly expanded its dominance. In his editorial column, Bierce attacked the National Guard, women, religion, dogs, lawyers, horse racing— but most of all, the Republican Party and everyone in it. Politicians felt a shiver of apprehension every time they opened the *Examiner.*

Today, Bierce was in, what was for him, a good mood. He clapped Jack on the back. "Have you stopped spouting that socialist claptrap since I saw you last?"

It was perhaps the sorest spot in their relationship. Bierce detested socialism, calling it the lowest form of radicalism, and he had shouted invective at Jack in an argument more than once. Jack was not here to argue on this occasion though. He grinned pleasantly. "No political theory today, Ambrose. Much more serious questions."

"If it's a job, we're fully staffed."

"It's not a job either."

Bierce examined him thoughtfully and called to the barkeep for another Sazerac. For a few minutes they chatted, for this was the first time Jack had seen Bierce since returning from the Yukon. Bierce finished his drink and called for another, motioning to Jack's glass at the same time. On the bar stood bowls of pickled oysters, salty fried shrimp and frogs' legs. Jack assuaged his hunger, well aware that the foods were selected to encourage more drinking.

"But what is it that's so serious?" Bierce wanted to know when the drinks arrived.

"Murder, Ambrose."

Bierce stopped with his glass halfway to his lips.

"The murders of these two saloon girls," Jack added.

Bierce sipped his Sazerac. When he put it down on the bar, he said, "Let me see now . . . you have some money or you wouldn't be here in Luna's—you'd be in one of those disgraceful hovels you usually frequent. You're not looking for a job so that means you have one—of some kind. You're a socialist do-gooder and eager to protect the working man and woman. Now what does all that add up to?"

It added up to something very close to the truth, Jack thought uncomfortably. He hoped he wasn't that transparent to everybody. It wasn't likely—fortunately there were few persons in San Francisco with Bierce's incisive mind.

"You're in a position to know a lot that never appears in the newspapers, Ambrose."

"Nonsense," snorted Bierce. "I have a lot of pages to fill. At the *Examiner,* we print everything we hear, everything we're told, everything we pay for, and then we make up the rest."

Jack grinned. "You're too shrewd for that. You guess a lot, you speculate a lot. You must have big, fat files on these murders like you have on every topic,

but you don't print most of it because you might point
a finger at some big name."

Bierce's eyes blazed and his mouth opened to hurl
a furious rebuttal. Instead, he laughed uproariously.
"You're a clever young fellow but you won't get me
that way. Naming names is my business."

Jack knew that was true. Bierce was undoubtedly
one of the great masters of the English language, but
tact was one of the few words that was absent from
his vocabulary. Still, Jack had sidestepped Bierce's curiosity for the moment. He had to try to hold that
position and not let the other suspect that he was
working for the mayor—another of Bierce's favorite
targets.

"So what's your interest in these girls?"

It was the question Jack had been expecting. It was
one he would be asked often and it was in his favor
that he could express his honest feelings even if his
answer was a little less than one hundred percent
truthful. He ate some more shrimp before he replied.

"I was born and raised here. It's my town. I know
a lot of the girls here and two of them have been
murdered. There may be more. I'm trying to find out
who's killing these girls and prevent further deaths."

"Isn't that a job for the police?"

Jack laughed out loud. "You—of all people to ask
that! I'm ashamed of you, Ambrose! You roast the
police force in your columns continually. You're un-
merciful. You call them incompetent, you call them
corrupt—"

"All right, all right. And it's true—they are. But
what can you do?"

"I don't know," Jack said. "When you write your
column, what can you do?"

Bierce examined his drink then turned abruptly to
Jack. "Why do you say there may be more killings?"

Jack knew he had to be careful. Bierce was shrewd
and clever. He was an expert at getting information

out of people. "It looks like part of a pattern. We haven't seen anything quite like this on the Coast before—not quite like it. No saloon wars going on right now. These girls are not from the dives and deadfalls. They're from two of the best-known music halls in the town."

"Does that mean something?" asked Bierce sharply.

"I think so but I don't know what."

Shouted voices came from a table. It was loud for Luna's, but a mere whisper compared to the raucous noises in the places Jack usually visited. He ate some frogs' legs and let Bierce think for a few seconds, then asked, "So what can you tell me, Ambrose? What do you know that will help me?"

Bierce was silent a little longer. "You haven't a hope in hell of finding the killers," he said at length. "But if you should—if by some slim, remote chance you should"—he stared hard at Jack—"I want the story!"

Jack drank some of his beer. "Why should I give you the story? You haven't given me anything."

Bierce chuckled. "I've taught you too well, youngster. All right, I'll give you something now. A warning, to start." He paused and Jack waited intently for him to continue. He had a great respect for Bierce's knowledge of San Francisco and all those in it.

"Now listen to this and listen well. The Big Three have gained an enormous amount of power since you went up to Alaska scrabbling for gold in that dirt. They were mighty before but they're like gods now."

Jack felt a little disappointed. Bierce's dislike of politicians and the masters of big business was widely known. He never missed a chance to lambaste them in his columns. Now, he seemed to be getting beyond dislike and into an unreasoning hatred, but Jack resolved to listen.

"I know my reputation for abhorrence of the rich and powerful causes a few people to laugh behind their hands, but don't you laugh, Jack. Beware of these men, for their machinations spread through this town like the tentacles of a giant octopus. Their fingers are in every pie. No business and no activity is out of their reach."

Jack felt a slight flutter of fear at Bierce's words.

"Are you saying the Big Three are behind these killings?"

Bierce grinned mirthlessly. "To quote you—'I don't know.' These men are known to you though, aren't they, Jack? They are Collis P. Huntington, Fred Crocker and Leland Stanford. They are never seen to do anything criminal and no one in this state would ever testify against them. They plan and they maneuver, they scheme and they plot. Others do the dirty work—and believe me, Jack, a lot of dirty work is being done!"

"It used to be the Big Four," Jack commented.

"Yes," Bierce agreed. "It was Huntington, Charles Crocker, Leland Stanford and Mark Hopkins. Hopkins died. Charles Crocker died and his son, also called Charles, took over from him. Not wanting to be confused with his father, he used his other name of Fred. So now it's the Big Three and they are immensely more dangerous than the original Four."

"But why would they want to kill two saloon girls?"

"I really don't know, Jack, nor have any likely leads appeared. Not the slightest reason for a motive. Nothing."

Bierce finished his drink. "Jack, there is one other name. This one may not be known to you. It is Walter Williams."

"Who is he?" Jack was intrigued. "I've never heard of him."

"Get your head out of those gold rush stories, Jack. Leave them to Bret Harte, he's better at them than you are anyway. You need to know the name of Walter Williams, for he is one of the most dangerous men in California."

"Tell me about him," Jack urged.

"Williams is a mercenary—but he's far more than just a mercenary. He doesn't just fight wars—he starts them. He's a professional revolutionary. When he was twenty-nine years old, he raised an army of three hundred men and invaded Baja California. He had complete control of it in less than two weeks. Those who had paid him to do it were not prepared for such speedy success and were not ready to back him up. As a result, that rich prize slipped out of their hands.

The next time he appeared, he was in the pay of a group seeking land concessions in Nicaragua. The Big Four played a large part in this. Williams gathered a few dozen men and pretended to be fighting for freedom in the civil war then going on in Nicaragua. Instead, he struck out on his own, seized the whole country and proclaimed himself president. He was hailed as 'the new Bolivar.' "

"Then what happened?"

"His backers—the Big Four, aided by Vanderbilt—were slow to give him the support he needed. They were fearful of his power, and dubious of his allegiance."

"Is he an ex-soldier?" Jack asked, fascinated. Here was a character to store in his mind, he thought, reaching for more frogs' legs.

"He was a lawyer. He was a newspaper editor too," Bierce smiled. "Those two professions give you an idea of the kind of villain he is! Gave himself the rank of colonel when he took Baja then promoted himself to general in Nicaragua."

"Why is he so dangerous?"

"Men who can't believe in themselves believe in Williams. He has an extraordinary control over his men. They will take any risks if he orders them. He is an utterly merciless killer and he trains every one of his men to be the same."

"The only reason that you would be warning me about him," said Jack slowly, "is that he must be here in San Francisco."

"He has been seen here," said Bierce. "Why? Nobody knows. He was here a short while ago. He disappeared and now he is back. During the time he was gone, something occurred . . . remember the Humboldt Wells incident? It must have been just before you left to go that godforsaken wilderness."

Jack remembered hearing about it. Humboldt Wells was a vital link in the Nevada section of the Central Pacific Railroad. One morning at dawn, a large band of heavily armed men had ridden into town, sealed it off and robbed all four banks.

"There were too many of them," said Bierce, "and they were too well organized to be outlaws. That was the conclusion of the Wells Fargo investigators. Their report said the whole operation was conducted with military precision and efficiency."

"Was any trace of the money ever found?"

"Not a sniff. Nor the men. There was never anything to tie Williams to it."

"But why would you think that the Big Three were behind that?" asked Jack. "They own the Central Pacific."

Bierce looked at Jack with unconcealed dismay. "Haven't I taught you any better than that? The Big Four pulled off many a coup like that. Trouble was I could never find enough on them to print. The Big Three are likely to be even more daring."

Jack declined another drink. The *Examiner* editor had little of further value that he cared to impart and he closed their conversation by asking Jack if he had another first name.

"In case I need it for your obituary," he added.

*   *   *

Jack went back to the Midway. It was a lull between shows and he found Flo selecting costumes. She gave him a wan smile. "Trying to stay busy and keep my mind off—"

"Yes, I know," Jack said, "but I have to talk to you and it's about what happened. It may be painful for you but the police are not likely to get any results," said Jack. "I've been asked to help. I know a lot of people on the Coast. I might be able to learn something and perhaps prevent any more murders."

"More? Oh, no!" Flo's hand flew to her mouth.

"I hope there won't be—I can't tell you any more than that."

"All right." That was one of the things Jack liked about her. She didn't pry. They sat on the same basket-weave love seat, still piled with clothes. Jack wondered again why she had a love seat in her dressing room, but this was not the time to ask.

"I remembered that Jenny had been in one of your classes."

"That's right. She was a fast learner and a good dancer." Flo's face clouded. "Jack, if I can help you find who killed her—"

"Thanks, Flo. What can you tell me about her? Where did she come from?"

Jenny had told Flo that she had worked in a saloon in Butte, Montana. She had hated the cold and seized the first chance to come to California. It was five or six weeks ago that she had arrived in San Francisco and the Midway had been her first job.

"She worked hard," said Flo. "She wanted to learn the hoochy coochy and she knew it would be difficult—it needs a lot of muscles that regular dancers don't use."

"I know," Jack agreed. "I've watched you."

Flo smiled. "Jenny was willing and anxious to learn the new dance. It took a lot of determination."

Jack knew that the dance came easily and naturally

to Little Egypt, but not all the other girls who wanted to learn it had the ability or the resolve.

"Did she have any particular men friends?"

"Several. She was very pretty."

"She was." Jack nodded. "Any particular men friends though?"

Flo thought; then her big dark eyes lit up. "I remember one—a sailor called Stefan, a big blond Swede."

"Does he come in often?"

"Not anymore, he went back to Sweden."

Jack grimaced. "That lets him out. Any others?"

Flo's calm countenance took on a look of distaste. "Yes. He worked at the docks. Always seemed to have plenty of money though I don't know how he got it. I didn't like him at all. He hit Jenny several times, hurt her bad once. His name was Spike. He had black untidy hair, mean looking. A funny thing though now that I come to think of it . . ."

"Go on."

"She seemed to know him well right from the beginning—and yet she'd only just got here."

"You think she had known him before?"

Flo nodded. "I think she must have."

"Does he still come in here?"

"He used to be a regular but—no, I haven't seen him since Jenny was killed."

"Thanks, Flo." Jack smiled at her. "I'll be back if I think of anything else."

"I can think of something right now," murmured Flo. She pushed a large hamper against the door, took Jack by the hand and satisfied his curiosity as to why she kept a love seat in her dressing room.

Chapter 5

It was late in the evening when Jack reached Grant Avenue, but time meant nothing on the Barbary Coast. A swirling white fog was rolling in off the bay and puddles of water were collecting on the uneven street. The gas lamps at each corner reflected eerily from the puddles, but their weak illumination did not reach to mid-block where it was dark and gloomy. Jack walked warily, knowing that a sandbag or a brass knuckle could materialize without warning from a hidden doorway. A murder a night was the average for the Devil's Acre, and the police were not even able to estimate the number of muggings and robberies.

Jack turned right onto Pine. In the next few blocks, most of the melodeons were lined up. It was becoming brighter as Jack walked on, for most of the establishments had brightly illuminated street fronts. The sidewalks were busy with men, miners wanting to spend their gold, seamen off the ships that packed the always-busy harbor looking for women, farmers in from the country looking for a good time and stevedores from the docks eager to gamble their meager wages into a nest egg.

Jack went into Molly's Melodeon first of all. He paid a bit, twelve and a half cents, to the tough-looking bruiser on the door and walked slowly up to the bar, his eyes searching the room. He saw no one who corresponded to Flo's description of Spike, the dockworker who had been Jenny's boyfriend and beaten her up several times. Jack was alert, too, for a glimpse of anyone he knew, anyone who might be a source of information.

Molly's Melodeon was a low-ceilinged, rectangular room with a bar along one side and a platform on an adjacent side. This served as a stage but it was empty right now, presumably a pause in the entertainment. Music from a piano and a squeaky fiddle were lost in the hubbub of conversation, argument, boasting and reminiscence.

There was no dancing in the melodeons, only liquor, gambling and girlie entertainment. The places were named after the musical instruments that equipped them when they first opened after the gold rush. It was a reed organ worked by treadles that operated a bellows blowing through the reeds. It had given way to one or two instruments, such as those whose output was now being drowned by voices.

Jack had to guess at the kind of place where Spike might be a habitue. The melodeons were the first to try and he might then have to go to the dance halls, then the concert halls, the beer dens and finally the deadfalls. It would be a steep decline through varying levels of vice and depravity.

He ordered a beer from one of the busy bartenders and meditated on his mission. He considered himself to be reasonably moral and with an abhorrence of deliberate cruelty, especially to women. So why did he spend most of his time in places like this, associating with the scum of the earth? He looked around the room. Many of the men here had probably killed and would not hesitate to do so again. Many would ill treat women, many would torture and maim and had not the least compassion for their fellow human beings.

Jack had been a hobo, had spent a month in jail, had watched a man being hanged, and had seen a woman flogged to death with a barbed whip. All of his experiences though had stemmed from a wander-lust and a desire to be in the open, see new sights, learn new things. Then the desire to write had taken over and now every minute of the day provided material for that writing.

He still had the burning urge to write, but at the moment he was an undercover police agent, and somewhere in this city of vice was a man who might know something that would help him track down the man with the slim-bladed knife who killed showgirls. The bartender came back for Jack's five cents. Jack knew him slightly, which was why the barkeep had not demanded the money when the mug of beer was placed before him.

"Seen Spike lately?" Jack asked. He put down a nickel and took a long swallow of the beer. It gave him a few seconds to observe the reaction.

"Spike Odlum? No, he used to come in regular. Had a run-in with one of the girls, boss told him to stay out of here."

This was more than Jack had expected. He now knew Spike's last name. The bartender's description of a run-in with one of the girls meant that he had physically abused her, which confirmed his character. It did not mean that he was necessarily a murderer, but he was Jack's only lead.

Jack finished the beer and pushed the mug back for another. As the pump creaked and the beer frothed, he said casually, "He owes me some money. I'd like to collect it. So he's drinking somewhere else now, is he? Know where?"

The bartender shook his head. "No idea—and don't want to know. He's a bad lot is Spike."

French Kitty's was the next stop in Jack's quest. It was one block over on the corner of California Street. She greeted Jack personally, a tall, dark, strikingly handsome woman who went under the names of Kate

Arlington and Katherine Neilson. Jack didn't believe that either was her real name, but everybody knew her as Kitty.

"So here's Handsome Jack! I knew you'd come back to me!" She greeted him with a warm kiss and an embrace that pressed her shapely body close.

She took him to the bar and bought him a drink. They chatted about friends and acquaintances. "Your friend Ambrose was in last week," she told him.

"I'm not surprised," said Jack. "I wouldn't even be surprised if you told me that Patrick William Riordan had been in here."

Kitty burst into a full-throated laugh. She threw back her head, emphasizing her ample breasts and the low cut of her tight dress. She was an enticing figure of a woman, but woe betide the man who tried to take advantage of her feminine charms. It was popularly believed that she carried a tiny one-shot Derringer in a strap around the top of her thigh. Nor was there the least doubt on the Barbary Coast that she would have any hesitation in using it and proceeding to bring all her womanly wiles into the courtroom to get acquitted.

"I'll have to invite him," said Kitty, still laughing at the thought of the Catholic archbishop of San Francisco entering her establishment.

Jack was not surprised that Ambrose Bierce had been in. His vitriolic friend frequented many of the drinking places in the city and was not deterred by the Barbary Coast and its reputation. "You should get Ambrose to bring the Tenth Cavalry with him the next time he comes. That would liven up your girls."

Kitty laughed again. The Tenth Cavalry was an all-Negro outfit whose fame as a fighting unit was equaled only by its notoriety when it came to women. Many in the military had been opposed to the creation of the Tenth and Bierce, always ready to oppose authority, was its staunchest supporter.

"Now that's something to think about," Kitty conceded. "If it was known that the Tenth was coming, half of my girls would quit on the spot and the other half would be at the door all evening waiting to greet them."

Jack regaled Kitty with an account of his meeting with Oscar Wilde and she listened wide-eyed. "I wish I'd been there. Oh, and another heavyweight is back in town," she said. "John L. Sullivan was in a few days ago."

"On your stage?" asked Jack.

"No, at the bar," said Kitty.

The former world heavyweight boxing champion had lost his title to Gentleman Jim Corbett some years ago and had been unable to regain it. He was a regular frequenter of bars and often did a stage act.

A couple of drinks later, Jack carefully broached the subject of Spike Odlum, repeating the story that Odlum owed him money.

Kitty was no fool. "Is that why you're looking for him?" she asked sagely, looking Jack in the eye. "You don't need the money, you've got a regular income."

Jack froze in lifting his glass, pretended to see something in it and removed it with a fingertip. Did Kitty know about his mission?

"Those stories of yours. They're selling well, aren't they?"

Jack sighed in relief, turning it into a rueful laugh. "Not well enough, I'm afraid."

"From what little I know of Spike Odlum, he may be a hard man to collect from."

"Maybe so," Jack said, "but I'm going to try."

Kitty gave him an enigmatic glance and called over one of the bartenders. She leaned over the bar and they conversed in low tones. A piano, a violin and a drum began to play. They played louder and louder and were obviously trying to get the crowd's attention prior to the dancing girls coming on stage.

Kitty turned back to Jack. "I thought he might have

been seen in the deadfalls by now," she said, meaning the lowest form of bar. "Seems he's got money though. Ike here says Odlum caused some trouble in the Best Idea. They threw him out but let him in again as he had become such a free spender."

Jack digested this with interest. As a dockworker, Spike Odlum did not make enough money to be a regular in places like the Best Idea, which charged a quarter admission, priced its drinks high and had some big-stakes games going. Someone was paying him, but who and to do what?

He conversed with Kitty until the girls came on. Kitty was called away to deal with some business crisis and Jack slipped out. It was after midnight and the sidewalk was crowded. An occasional drunk stumbled and fell. He was left there by others who stepped over him. Perhaps a hungry thief would pretend to be helping him while rifling his pockets. Not for the first time, Jack wondered at the absence of police. Wasn't this the most crime-ridden city in the world?

The Best Idea was on Stockton Street. It was only one block in the direction of leaving the Barbary Coast and entering relatively staid San Francisco, but it was reflected in the marginally less lascivious concert saloon that Jack entered. Spike Odlum must be trying to better himself, he thought, but then a more likely explanation was that with more money, Odlum could afford to spend more.

The show was already in full swing here. A trombone blared above the piano and the violin while the crowd, all men, thumped their glasses and bottles on the tables, more or less in time.

Eight girls twirled their black skirts as they came to the edge of the small stage and then went back in unison. From the music, Jack knew that this was the first part of the cancan, brought from Paris a few years earlier and a natural for the Barbary Coast shows.

The girls were all attractive and good dancers. Skirts flicked high and gave the impression that the girls wore nothing beneath. The audience grew noisier as the dance got faster. Jack, ever the voyeur in search of copy for his stories, noted the bulging eyes, the eager faces, the stamping feet and the shouts of encouragement.

The dance became a frenzy and the girls squealed louder as their skirts flashed higher. Tension gripped the audience, mounting until it seemed it could terminate only in an explosion.

The trombone blasted final screeching notes and as the crowd roared approval, the girls turned their backs to the audience, bent forward and flipped their skirts over their heads, removing the doubts that had been in the minds of every man in the audience.

Chapter 6

The applause was deafening. The girls came back on stage to take a bow and the yelling and whistling grew even louder. They tried to leave the stage but hands from behind the side curtains pushed them back. The musicians started up again and the girls lined up and did one more—greatly shortened—version of the can-can. They ended as before and by now, those from the nearer tables had crowded forward.

The vociferous shouts of approval demanded yet more but the girls scampered off and left their audience on its feet. When it was clear that the girls were not coming back on stage, the noise began to abate. Seats were resumed and waiters were able to move between the tables again.

Jack studied them, table by table. He was about to conclude that he had to move on to another place when a movement caught his eye. A man had left a table and was heading for the door. Jack could see him clearly now. Black-haired, mean-looking—he fitted Flo's description precisely. But black hair was not uncommon and the Barbary Coast must have more mean-looking characters than any other square mile on the face of the earth. He had to be sure.

He waited till the man reached the door then made his way down the bar. The two bartenders on duty at his end were new to him—it was a transient job at best. The third one, however, at the far end, he recalled from a different place, the White Swan. What was his name . . . ?

Jed, that was it. Jed saw him and nodded. "Hello, Jack, what'll it be?"

"Still got one down there, Jed, with some friends," Jack said, waving vaguely down the bar. "How long you been here?"

"Just a week. Pay's better."

"Good. Listen, didn't I just see Spike Odlum in here? With all this crowd . . ."

"You did. Left not a minute ago."

"I owe him a drink," Jack said quickly. "Know where he went?"

"He didn't say. He often goes to Murderer's Corner about this time of night though."

"Thanks." Jack hurried out into the night.

The fog was thicker now. It would probably be gone before dawn but it twisted and twirled in the streets, weaving a mosaic of black and white. The air was damp and cool as Jack looked for Spike Odlum. He saw him on the other side of Stockton, heading in the direction of Washington Street.

Murderer's Corner was the name for Jackson and Kearny Streets. It was no longer quite as dangerous as its name suggested, but only because the more perilous locations on the Barbary Coast varied from week to week.

Jack speculated that Spike Odlum's destination was the Opera Comique. It was the kind of place that would attract a man of his character. It employed French and Spanish women, not only as performers but also as "pretty waiter girls," as they were known. It was popular as having the most obscene shows on the Coast. It was a little pricier than most but Odlum's newfound income seemed to support a higher level of lifestyle.

The sidewalks were not as busy but a fair number

of figures hurried or stumbled along despite the hour. Jack kept a sharp eye open as he always did. He knew that his robust build might deter some assailants but he took no chances.

Odlum went past Washington Street. The next was Jackson, but instead of turning right to go to the corner of Kearny, where the Opera Comique was located, Odlum went straight ahead. The streets were still bright from the dazzling fronts of saloons and melodeons. Bursts of raucous music, laughter and shouting surged through the night as Jack walked on. He was careful to keep a good distance from his quarry and wherever possible, he walked near a knot of men so as to appear one of them.

The pursuit continued. Odlum glanced behind and around him now and then but Jack was sure that he did not know he was being followed. Odlum was merely observing the same vigilance against thieves and muggers as was Jack himself.

They passed Pacific Avenue and Broadway. Jack had to slow his pace and stay farther back, for the streets were more quiet here and some blocks had only one or two saloons or bars. Telegraph Hill was not far ahead and to the right, but the low-hanging fog obscured it. Where could Odlum be going? Soon they would be out of the Devil's Acre and Odlum would be out of his milieu.

Jack crossed Union and Filbert, keeping to the other side of the street, seeking shadow where he could and stopping for a few seconds periodically. Odlum was still being cautious but not looking back. He must be getting near his destination, thought Jack.

At the corner of Greenwich, Odlum stopped. In front of Jack, two men stood, swaying and mumbling barely intelligible conversation. Jack went up to them quickly and flung an arm around the neck of the nearest. The man hiccuped and looked blearily at Jack, who gave him a reassuring grin. It was then that Odlum looked back but all he saw were three drunks.

Jack swayed in time with his two companions. Odlum crossed the street to where several buildings had fallen down. It was not an uncommon sight, for the city was lax in enforcing codes and fly-by-night construction companies abounded. The rubble had been piled high and a large shed had been erected on the leveled ground. Spike Odlum crossed Stockton and Jack lost him in the dark shadows.

Staying close to the walls of the buildings, Jack moved nearer but Odlum was not to be seen. Jack waited, hoping to see him against the fog that here was white and wispy. After a few minutes, he came to the only conclusion possible. Odlum had gone into the shedlike building.

Jack listened at the door. Voices sounded loud but he could not make out their trend. They did not sound like the crowd at a music hall or any show of that kind. Perhaps it was a meeting, some committee? It must be of an unofficial nature if so. Jack was an ardent socialist and had taken part in many political meetings and rallies in Oakland and San Francisco. He did not recall ever attending one in a building like this.

He tried the door handle, pressing on it slowly. The door opened a few inches. Someone on the other side pulled it sharply. The door opened all the way.

Several men stood just inside. All were well dressed. Some of them turned to look at Jack but their interest was casual.

It was warm after the chill of the foggy night air and the oil lamps on the walls cast cheerful flickering shadows. Jack could hear voices on the other side of a curtain. It sounded like a considerable number of people but the voices were not raised. Instead, they had the hum of conversation with an air of expectancy for some approaching event.

The man who had pulled the door open had a big stomach and a red face. "Come in, come in," he invited warmly. "We have been waiting for you." He tugged at Jack's arm and closed the door behind him.

Bewildered, Jack was trying to figure out just what this place was. The space they were in was small and must be only a tiny part of the large shed. A heavy curtain blocked the view of the rest of the building.

"I'm Arthur Edgerton," the man said. "This is David Harker and Wallis Fields." They looked like businessmen in cutaway coats, dark trousers and haircuts that looked like the work of a professional barber—unlike Jack's own handiwork on his unruly curly brown hair.

"You're going to be first, I believe," said the man calling himself Edgerton. "Come along. Might as well get started."

He led the way to a gap near the end of the large curtain. Still bemused, Jack followed, his curiosity as a writer aroused. He had not seen Spike Odlum since he had entered and supposed he must be among the crowd behind the curtain.

They went into another small area. It had low benches, racks hung with clothes and shelves on one wall with bottles and jars containing various colored liquids. A small man greeted Jack with a toothy smile. He was thin and bony but moved quickly. "You're the first, eh? All right, let's get you ready." His grin widened at Jack's baffled expression. "I'm Spider," he said as if that were explanation enough.

"Look," said Jack, finding his voice finally. "I don't know what this is all about but there must be some mistake. I'm not the man you're—"

"Come on now." Spider had Jack's jacket off and was unbuttoning his shirt. "They all get a bit nervous about this time."

He felt Jack's arm. "I can tell you've done this before." He reached up with a clawlike hand and felt Jack's jaw, then examined his ears. "You're in good shape."

Jack grabbed his shirt as Spider pulled it off and was about to toss it onto the rack. "Now wait a minute. Will you tell me what this is all about?"

Edgerton had been observing all this with an unconcerned attitude but now he came forward. "Look, lad, you want to earn thirty dollars, don't you?"

"Thirty dollars?"

"Ten dollars a round—but I can see that'll be no problem for a fellow like you. Go three rounds easy as pie."

It was a prizefighting arena beyond the curtain.

Jack felt a mild relief after the uncertainty. He knew of places like this, had even attended some of them. Since the Marquis of Queensberry rules had been brought in some years earlier, boxing had reluctantly changed from a ferocious bloodthirsty battle to a sporting event that was attracting increasingly larger crowds. Three-minute rounds and the use of gloves were the two changes that were revolutionizing boxing, and when John L. Sullivan had defeated Jake Kilrain in Richburg, Mississippi, that had been declared the last bare-knuckle fight.

But there still remained those who missed the brutality, the blood and the broken bones of bare-knuckle fighting. Some of these were here tonight and it looked as if Jack had been mistaken for one of the contestants. It was not surprising, for he had the look and the build. He had done a considerable amount of boxing but that had been all amateur.

"Three-minute rounds, that's all they are," said Edgerton, who was evidently one of the promoters. "We try to stay with the times. We have adopted the Marquis's idea of three-minute rounds. It's an improvement in a way. Lets the fighters get their breath so that all the time they're out there, they're fighting hard. The old way, where they fought until one of them had won, well, some still want to see it but we try to be modern." He gave Jack an oily smile.

Jack, meanwhile, was musing over his five dollars a day as an investigator for the mayor. That could get him killed. Here, on the other hand, was thirty dollars for nine minutes' work! What if it was bare-knuckle? Jack had fought that way before. He could even recall thinking that it was sissified to wear thick padded gloves. And the worst that could happen would be a few bruises and a little blood.

In his boxing days, Jack had lacked the killer instinct and knew he did not attack his opponent enough. He preferred the methodical defense, waiting until an opening occurred for a winning blow. That was also the ideal strategy for a contest such as this one. So why not?

He let Spider take off his boots and fit him with a pair of thin, tight-fitting light shoes. Edgerton's smile widened. His reminder of thirty dollars had done the trick. The lad had been reluctant at first but now he was hooked. He eyed Jack's bare chest and strong arms appreciatively. Three rounds? Well . . .

From the arena came a few catcalls and some whistles.

"Customers are getting restless," Edgerton said, his smile still in place. "Is he ready, Spider?"

The little man nodded. "Sure he is."

Edgerton turned and went out. Spider patted Jack on the back. "Watch out for his left. He's got a longer reach than you."

"Who am I going to—"

Edgerton came back before Jack could finish the question. With him came a big man, bare to the waist like Jack. He had a strange haircut. His hair was shaved from the ears and up both sides of the head, leaving only a strip of hair from back to front about three inches wide. Jack had seen that haircut before in newspaper pictures.

It enabled him to identify his opponent instantly.

It was John L. Sullivan, the last bare-knuckle heavy-weight champion of the world.

Chapter 7

It was a standard-size ring, twenty feet by twenty. That was the first thing Jack noticed. It would be important in fighting a defensive battle, for he would need all the space he could find to maneuver and there was no doubt that was what he would have to do. The former heavyweight champion of the world! Not only that but the winner of the last bare-knuckle championship fight!

There was a stubborn streak in Jack that his stepfather had warned him about. "Long as you recognize it," John London had said more than once, "then you can deal with it." Jack recognized it now. Was it stubbornness to go through with this fight? Or was it an acknowledgment of it to duck out?

No, it was not a matter of choice. Jack was no quitter, regardless of the odds against him. When he had been a law-enforcement officer with the California Fish Patrol, he had once faced five Chinamen, every one with a knife. In the Klondyke, he had been crippled from the waist down for weeks with scurvy. In the Erie State Penitentiary, he had fought empty-handed against a crazed Polack with a broken table leg. Quitting was not in his nature. He was in this fight.

It was a professional-looking ring. As he climbed in, he noted that the ropes were one-inch diameter, maritime-quality manila. The corner posts were well wrapped and the canvas floor had a little give but was solidly padded. A few cries of encouragement went up, cheers for the underdog, thought Jack.

Oil lamps hung from the ceiling, illuminating only the combatants in their square zone of conflict. They left the crowd in near darkness and all Jack could see was that the shed was packed with indistinct figures. He had not forgotten that he had followed Spike Odlum here but there was no chance of seeing him in this dim light. Movement from row to row was men collecting gambling money. If anyone was betting on him, Jack wondered what the odds were.

His opponent, the great John L., appeared and the reaction was tremendous. He had been a popular champion and was still a well-known and well-liked character of national importance. The referee was a short, tubby man in a red shirt. His face showed signs of fistic battle and he was lively despite his girth. He rattled off a few sentences that presumably were fundamental rules of the contest. John L. did not appear to be listening and Jack was too tense to concentrate.

The fight began.

The first round was the longest three minutes Jack could recall. He weaved and ducked, dodged and slipped while he yielded ground but did not back away too obviously. He quickly learned that parrying was not an effective defense. The power of the ex-champion's blows was already numbing his arms and shivers shot through Jack's body.

Clinches were to be avoided too. The long arms of Sullivan could swing way out and then come in to jab with ferocious intensity. Continuous movement was Jack's best ploy and he used it to the full while trying to maintain a semblance of a contest to please the crowd. A loud voice in the front rows kept urging him to "Get in there and punch him!" but Jack's chances of doing that were few.

The first round ended and Jack gratefully let a sec-

ond pour water over his head. He drank some and
spat into a bucket. "Ye're doing great, kid," said the
second, and Jack saw then that it was Spider. Over in
his corner, John L. Sullivan was unmarked and not
even out of breath. He chatted with his second as if
he were at a garden party.

Round number two was tougher. The crowd was
behind Sullivan, urging him to finish the contest. Their
shouts echoed from the low roof of the shed. In a
fight for the championship he might have done so, but
he was treating this merely as a diversion to make
some money and be seen. He satisfied the crowd by
drilling a straight left into Jack's face, but Jack had
managed to ease back and avoided receiving the full
weight of the blow. Sullivan followed up with a tattoo
of body blows that stung but might have been much
harder.

The crowd was frantic for blood in the third round.
Jack went down to a right hook. He saw it coming
but could not get out of the way. He would have gone
down again but for his effective use of a forearm block
that brought a nod of approval from the champion.
Sullivan seemed to be looking down at the front row.
He must have received a signal, for he stepped up the
fight to a level beyond Jack's capability. A jab under
the lower ribs left Jack gasping for breath, a jolting
left crashed into his jaw then a right followed at the
speed of light. Jack's world dissolved, spiraling down
into blackness.

When he recovered, Jack was in the small dressing
room. Objects swam slowly into focus. He was pain-
fully aware of a feeling that his entire middle had been
paralyzed and his jaw seemed as if it were the size
of a watermelon. Spider's face looked misshapen and
grotesque but it straightened out as Jack's vision adjusted. "Okay, kid?" Spider asked solicitously.

Jack tried to nod but he grimaced, convinced that

his head would fall off if he persisted in the intention. "Just take it easy," Spider told him. Jack did. He took it so easy that it was some time before he came out of the deep sleep. The world seemed to consist of noise as full consciousness returned, but he realized it was final applause coming from beyond the curtain.

"That's the end of the last bout," Spider said and grinned. "John L. is taking a big bow—well, a lot of big bows. He knocked out all four of you."

"Aw in 'e sird 'ound?" Jack muttered.

"That's right, kid. All in the third round."

Normality was returning fast. Jack struggled to sit up. On another cot, a young man about Jack's age was still groaning and his limbs twitched. Spider helped Jack up and onto his feet. He staggered but regained his equilibrium. Every inch of his upper body ached and his jaw felt as if it would fall off. His legs were weak from running and dodging.

"I'm okay," Jack said unsteadily. "Where's my money?"

Spider grinned. "Yeah, you're okay, all right. Mr. Edgerton will be in any minute with your thirty bucks. They'll want you to go out there and talk to some of the crowd. There's one fellow in particular wants to talk to you. There's some ladies too." Spider winked. "They like prizefighters."

"Is that right?" Jack doubted if the word *ladies* was fully appropriate.

Edgerton came in at that moment and the noise of the enthusiastic crowd spilled into the small room.

"Well done, lad." He peeled three ten-dollar bills from a thick stack and handed them to Jack. "We might get Bob Fitzsimmons here one of these days. How would you like three rounds with him?"

"I don't think so," said Jack through puffy lips.

"Might raise it to fifteen a round," pressed Edgerton.

"Going back to my regular job."

Edgerton grinned, showing a lot of teeth. "John L.'s a great champ, isn't he? Could have really messed you up, you know that, don't you?"

Jack did know it. He was well aware that Sullivan could have turned his face into a mangled mess and broken a few of Jack's ribs had he been as vicious as many of the prizefighters of the day. He was lucky that Sullivan was one of the few sportsmen in the game.

Jack's head was clearing fast and he was glad Edgerton was not going to ask him what his regular job was. "Law-enforcement officer" would not have been a judicious response.

"Has the other kid come around yet?" Edgerton asked Spider, who glanced at the other cot and shook his head.

"All right," said Edgerton, beckoning to Jack. "Come with me. People want to meet you."

In the auditorium, nobody had left. They stood in small groups, eagerly discussing the bouts. The bookmakers moved among them, paying out on bets, most of which had been based on how long the various contestants would last against the ex-champion.

Edgerton led the way to the first row. He stopped before a man probably in his mid-thirties. He was short, barely up to Jack's shoulder, and slender in build. He had light reddish hair and freckles on a pale face. He wore an old black suit and a long black coat that Jack thought made him look like an undertaker. On his head was a floppy black hat, and he wore black gloves. A gold cross hung on a thin gold chain around his neck.

It was the eyes that caught Jack's full attention. They were large and staring, light gray in color, so light that Jack felt he was looking right through them into the man's soul.

"This is General Walter Williams."

Jack felt a tremor run through his aching body at

the name. This was the man he had been warned about in Luna's.

The words of Ambrose Bierce came into his mind immediately. "One of the most dangerous men in California," Bierce had described him. "A mercenary—but far more than just a mercenary. He doesn't just fight wars—he starts them."

"What's your name, son?" Edgerton asked, and Jack gave it, his tired brain not pausing to think.

It didn't seem to matter. Jack's name meant nothing to Edgerton and Williams's expression did not change one iota.

"You put up a good fight out there," Williams said in a thin, reedy voice. Unimposing as his voice was, it was cold as ice and the unmistakable Tennessee accent made it not one whit less terrifying. Jack felt a shiver of repulsion but suppressed it, saying, "John L.'s a hard man to beat. I was lucky to get through the first two rounds."

"All four of you did," Williams's chilly voice went on. "John L. could have taken you all in the first round had he wanted. All at the same time if he had felt like it."

The lifeless eyes bored into Jack, but behind them Jack sensed a brilliant intellect. Any man who could seize control of a country the size and importance of Nicaragua and make himself president of it must be a man to reckon with. "The new Bolivar," Bierce had called him, and Jack respected the newspaperman's opinion.

He also recalled the further words of Bierce, "An utterly merciless killer."

Walter Williams was clearly not a man to argue with and Jack did not intend to cross him. He nodded in what could be taken for agreement as to the invincibility of Sullivan and waited to see what Williams wanted to talk to him about.

"I hear you've been making inquiries," Williams went on tonelessly.

"Inquiries?" Jack raised an eyebrow as if he did not understand.

"About dance hall girls."

Jack's head had cleared by now and he was in full possession of his faculties. Just as well, he thought, for it might be more critical to show some fancy footwork now than it had been in the ring.

"That's right," he said evenly.

"Why?"

Williams's question was like a stone dropped into a pond.

Jack looked steadily at him. "I knew Jenny Morris and Lola Randolph."

"Did you know them well?"

"Very well," said Jack.

Not a flicker of emotion showed in Williams's face. "What have you found out?"

"Nothing useful," Jack said. He felt he had better elaborate on that. Williams was not going to be an easy man to lie to or to evade. "I haven't found out if there's any connection yet with the murder of Lola Randolph."

"Do you think there is?"

"They were both showgirls. That's the only thing they have in common."

Jack felt Williams's gaze boring into him. He had a momentary flash of fear that he could not hide the truth from this man. He suppressed the thought instantly, not wanting to let it show on his face. The newspapers had not mentioned the fact that both girls had been killed with a similar—probably the same—thin-bladed knife. It was vital for Jack not to let Williams know that he had that information.

"What's your next move?"

Jack was thinking fast. Williams knew that Jack had been making inquiries about the girls. How much more did he know? Bierce's warnings about the man suddenly became of great value and Jack decided to go along with his friend.

"I already made it," Jack said. "I followed a man who I was told had known Jenny Morris, one of the girls. I followed him here tonight."

"Here."

"Yes. Then I was dragged into that fight. They mistook me for someone who didn't show up, I guess."

"You see the man now? Look around."

Jack did so, rapidly trying to decide what to say if he saw Spike Odlum. It did not become a dilemma. Jack could not see the man.

He had barely turned back to Williams to give him a negative answer when Williams said, "He didn't have anything to do with the death of either of the girls."

Jack played the innocent. "Who didn't?"

"The man you followed."

Jack did what he should do. He was silent for a few seconds, then he said, "You know this man?"

"I know who he is. I can assure you he did not kill either of those girls."

Jack shuffled, shrugged. "If you say so."

"I do say so." Frost glistened on the words.

"Saves me wasting my time then. I can look somewhere else."

"You can help me," Williams said. "If you find out who killed either one of those girls, tell me."

Jack eyed him for a moment.

"I have my own reasons for wanting to find him," said Williams, but the way he said it did not encourage Jack to ask what those reasons were. "How much did you get for that fight tonight?" Williams went on.

"Thirty dollars."

"Here's what I'll do. I'll give you fifty dollars for any item of information that I consider really helpful and a hundred dollars if it means we catch the killer."

Jack felt a flood of relief. Williams evidently did not

suspect him of being any more than a young man in
need of money—like thousands of others here in
San Francisco.

"More than you make with those stories," Williams
said, and Jack's relief was temporarily suspended. Williams knew that much about him. He hoped it was all.

"Where can I get in touch with you?" Jack asked,
hoping he was allowing a glint of avarice to show at
the mention of a hundred dollars.

"Leave a message at the bar of the Bella Union. It
will reach me."

The Bella Union was a melodeon but as upper class
as any melodeon could ever be. It attracted a wealth-
ier clientele and put name performers on the stage.
The girls were more attractive than most of the Bella
Union's rivals and wore more elaborate—and scant-
ier—costumes.

Jack nodded. Williams turned and walked away
without another word. Jack watched to see who he
approached but lost him in the crowd. A bosomy
blonde woman with a tower of hair and heavy makeup
took him by the arm. She smiled and said, "I thought
you were wonderful out there. Easily the best of the
four. Weren't you afraid of that huge man?"

"Well, he was the world champion," Jack said.

"Yes but those muscles . . ." She still had hold of
Jack's arm. She squeezed it and giggled. "Still, you're
not so bad yourself . . . listen," she went on, "some
of us are having a little party at my house. Why don't
you come along with us? I live just up on the hill."

Other thoughts were crossing Jack's mind. Williams
had mentioned dance hall girls, but then he had offered Jack a hundred dollars if "we catch the killer."
Was he just assuming that the same man had killed
both girls? Or did he already know more than he had
divulged? Well, Jack didn't doubt that. Williams was
a man to play his cards close to his chest. He appar-

ently knew about Spike Odlum too—but was he shielding him?

Another uneasy thought appeared. Had Spike deliberately let Jack follow him here? At Williams's bidding?

"I'm Maisie," said the blonde woman. "Shall we go? What's your name?"

Chapter 8

Bone-weary, every muscle aching and mentally fatigued, Jack pondered for a few seconds whether this invitation would lead to the therapy he needed or whether to invent some excuse to go home and fall into bed.

People were filing out of the auditorium now. The oil lamps had been turned up to help the exodus and it was easier to see the faces of those who remained. One figure that immediately caught Jack's eye was the black-clad, self-styled "General" Walter Williams. A man stood near him. Jack had not noticed him before but could see now that he was some kind of bodyguard. His eyes flickered constantly and his body was tense, his hands poised for movement.

He had an unusual appearance too. He wore a military-type jacket from which the epaulets had been removed and the buttons replaced. The pockets were gone too, facilitating rapid hand movements. On his head was a bush hat of the style copied by many after being worn by Teddy Roosevelt's Rough Riders. His face was hard as granite with a thin nose and a slit of a cruel mouth. He turned sharply to inspect a man pushing close to Williams, and as he did so Jack noticed an unusual accoutrement—from a wide leather belt around the waist of the modified military uniform hung a Navy cutlass.

Williams was talking to Fields, one of the two businessmen who had been with Arthur Edgerton before the fight and who was presumably another of the backers of these pugilistic events.

As Jack watched, a messenger boy came in waving an envelope and making the most of his fleeting importance. He spoke to Fields, who motioned to Williams. Ripping open the envelope, Williams read its contents quickly. Jack strained his ears to hear what Williams said to Fields.

"I find I have an urgent appointment. Will you have one of your men get me a cab?"

Maisie was engrossed with a young man who sported an ear that was heavily bruised and swelling rapidly. He was evidently one of the other contestants who had shared the ring with Sullivan. Jack did not think she would miss him and slipped past knots of people still discussing the fights and headed for the door.

An older man with the misshapen features of a one-time prizefighter was in charge of transport arrangements, it seemed. He had lined up several cabs and waved the first one forward. The horse trotted smartly to the door and Jack watched Williams and his bodyguard climb in. He tried to hear what instructions Williams gave to the driver but the thin, reedy voice did not carry.

"A cab for me too, if you will," said Jack to the ex-pug in his most authoritative tones.

He sat back against the cushions, wondering where they were going. The driver merely nodded when Jack told him to follow the vehicle in front and they rattled over the uneven street. Who was powerful enough to command a man like Walter Williams to come to him at a moment's notice at nearly four o'clock in the morning?

They went along Lombard Street and turned on Powell. Morning breezes were already beginning to gust gently through the streets and brush away the fog, but a few tendrils remained. It was a short ride and after a few moments of uncertainty, their destination became obvious to Jack. They were heading toward Nob Hill, one of the most exclusive neighborhoods in San Francisco.

The native San Franciscans often referred to it as "Nabob Hill." The bonanza kings, the railroad pioneers and the bankers lived up there. Mark Hopkins's home was said to have cost two and a half million dollars to build. "More than the national budget of Belgium!" Ambrose Bierce had written in one of his scalding columns. A few of San Francisco's politicians could have afforded to live up there, but chose slightly less expensive neighborhoods lest questions be raised as to the origin of the money.

Jack knew that the cab had approached it by an initially circuitous route because the climb from Kearny Street was at an angle of nearly forty-five degrees. No wheeled vehicle could ascend from that direction, which had been why the first cable car track was laid there more than twenty years earlier.

The air was already clear up here as the last of the night fog crept out of the streets and into the bay. Ahead, the other cab slowed abruptly. The gap between them closed as the hack behind slowed too.

"No, no," Jack called out. "Go on past, slowly."

As they went by the front of the huge mansion, Jack saw Walter Williams alight. A guard by the gate came forward to identify him.

"Keep going," said Jack. He knew who owned that mansion. Most of the inhabitants of San Francisco knew who lived there. It was the home of Collis Potter Huntington, one of the Big Three and one with the reputation of being the most ruthless man in California.

It was almost noon when Jack awoke. His body seemed to be on fire and he groaned in agony as he tried to stretch his legs and flex his arms. But he was young and strong and the pain subsided after he forced himself to get out of bed and walk around. He hobbled to the small stove, where he made himself a mug of strong black tea.

While he drank it, he thought over the events of the previous action-packed night. The fate of the two showgirls was uppermost in Jack's mind. What could be General Walter Williams's reason for wanting to find the killer of the girls? How did he know that the same man had killed both girls?

The second question was easier to answer than the first. A man with his influence could readily gain access to police files. Jack could not even guess at the answer to the first question. Then came the later puzzle—what was Williams doing at the mansion of Collis P. Huntington at four o'clock in the morning? Did their meeting have any connection with the girls' deaths? The latter connection seemed improbable. The devious schemes of the Big Three were sketched on a much bigger canvas. Their machinations were national and often global.

So now what? Jack made himself another mug of tea and sipped the strong brew. His next course of action became clear. He needed to talk to Ambrose Bierce again. The wily old editor knew far more than he ever divulged and quite a lot more than he ever printed. He might be able to make some meaning out of last night's clandestine meeting on top of Nob Hill.

It was too early to catch him at Luna's and Bierce detested being interrupted in his office routine. Another alternative occurred to Jack—he could visit Little Egypt after her afternoon dance classes. A stab of pain went through his shoulder as he lifted the mug of tea and he reconsidered that pleasing possibility. Perhaps other parts of him were similarly impaired by his ordeal in the ring. It might be better to postpone that visit for a day or so.

He could write. He had cut down on his writing time since undertaking this mission for the mayor, but here was a good opportunity to catch a few hours. He had been turning over in his mind an article about a further experience in the Klondyke. He pulled out his diary and set to work.

"Well, my young friend, what brings you back so soon?" was Bierce's greeting. Jack had written all afternoon and had done a few exercises that were uncomfortable at first but had largely soothed his aches. It was about seven o'clock and the bar at Luna's was still quiet. Jack knew that Bierce liked to come here after his day at the newspaper office so this was a good time to talk to him.

"If it's literary advice you've come for, I've given up teaching," Bierce said. "Besides, you couldn't afford my classes despite the money you made last night."

Bierce chuckled at Jack's sudden glance. "I'm a journalist, remember? It's my job to know these things. I'm surprised to see you survived three rounds with the great John L. though. He must be getting old and weary."

"My bruises don't agree with that," said Jack. "No, I need your opinion on something that happened after the fights last night."

He had decided to tell the newspaperman everything—except about his mission for the mayor. He stressed again his determination to learn who had killed the two showgirls and he was relieved that the astute Bierce did not press him on that point.

He told of following a known abuser of Jenny Morris, recounted his fight in a few words and then told of his cab ride and its ending in General Walter Williams going to Nob Hill for a meeting with Collis P. Huntington.

Bierce's cynical expression forsook him for once.

He took an extra sip of his Sazerac to cover this slip in his usually invulnerable facade. "Well, well," he said slowly, "you did have a busy night. I need another Sazerac after that. You can pay for it with your easily earned money."

Jack grinned. "It wasn't that easy. I was lucky it was John L. though. Some of those other man-eaters would have had me in St. Francis hospital today instead of being here having the pleasure of buying you a drink."

He paid for two more Sazeracs. It was a drink he only indulged in when he was flush with money and such occasions had been rare recently.

"Incidentally," Jack went on, "Williams has a bodyguard. Strange-looking fellow, wears a cut-down military uniform and a bush hat. He carries a—"

"Yes, Jack, I know who he is. They call him Captain Cutlass. You'd do well to give him a wide berth. He's a cold-blooded killer."

"That uniform—"

"That's what it is. The one he wore when he was one of Teddy Roosevelt's Rough Riders. Some say he killed more men than Bucky O'Neill."

Jack nodded. That meant a lot of men. Bucky O'Neill had been the sheriff of Tombstone, Arizona, before volunteering for the Rough Riders and was probably the deadliest shot in the whole unit. "Does this Captain Cutlass really use that weapon?"

"He most certainly does. He often uses it a lot before killing his victim. Roosevelt had him court-martialed for excessive cruelty in torturing prisoners that way."

Bierce finished his earlier drink and moved the fresh one closer. "You have unearthed some fascinating information, Jack. What do you intend to do with it?"

"My intention was to tell you about it and ask you what I should do with it," retorted Jack.

Bierce chuckled. Often when he did so, he bore a striking facial resemblance to an opera singer's portrayal of Mephistopheles. He knew it and capitalized on it. This was one of those occasions.

He regarded Jack intently. "I suppose I can trust you," he said slowly. "Can I?"

"That's for you to decide. I hope you can."

"You realize that what you have learned is potentially more dangerous than a worn-out Derringer with a hair trigger?" Bierce asked.

"Certainly," Jack said. "That's why I came to you."

Bierce grunted. "Want to bring me in the line of fire too, do you? What happened to friendship?"

"Wasn't it you who said, 'Greater love hath no man than this—that he lay down his friends for his life'?"

"Probably." Bierce shrugged. "Sounds like me."

He stared up into the massive mirror above the bar. It gave him a full view of the room behind him. The room was nearly empty and there was no one within earshot except the white-aproned bartender who was reading a newspaper. Bierce beckoned him over. "Charlie, there are a few glasses down at the far end of the bar that need polishing."

Charlie was accustomed to Bierce's ways, including the more eccentric ones. He winked. "So there are, Mr. Bierce, so there are. I'll take care of those right away."

"And don't let me catch you reading that irresponsible rag again," Bierce rapped, nodding to the bartender's newspaper. "It contains nothing but lies and misleading information." It was the *San Francisco Chronicle.* It considered itself a competitor of Bierce's *Examiner,* but Bierce steadfastly refused to admit that it was even in the same business.

Bierce watched until Charlie was down at the far end of the bar. "There's a man you should talk to. You'll have to do it right away because he won't be in town much longer. He knows a lot more about the—well, about this kind of thing than anybody else, including me. You'll enjoy talking to him anyway. He fancies himself as a bit of a writer—you know, like you."

Jack grinned. "All right. What's his name?"

Bierce ignored the question. "He has been putting together a dossier on the Big Three. He has been assembling intelligence on them since they were the Big Four. He'll tell you that they're even more dangerous now than they were then. What you have to tell him will be very helpful to him. In return, he may confide in you—that I can't say for sure, but he may."

Jack waited for Bierce to go on.

"He has written material for the *New York Sun* for some years." Jack knew that the *Sun* was another paper on Bierce's list of those to be detested, but then that applied to virtually every journal in print. "He writes regularly for the *Times* of London too."

"Have I read anything he's written?" asked Jack.

"I don't know," Bierce said carelessly. "You read rubbish like Ouida, H. G. Wells and Joseph Conrad, as I recall. Still, you may have read some of his fiction—"

"Such as?" prompted Jack.

"Oh, he wrote a story for children. He called it *The Jungle Book.* Then he wrote *Soldiers Three,* that would be more your style, full of excitement and mindless adventure. *The Light That Failed* was a bit better. Does your education extend far enough that you have heard of him?"

"Oh, yes." Jack nodded "You mean Rudyard Kipling."

Chapter 9

The train from the central station in San Francisco the next day carried Jack London south, stopping at several small townships and skirting Lake Pilarcitos. It headed out to the Pacific Coast from there and with several more stops still to come on its journey to Los Angeles, it deposited Jack in San Sebastiano.

Jack had made an early night of it after leaving Bierce at Luna's. A few extra hours of sleep had almost restored him to his normal vigor, and with a letter of introduction from Bierce in his hand, he had boarded the first train south. Fishing nets hung drying and the tang of sea and fish were strong in the soft air of the sleepy little village. There was no cab service, Jack learned, but he managed to get a ride on a cart making a delivery to an army post. The driver, an old Mexican, made deliveries to Kipling, he said, and the house on the cliffs where the writer lived was not far off his route.

It had the look of a farmhouse but there was no farm and its position among the jagged rocks on the ridge made it unlikely there had ever been one. Layers of vines covered much of the outside. It must have been built to satisfy one man's requirements, thought Jack as he walked up the path leading to it.

Rudyard Kipling did not look like a well man. His complexion was pale despite the days he had been here in the California sun. His eyes were lackluster behind the round spectacles and his hair was lank and lifeless. Nonetheless, Jack sensed a vibrant energy in him and felt a genuine thrill at meeting such a great name in the writing world. Kipling had long been one of his idols and he had read everything the other had written. Their embracement of socialism was a further bond of understanding between them.

Inside, the house had a well-worn but serviceable air about it. The stone-flagged floors and the high, beamed ceilings kept it cool. The walls were adobe but inset with flat stones. The fireplace was huge and was blackened from use, both cooking and heating, judging by the numerous fire-irons and the spit.

They sat in a room with a fine view of the Pacific Ocean. The fishing boats had not yet come in with their catches and the blue water was living up to its name. Bierce respected Kipling greatly. Jack knew that, regardless of Ambrose's habitual way of putting down almost everyone, including friends. Bierce had not prepared him for Kipling's appearance however. Jack had seen photographs of Kipling and knew what he looked like, but he was saddened to see that the bushy mustache and eyebrows had strands of gray while the hair had receded from the already high forehead. All this despite the fact that Kipling was little more than ten years older than Jack. "Ruddy has inflammation of the lungs," Bierce had told him. "It is a recurrent ailment. He recovers for a while then it returns."

He was a quiet-spoken man, not exactly shy but not as outgoing as Jack had anticipated. Perhaps that was just his English manner, Jack thought. Still, for a newspaperman, it seemed out of character.

Kipling greeted Jack in a friendly manner. They both read Bierce's letter. It was longer than Jack had expected and Kipling paused a couple of times to glance up at Jack and nod. He finished reading then went back to confirm a couple of points. He set the letter aside, reached for his pipe and filled it. After he had lit it, he said to Jack, "So you're a writer, eh?"

His manner grew markedly more cordial as Jack described his background as an oyster poacher, a law-enforcement officer, a gold miner in the Klondyke, a sailor, a hobo and a prizefighter. He omitted mention of stoking boilers, trying to sell sewing machines and cleaning carpets.

Kipling gave him a keen look. "A wonderful background for a writing career. And for such a young man."

"I know your background too," said Jack, becoming emboldened by the other's increasing affability. "India was a wonderful place to be born and live. So much material there to draw on." He added hastily, "Of course, you had to be able to write too." He thought about telling the other how he had copied out some of Kipling's works, word by word, in the hope of acquiring some of his skills, but decided not to mention it.

"I was fortunate in that by knowing other writers," Kipling said, "I was voted in to the Savile Club in London and my association with its members improved my work vastly."

"Who were they?" Jack asked.

"Thomas Hardy and Henry James sponsored me. Andrew Lang was a strong influence on my work and Rider Haggard became the most influential of all. He and I worked closely together."

"I didn't know that."

"Oh, yes, we read each other's work and not only made changes but suggested major redirections. We never collaborated on anything—at least, both of our names never appeared on any work—but we were closer than many collaborators."

"That interview with Mark Twain really made your name famous in this country," Jack said.

"Ah, that interview!" said Kipling with a soft laugh. "I had had no contact with him before that. I didn't tell him I was coming. He was living up there in New York State at the time and I just dropped in and told him I wanted an interview. I thought he was going to throw me out but he didn't and we have been friends ever since."

"Of course, you were known already in this country from *The Jungle Book*," Jack told him. "It was very popular here—and so were all your India stories after that."

They chatted on, Jack telling of his desire to see England soon and study how socialism was working there. That piqued Kipling's interest and he told Jack of his own attraction to socialism and how he came to write his own book on it. Kipling told Jack of his other American acquaintances, including Theodore Roosevelt, then finally he tapped the letter from Bierce. "Ambrose says you have some information that I might find useful."

Jack told him the same story that he had told Bierce. Again, he left out his assignment from the mayor but told everything else, how General Walter Williams had received an urgent message after the prizefight, and how Jack had followed him to the mansion of Collis P. Huntington on Nob Hill.

"Have you heard of General Walter Williams?" Jack asked.

"Oh, yes, indeed. His activities in Nicaragua have been of grave concern to Her Majesty's government. The country adjoins vital British possessions. More significantly, at the present time—perhaps even as we speak—the United States Congress is discussing a canal across Central America to join the Atlantic and Pacific Oceans. A route through Nicaragua is the most probable, being much the shortest route. As you may know, digging began on a canal through Panama in 1882 but the company went bankrupt."

"So Williams, as the former president of Nicaragua, is very well known to you!"

"Precisely." Kipling puffed smoke clouds. "And if the Big Three are behind him, that makes him triply dangerous."

"In what way?" Jack asked.

"Walter Williams has been president of Nicaragua once. Why not again?"

There was a silence as both men assessed the Pandora's box their conversation had opened.

"What can I do?" asked Jack.

Kipling rose and went to the window. He puffed his pipe and stared out at the placid ocean. He turned and said solemnly, "I'm going to confide in you, Mr. London—"

"Jack, please call me Jack."

"Very well, Jack. I have been in this country many times. I lived in Vermont for four years. I have had many journalistic assignments from newspapers in New York and elsewhere. I have also written extensively for the *Times* of London, which reports widely on American affairs."

He came back to his chair. "One series of articles on American pioneers turned out to be very much more far-reaching than that. It touched nerves on some subjects that certain papers were afraid to print. It led to revelations about railroad builders in particular that could clearly have enormous repercussions."

Jack nodded. He was absorbed in Kipling's words and had been wondering where he was headed. Now it was becoming apparent. Jack realized why Kipling was such an astute reporter. "I can see why you and Ambrose have so much in common."

"Yes, 'the implacable enemy,' that's how these men have described Ambrose. He and I keep our association sub-rosa as much as we can but we both have the same aims." His eyes twinkled for a moment. "You may hear stories about us being bitter enemies. They help to conceal our mutual interests."

"I see now," Jack said, "why Ambrose knew that you would be interested in knowing about Huntington's nocturnal visitor."

Kipling tamped his pipe. When it was burning well again, he continued, his eyes behind the glasses taking on an intensity. "Jack, these are three men who shape America—and indirectly, the Western world. Oh, they have done good things—such as uniting Eastern and Western America by means of the transcontinental railroad, but that is only a tiny part of what they have accomplished.

"The Big Three own the whole waterfront of San Francisco and Oakland. They control all the water traffic in the Bay Area, all the shipping that goes in and out of it and the river traffic in the hinterland.

"Soon, they will direct the movement of all ocean vessels along the western seaboard of America. This is why your information about Walter Williams's activities is so vital. Command of the Nicaragua Canal, linking the Atlantic and Pacific Oceans, will make these three men, the Big Three, masters of the globe."

Jack was absorbed. He had no idea that the tentacles of the Big Three had such far-reaching ramifications.

Kipling sucked his pipe stem reflectively. "Jack, I have told you something of what I have been able to piece together so far. I wish I could continue but I have to tell you that I cannot take my investigations any further."

"Why not?" asked Jack, astonished.

"I leave San Francisco in two days' time for New York. From there, I have to return to England." He nodded at Jack's surprise. "I know—but it is not of my choice. I have to go to South Africa. There will be war there soon."

"War?"

"The press is not aware of it yet but it is coming. Friends in Whitehall know it. They want me to report it—at least, that is the ostensible reason. In truth, they want me to whip up public opinion, make war acceptable to the British people and to the Empire." He removed the pipe from his mouth and regarded it intently. "Between you and me, my duties will go further. I call it 'The Great Game.' " He waved the pipe in Jack's direction. "I'm sure you can interpret what I mean."

Kipling meant a blend of espionage and diplomacy, blurring the lines of distinction between them and making full use of newspapers to sway public opinion. Jack understood that.

Kipling replaced his pipe and blew more smoke. "There. I have told you what I cannot do. It must be becoming obvious that I am outlining to you what you must do."

Jack was elated at the thought of the great Kipling turning over an assignment like this to him but he was concerned about his own assignment too. The other showed his perception again. "You can still carry on with your personal crusade. Who knows? It is not beyond reason that the Barbary Coast is the crucible where both of these plots have their evil origins."

He was studying Jack shrewdly, trying to make up his mind on some point. "Keep in touch with Ambrose. He knows I have to leave and why—that's why he sent you to me so promptly. There's a name I want to give you. He was a deputy sheriff in Dodge City, joined the Pinkertons and then spent some years as an agent for Wells Fargo. He hires out to various law-enforcement operations and he has been very useful to Ambrose and me. His name is Wesley Montague and I'll give you his address in San Francisco where he is living at present."

Kipling puffed his pipe, trying to make up his mind about something. "One other point," he said. "You live in San Francisco, you probably pick up all the gossip around the harbor . . ."

"Yes," Jack agreed.

"Have you heard talk about a freighter that docked under very mysterious circumstances recently?"

"What sort of mysterious circumstances?"

"I'm not clear—" He waved his pipe in the air. "This may be nothing. It may be some cover-up of damage to a faulty vessel, some salvage affair—I don't know."

"I don't know of anything like that," Jack told him.

"Well," Kipling said, "keep this in mind. You may run into some mention of this vessel." His eyes twinkled for a second. "I suppose all writers perk up at any happening that sounds mysterious."

He rose. "Now, let me show you around. I have a pleasant garden out in back. My wife is visiting her cousin for a few days but she'll be rejoining me tomorrow. In the meantime, I have a Mexican woman who is an excellent cook—as long as you like Mexican food. She'll prepare us some lunch and afterward, Tomasito will pick you up on his way back from the Army post."

Chapter 10

The train arrived back in San Francisco at five thirty that evening. Jack wanted to talk to Wes Montague, the lawman, as soon as possible. He figured that the ex–Wells Fargo agent would be out later in the evening, combing the bars and dance halls for gossip just as Jack himself intended to do. So this might be a good time to catch him.

Kansas Street was out near the wharf but in a reasonably respectable residential area. Dock workers would not be able to afford to live here. It probably suited clerks and foremen working at the docks and many merchant ship officers.

The houses were two stories and built in one long line from corner to corner, block after block. Stairways led from the street to the upper floor and Jack took one of them to number 110. He knocked at the door. There was no answer. He tried again with the same result.

He was about to leave, assuming that Montague was not here, when he heard a noise like a slamming door. He thought it came from inside number 110 but could not be certain. He rang the bell, and when there was no response he tried the knob. It turned, the door opened and he went in.

It was dark inside. Heavy curtains covered the windows and Jack was tempted to open them but did not. He fumbled his way through a doorway and into another room. It had a window that allowed some light, just enough that Jack could see a small table, a stove and some cupboards. An oil lamp stood on the table. Jack debated then lit it with the matches alongside it.

From the light it provided, Jack saw that there was only one other small room. It was a bedroom. A body lay there on the floor beside the bed, facedown.

It was a man and he was dead. Jack didn't recognize him. At first, that was because of his injuries; his face and head were battered. When Jack regarded him more carefully, he knew he had never seen him before. He was tall and well built and Jack supposed him to be Wesley Montague.

That noise he had heard . . . had it been a door slamming? He entered the adjoining room cautiously. It was empty, but Jack saw that a door led down to an alley at the rear. Presumably the assailant had left hurriedly on hearing the knock at the door. Or had it been one of the final blows that had killed Montague?

Jack moved the lamp closer and examined the head carefully. He had seen many dead and dying men and something bothered him about Montague's head wounds. What was it? Then it came to him—the blows had been strong and had done considerable damage but there was little blood. In particular, one blow on the bone in front of the left ear had made a deep impression but little blood dribbled from it. Jack went over the head and neck inch by inch. He was about to give up when he found it.

A tiny incision at the base of the neck, less than an inch long. It had hardly bled either, but Jack had expected that as soon as he found it. This was the cause of death—Montague had been killed with the same thin knife that had been used to kill Lola Randolph and Jenny Morris, then he had been beaten up in an attempt to hide the fact that the same person was responsible.

He listened, but could hear nothing. He went through the pockets of the dead man but found nothing to show his identity. He looked through the room. A chest at the side of the bed held only a few clothes, all men's. He moved through the rest of the small abode but Montague's possessions were scanty.

Jack took the lamp with him and went back into the room with the table and the stove. There was coffee on the shelf and some cans of food. The heel of a bread loaf was in an old tin. Montague had probably done as Jack did—eaten as much as he could of the free food in the bars and dance halls.

Jack didn't know where else to look. There seemed to be no likely hiding places, and as a lawman who worked undercover Montague was surely careful about leaving revealing papers where a thief might find them. One thing that bothered Jack was that he could find no gun. A lawman without a gun?

Jack was about to leave when he noticed the cloth covering the table. It had no meaning before but now he found it to be out of place. This was not the kind of dwelling to have a cloth on the table. Only the more luxurious homes and the better restaurants had such a thing.

The only place Jack saw them was in the concert saloons. Many had secluded alcoves where men could bring their mistresses and enjoy a clandestine supper. Every opportunity to display wealth and luxury was taken—champagne, the finest crystal and china, silver cutlery—and a sparkling white tablecloth.

This one was much bigger than the table, and Jack went to each side in turn, lifting it up until he found what he was looking for—on one side, near the edge, was embroidered a name, The Duke of York.

Jack knew it. It was not one of his favorite haunts, for the entrance fee was a quarter and the drinks were high-priced. It was reputed to have one of the best shows on the Barbary Coast and its showgirls were renowned for their beauty and appeal. They were also renowned for their sexual prowess after the show was over, and the upstairs bedrooms were said to have mirrors on the ceiling, thick carpets and magnificent four-poster beds with silk sheets.

It was possible that Wes Montague had taken one of the tablecloths after one of his visits there. The visit could have been for business or for pleasure. Yet somehow Jack thought that was a little out of character for the professional lawman. Would he be concerned about having his kitchen table covered with a cloth?

Yet Montague must have been at the Duke of York, and the cloth was not old so his visit had been recent. Jack debated whether to take the cloth but finally decided to leave it. If the police were no more diligent or successful with the solving of this murder than they had been with the murders of Lola and Jenny, the tablecloth wouldn't help them.

It was still too early to start the evening patrol of the bars and saloons. Only a few gawking out-of-towners would be there, eager to be able to describe to their neighbors back home how vile and wicked the Barbary Coast was. Few of them would be found there after midnight, when their eyes would pop out of their heads.

Jack decided to put in about three hours of writing before going out. It would not be easy to concentrate but he had learned to write on pitching schooners, in prison cells and in railroad hobo camps.

He put out the lamp and felt his way to the door. He opened it cautiously and peered both ways. No one was to be seen. He trod softly down the stairs and out onto the sidewalk. He was turning when out of the corner of his eye he caught a glimpse of movement across the street. It was on the edge of the pool of light cast by the only streetlamp. It seemed to be a dark-clad figure but he had had no opportunity to see any details. Now it was gone. He stood still and waited, his pulse throbbing.

He could be shot from across the narrow street and he was equally at the mercy of an expert knife thrower. It was not easy to remain motionless but he forced himself. Nothing moved. Two sailors, drunk already despite the early hour, came swaying and staggering into sight around the corner. Jack scrutinized them as they came closer. They could be muggers—masquerading as drunken sailors was a popular cover—but they went on by, mumbling incoherent words to one another.

Jack was watching the place across the street the whole time but still could see no one. He walked off at a fast pace with a glance over his shoulder now and then. He reached Filbert Street, where there were lights and people, and breathed a sigh of relief.

Jack had trained himself to forget all intruding elements when he wanted to write, but he was only human and the intermittent thought crept in even when he was imagining himself back in the icy hell of the Chilcoot Pass in the Klondyke. He had had frostbitten fingers and toes there and had been lucky not to lose any.

The main thought was that the killer of Lola and Jenny was also the killer of Wes Montague. That tied together his investigation of the murder of the two dance hall girls and the conspiracy that involved General Walter Williams and Collis P. Huntington—the conspiracy that both Ambrose Bierce and Rudyard Kipling believed to be monstrous. Was that too convenient?

He forced his mind back into snow drifts four feet deep and a wind that cut like a blade. Danger awaited him in the mining town ahead, but in the meantime two dogs had died and . . .

Jack's self-imposed quota was one thousand words

a day and he usually came close. Today was not one of those days though, and he reluctantly stopped at about four hundred.

When he went out, he headed for Pacific Street. He was trying to decide which dive to enter first when he was almost hit by a flying body.

"Don't come in here and try any more o' those tricks or I'll tear yer head off and feed it to my dog," snarled a big man with a massive pair of shoulders and long arms.

His victim lay twitching on the street, and the man who had thrown him there stopped and stared. "Jack, me boy! Ye're a sight for sore eyes! Is it coming in fer a drink ye are?"

The place was O'Hara's and the big Irishman who owned and ran it hired mainly Irishmen, mostly as big as himself if he could find enough of them. Jack had been in a few times but found the place a little too rough and raw for his taste. Still, he found it hard to refuse the offer and thought he might pick up some tidbits of information.

"Hello, Shaun. No, I'm not coming in if that's the way you treat your customers." The man in the street was sitting up, muttering and trying to focus his vision. He struggled to his feet and staggered back to the entrance.

Shaun Gilligan met him with a flat hand in the face that sent him lurching back across the street, where he fell into a half dozen tough-looking miners who delightedly accused him of attacking them and set about teaching him a lesson.

Shaun bellowed with laughter, grabbed Jack's arm and pulled him into O'Hara's. The place was lively. A sign over the bar read "Anything Goes," and Jack knew that O'Hara meant every letter of it. About fifty girls were employed here and they were among the most brazen women on the Barbary Coast. In many dives on the Coast, the drinks served to the waiter

girls and the female performers were innocuous, and
most of the drinks that the men bought them went
into the many big brass spittoons that were scattered
so liberally everywhere.

At O'Hara's though the girls were given real liquor,
O'Hara believing that their antics were more amusing
when drunk than when they were sober. Any of the
girls who did not respond accordingly to the liquor
would be given cantharides for stimulation. Most of
them drank beer, knowing the powerful effect of
O'Hara's rotgut whisky.

The waiter girls wore very short skirts, silk stockings
and blouses so thin they were transparent. Until a
month ago they had worn nothing above the waist,
but the police had ordered them to mend their wicked
ways in that regard. They had yielded to the law—to
the delight of the customers, who found the thin
blouses more tantalizing, particularly as they were
never buttoned.

"Time for me five-minute break," said Shaun.
"Let's have a beer."

They joined the throng at the bar, Shaun getting
preferential service. "So what are ye into now, Jack?"
he asked. "Back to yer oyster poaching?"

"No, Shaun, I'm working a personal grudge," Jack
said, half emptying his mug.

"And against who might that be? Not a friend of
mine, I hope!" He laughed at his own joke and Jack
joined him.

"I don't think so. You see, Shaun, I knew the two
girls who were killed."

"Which ones?" asked Shaun. It was a reasonable
question. Murder in a variety of forms was an every-
day part of life on the Barbary Coast and it was difficult to keep up with all the victims.

When Jack explained that he meant Lola Randolph
and Jenny Morris, Shaun became solicitous. Two girls
being murdered had no significance for him, but when

he heard that they had both been showgirls he was sentimental in the traditional Irish manner. These girls were considered by those who worked on the Coast as "their own," and they were fiercely condemning of those responsible.

Jack explained that he was angry at the police for not doing enough to find the killers of the two girls, and as he knew many people and places in the Devil's Acre, he was taking a personal interest.

" 'Tis a good lad ye are, Jack," Shaun said. "Are ye having any luck?"

"Do you know Spike Odlum?"

"Aye, he comes in here once in a while." His face tightened. "Is he mixed up in this?"

"I don't know, but he may know something that would help."

"He's a bad character," said Shaun, shaking his head. "Knocked one of our girls about once."

"Let me know if he shows his face in here again, would you? I'd like to talk to him."

"That I will, that I will." Shaun was enthusiastic about the idea. "If you need any help persuading him to tell you what he knows, I'm yer man."

Jack bought Shaun another beer, then despite the pleading of a pretty waiter girl who could not have been more than sixteen to take him upstairs, he left and headed down Vallejo Street toward the Duke of York.

Chapter 11

The Duke of York was one of the most popular resorts ever operated on the Barbary Coast. It was the favorite haunt of the young bloods of the town whenever they wanted to see life in the raw—or at least what they regarded to be life in the raw. No sailor, American or foreign, considered his shore leave to be complete unless it included a visit to the Duke of York. It was usually their first night ashore, they had their pay in their pockets—and it needed a full pay packet to whore and gamble in the Duke of York.

It had been one of the first places to be built during the Yukon gold rush in 1849. It had been destroyed six times by the great fires that devastated San Francisco during the ensuing forty years. Now it was "bigger and better than ever, more grace and beauty, replete with music and dance, bounding with fun and frolic." It was "unapproachable and beyond competition." At least that was how it was described in the dodger that was handed to Jack on the sidewalk by an elderly man with a wooden leg. Jack read the leaflet with a smile, looking through the names listed, for these often included well-known entertainers.

A show was just starting. Jack paid his twenty-five cents but the semicircular bar at the back was too crowded. A waiter girl took his arm. "There's a small table up near the stage. We usually charge a quarter for it but—"

Jack gave her a quarter and followed her past the curtained boxes surrounding the floor. Tables could accommodate from two to twenty persons. Most of them were occupied; it would be the later performances that would see them fully filled, for the shows would go on into the early hours of the morning. The waiter girl took his order for a whisky and a beer chaser and gave him an inviting smile.

A piano, a violin, a trumpet and drums formed the orchestra, which began to play with extraordinary vigor. The tune was the popular "Two Little Girls in Blue" by Charles Graham, a catchy melody. A drop curtain rose slowly. On the left side of it were paintings of satyrs chasing naked girls, and on the right side were paintings of the same satyrs catching the girls.

The stage was large and on it was a row of girls, all in virtuous, frilly blue gowns that covered the girls very completely, as was evident from the scattered and subdued clapping from the disappointed audience. All the girls were extremely attractive and spun blue parasols provocatively as they went into their dance.

Cries from the crowd urging them to raise their skirts higher were met with saucy smiles and slight shakes of the head. Their dance became more animated as they formed separate lines and wove in and out between each other. Then came disaster. Two girls collided. Both stopped dancing and mouthed wordless insults at each other. The other girls moved around them, trying to maintain their dance. The feud between the two grew more heated. Arms waved and heads jerked. Then one grabbed at the other and pulled away half of her dress. The other snatched with both hands and dragged off a skirt.

The audience was responding with laughs and shouts, urging the girls on. The other girls joined in now, their dance forgotten, taking sides with one or the other of the combatants. The orchestra played

louder, the tune now "It's Gonna Be a Hot Time in
the Old Town Tonight."

Blue garments filled the air and covered the stage.
The girls were revealed in skimpy blue undergarments,
and as the skirmish continued they started to grab at
those too. The encouragement from the crowd got
more frenzied and whistles blended unmusically with
the orchestra. The violinist appeared to be their leader
and he waved his instrument and bow in the air for
attention. The music stopped and the girls gradually
ceased struggling.

This was highly unpopular with the crowd but the
violinist rapped his bow on his music stand and waved
to the girls. They kicked the dresses into the wings,
formed two decorous lines and began to dance to the
music of "On the Sidewalks of New York."

Jack's table was only feet away from the stage and
he was enjoying the show. He looked from one girl
to the other, admiring each of them in turn. He noticed that one girl from the middle switched places
with another so that she could be at the end and close
to Jack. Her gaze met and locked with his. She was
exceptionally lovely with high cheekbones, flashing
eyes and dark hair. She had long, shapely legs and
kicked them provocatively toward Jack as the orchestra segued into "Ta-rara-boom-de-ay."

The song had originated in a saloon in St. Louis
where the girl entertainers were all colored, and when
it was sung it was usually to obscene lyrics. The audience knew it was also a dance of utter abandon and
cheered on the dancers.

The dancer nearest to Jack had an intelligent look
that was uncommon on the Barbary Coast. Most of
the women who came here did so for reasons of selling
their femininity. Intelligence, even in a better class
place like the Duke of York, was not too common.

Perhaps it was the writer in him that noticed that
intelligence, Jack thought. Until that quality caught his

attention, it had been her unusual good looks and sensual body that had drawn him.

The dance ended in a riot of flailing limbs and outthrust breasts, of darting eyes, dazzling smiles and parted red lips. The orchestra outdid itself, even managing to be heard intermittently above the roar of the crowd. Many were on their feet applauding and Jack found himself among them. The girl at the end, bosom heaving, smiled at the crowd then in Jack's direction. Or so he thought. She probably smiled that way as part of her profession.

They took two bows and the orchestra played them off with "Everybody's Sweetheart." Most of the girls exited by the side curtains. A few went into the crowd, and to Jack's astonishment the dark-haired girl at the end of the line came down the few steps at the end of the stage and walked to his table.

"Buy me a drink?" she invited. It was said with a friendly smile, quite unlike the brazen approach of the bar girls found in most of the places. Up close, she had a smooth complexion that had not yet been blemished by liquor or disease and she stood naturally, as if unaware that she was naked except for three tiny fragments of blue cloth.

"Sure," said Jack, his throat dry. She was probably three or four years older than him but Jack had known older women. None as exciting as this one though.

She was about to sit, then paused. "I have a better idea. Let's go upstairs. Perhaps we can find a quiet place."

"Okay," said Jack, hardly aware of his own voice.

She led the way up a staircase at the side of the stage. It was not well lit and Jack found himself becoming even more aroused by the flicker of bare limbs before him. A long corridor had several doors and the girl opened one of them. "In here."

Jack went in. The room contained only a bed, a rack of clothes and a couch. A kerosene lamp gave

out an orange glow. Jack heard her close the door
behind him and he turned . . . to find himself looking
at a large pistol that was aimed directly and steadily
at him.

It was like looking into the muzzle of a cannon.
Jack froze. The muzzle seemed so big that there could
be no escape from it. Wherever he moved, the pistol
would end his life.

"Why did you kill him?"

The voice that had been so inviting before was gone.
This voice was brittle as old glass. When Jack didn't
answer, she jabbed the gun at him and he flinched
instinctively.

"I didn't," he croaked.

"I saw you there," the girl said harshly.

Jack's panic was subsiding now after that first terrifying moment. He took a few seconds to gain control.

"That was you I saw across the street," he said
slowly.

She did not answer but he knew he was right. "He
was already dead when I went in," Jack went on, then
the pistol in her hand reminded him of something—
something he could use to prevent the girl from pulling the trigger. "I thought it was strange that he was
a lawman and didn't have a gun in the house." He
nodded at the weapon in her hand. "That's it. You
took it." He was recovering quickly. "You killed him."

She was breathing deeply. The emotional stress of
having a man's life depend on a squeeze of the trigger
was telling on her too. Jack concentrated on watching
her near-naked breasts heave.

"I certainly didn't kill him," she said haughtily as if
that were obvious. "So you must have," she added,
and the glint that . had been in her eyes at first
returned.

"I didn't even know him," Jack said firmly. "Was
his name Wes Montague?"

She did not appear convinced. "You know it was."

"No, I don't know that. I went there to see a man called Wes Montague. I had never met him. I found a dead body on the floor."

Jack let out a long-pent-up gasp of air. "I'm going to sit down," he told her. The pistol jerked but he ignored it, sure that there was enough uncertainty in the girl's eyes. He moved slowly over to the couch and sat, still facing her.

"How do you know he was dead unless you killed him?" Jack was determined to keep the initiative.

"I found him like that. Then the knock came at the door. I waited. It came again."

"That was me," Jack confirmed.

"I went out the back. I didn't want to be found there with his body."

"What was your interest in him?" Jack asked.

"He was my husband."

"You weren't very concerned about him, you—"

"We haven't lived together for two years."

"What's your name?" Jack asked.

She waved the pistol, making a negative gesture. "That's enough questions. Why did you want to see Wes?"

It was the query that Jack had been expecting. He still wasn't sure how he was going to answer it. His associations with the mayor, with Bierce and with Kipling could not be divulged, yet she was the one with the gun. He had kept her talking long enough that the first impulse to shoot him had passed. Perhaps there had not been such an impulse, but it would have been foolhardy to take that chance.

Jack was also aware that she was extremely desirable, the more so as she was clad only in those tiny scraps of blue material. He was conscious that his desire was apparent, which was why he had wanted to sit down.

For the first time, she seemed to feel his eyes on her body. Keeping the pistol aimed steadily at him, she reached for the rack of clothes, felt along it and pulled off a crimson robe, draping it over her shoulders.

It was not an easy maneuver with one hand. Jack could not repress a slight smile. Her body remained exposed. Angrily, she pulled the robe across.

"I want to know why you wanted to see Wes," she snapped.

"I'm investigating a certain matter," Jack said carefully. "I was told to talk to a Wes Montague as he was investigating a case that might be connected."

She tossed her head disdainfully. "Why should I believe you?"

"It's the truth," Jack said with all the candor he could muster.

"What are you investigating?"

"I can't tell you that."

"Why not?" she flared.

"It might put other lives at risk—anyway, for all I know, you killed him. Women have killed husbands before."

"That's absurd. All those blows to the head—only a man could have done that."

"Those blows didn't kill him."

Jack's matter-of-fact statement caught her unawares. "Then what did?"

"A thin-bladed knife in the throat."

He was not sure why he told her. She had probably not examined the body minutely enough to confirm the truth of what Jack said and she couldn't know that this was the same murder method used to kill Lola and Jenny. It had not been necessary so why had he told her? Was it because in addition to being extraordinarily attractive, she now had the look of a young, vulnerable girl?

He had gone this far, he might as well go a little further. Besides, she still had that pistol in her hand. The thought seemed to occur to her at the same time, or perhaps the weight of the big weapon began to tell. She walked over to the bed and sat. She rested the gun on the bed too but kept her grip on it.

"It's the same way that other murders have been committed," Jack said. "Other murders that I am helping the police solve."

She eyed him, trying to decide. "Can you prove that?"

Jack was tempted to say, "Ask the mayor," but decided against it now that the worst of this encounter was over. Asking Kipling was equally untenable.

"Yes," he temporized, "if necessary."

"What is your name?" she asked.

"Jack London."

To his surprise, she nodded. "I remember now. You looked a little familiar. You were at Berkeley University as a special student."

"You were there?"

"I was working in the office. What were you taking?"

"Writing."

"Are you still writing?" she asked.

"I came back from the Klondyke and I'm writing now, yes. Sold a story to *Overland Monthly*."

"You still write after bringing all that gold back from the Klondyke?"

"Gold?" said Jack with a laugh. "Four dollars and fifty cents worth of it, that's what I brought back."

"My name's Nancy. I go by my own name, Nancy Prescott." She looked at the big pistol by her side. "I guess I'm not going to shoot you after all."

"I'm glad," said Jack. "I haven't finished my investigation yet."

"That the only reason?"

"No. If you'd shot me, I wouldn't have had the chance to get to know you."

She pushed the gun aside, letting go of it for the first time. "Don't get any ideas. This was Wes's gun but it's mine now."

"Do you care about finding out who killed him?"

She looked away. "While he was with the Pinkertons, it was fine. But when he took that job with Wells Fargo, it took him all over the country. I wasn't ready for that—anyway, I found out that he had a woman in Carson City. We had a fight and he left. I worked at the university for a while then another girl and I had a try-out for dancing jobs. We were hired and given lessons—by a top dancer. She used to be called Little Egypt, you must have heard of her."

Jack nodded.

"She's great."

Jack nodded again.

"Then I got a chance here. The pay's better and they—well, they don't expect as much of you."

Jack knew what she meant. In some of the lower places, after the show, a girl might be expected to have intercourse with twenty or thirty men a night.

"This business about Wes—I mean, he treated me rotten but he was my husband. If I can help find out who killed him—"

"Anything you can tell me might help. For a start, what were you doing at his place? You said he'd left."

"Over a year ago. He came back to San Francisco last month. He looked me up, just for old times' sake, then he came to see me here at the Duke of York last Friday and asked me to come to his rooms. Said he had some things to give me. For safekeeping, he said."

"Couldn't he have given them to you when he visited you here?" Jack asked.

"He said it wasn't safe to be carrying them around."

"Did you find them?"

She shook her head. "There was nothing. I found him dead, looked all through the place but nothing."

She must have caught Jack's expression. She shrugged. "I hadn't seen him for over a year. We were practically strangers. It was a shock to find him dead—

killed, but then that had always been a possibility in his line of work. It may sound callous not to go rushing out for the police—"

"I understand," Jack said though he was not sure he did. "Do you know anything about the case he had been working on?" he asked.

"It was something big, very big. I don't know if this has any meaning, but Wes used some word, I forget what it was, then he said, 'That's what comes from talking with Limeys.'"

To Jack, it was confirmation that Wes Montague had been working with Rudyard Kipling, although the point had not been in doubt. "Anything else?" he asked.

"Well, he said, 'Hey, you're a California girl'—I was born in Santa Barbara—'where's Vermilion Bay?' I told him I had never heard of it."

"I'm a Californian too," Jack said. "I haven't either. Did he say why?"

"No."

"Anything else you can think of?" Jack pressed.

She thought, a finger against her lips. She made a pretty picture, thought Jack, in that crimson robe.

"Ah," she said suddenly, "he was asking me what kind of men came into the Duke of York. I said something about sailors and he said, 'Beware of any man who calls himself a captain.' He might have been joking—I thought he was at the time. But now I'm not so sure."

"I don't know either," Jack said.

"You'd better get out of here," she said, standing up. "I have another show coming up."

"Will I see you again?" Jack asked.

"Any time you want—it only costs a quarter."

"That's not what I meant, I—"

"Sure, I know what you meant. I don't know. One thing at a time."

He got up from the couch and moved toward her, but keeping a little distance between them. She reached the door first, pulled it wide open and said, "Be careful."

"You too," said Jack.

Chapter 12

Jack was busy scribbling away the next morning in his room on Sixteenth Street in Oakland. His body was there but his mind was in the Klondyke, and he was intently describing the thrill of finding the first grains of gold when there was a loud rapping at the door.

He was instantly alert. Finding Wes Montague's dead body had brought him to an unpleasant awareness of deadly and powerful forces at work in the city. Once again Ambrose Bierce's sober warnings rang alarm bells and Kipling's endorsement of them set Jack's nerves tingling.

His small room had no window out onto the street so he could not see who was there. He rarely had visitors, as his friends knew when he was writing and left him alone. He went to the door and listened. He heard the shuffling of feet. It sounded like only one person. The whinny of a horse followed. That meant a cab. He opened the door.

The driver was an older man with stooped shoulders and rheumy eyes. "You Mr. Jack London?" he wanted to know.

"I am," said Jack. Not many people called him "mister."

The other regarded him for a moment then nodded. "You look like what I was told. Mr. Townrow sent me to get you."

"Now?"

"Said I was to pick you up and take you to him. He wants to have a talk with you."

"All right," Jack said. "Just a minute." He hastily put away his papers and put on his seaman's jacket. It looked gray outside and a blustery wind was throwing sprays of fine rain.

They set off into town. The streets were active with loaded delivery carts, wagons full of produce and loaded buses. They passed city hall and to Jack's surprise, stopped in front of St. Dominic's Church.

"This is where he said to bring you," said the driver.

It was cold and damp in the church. Candles flickered and light streamed in through a large window of red, green and yellow glass. A woman in a black shawl was changing the flowers on the altar. On one side of the center aisle at the back of the church were half a dozen people. On the other side, on the back row, was one man.

Jack went and knelt alongside the solitary man.

"I would have thought you'd be on the other side, waiting for confession," Jack said in a low voice.

Ted Townrow smiled and turned to him. "If I were over there, I'd be the father confessor—yours, Jack. In fact, that's why we're talking. What do you have to tell me?"

Jack had known that Ted Townrow—and through him, the mayor—would be wanting an accounting of his activities sooner or later. He had wondered what he should say without coming to any firm conclusion.

"Nothing conclusive so far," he told Townrow. "There is one man who is known to have beaten up Jenny Morris. I finally ran him down but he disappeared and I haven't been able to find him again."

"What is his name?"

"Spike Odlum."

Townrow shook his head. The smell of incense was faint in the air. Footsteps clattered on the stone floor as a woman left the confessional.

"Doesn't mean anything. What else?"

Jack did not want to mention Kipling, who had abjured him to tell no one of their meeting. That would lead to mention of Bierce and Jack knew that his name would inflame both Townrow and the mayor. Ambrose delighted in roasting all those in public office, and from the mayor on down, all those in city hall in San Francisco were targets.

Kipling's reference to his allegiance to higher levels of government than city or state had impressed Jack immensely and he was not going to break that confidence. At the same time, his own determination to find the killer of the two showgirls was undiminished and he wanted to continue with that investigation.

"Not much. San Francisco is a big city."

"You can surely confine yourself to the Barbary Coast," retorted Townrow. "That's only a few acres."

"Maybe, but there are five thousand bars, saloons, dance halls and deadfalls in it."

Townrow knew that was true. Three thousand of them were licensed and it was estimated that at least two thousand more operated illegally. He glanced behind. A woman had entered. He watched her go to the confessional boxes and kneel outside one of them. He lowered his voice a notch further.

"There was another murder yesterday. One that may be connected."

"Another girl?"

"No, a man. A lawman called Wes Montague. Did you know him?"

"No, I didn't," Jack said truthfully. "How is his death connected?"

"He was killed with the same type of knife and in the same place, the side of the throat. The killer had beaten him about the head to try to disguise it."

"Did he have any relationship with the two girls?" Jack asked.

"Not that we've been able to find out yet. You

should keep it in mind though. You might run across his tracks."

"Is it reported in the papers?" Jack asked. "I haven't seen one this morning."

"No. It will be in tomorrow's papers but we're keeping out any mention of the cause of death."

"Who did he work for? You said he was a lawman."

"He was with the Pinkertons and then he was an investigator for Wells Fargo. He seems to have been taking individual assignments recently, made more money that way probably. We don't know yet who his clients may have been but we're working on it."

They chatted a few moments longer but neither imparted anything of further value. "We'll leave separately," Townrow said, "you go first."

Jack went out of the church into a fine drizzle of rain. Townrow could at least have provided a hack to return him to his rooms, he thought. He was wet through when he arrived back, but his condition was forgotten when he saw that the mailman had left a letter for him. It was from *The Black Cat*, an Eastern magazine to which Jack had sent a short story. How long ago had that been? So long that he had forgotten it.

After a long string of rejections, Jack was not optimistic as he tore open the envelope. The editor, a man named Umbstaetter, started the letter with "I find your story more lengthy than strengthy," but then Jack's disappointment turned to glee as he read on, "If you will give me permission to cut the four thousand words in half, I will send you a check for forty dollars."

Forty dollars! That was double the figure he had expected. He sat down, bursting with excitement, and wrote Umbstaetter a letter accepting his offer. The fine rain had stopped when he went outside. He ignored his damp clothing and hurried to the post office on Folsom Street.

He felt a glow of satisfaction when he came down the steps after mailing the letter. Forty dollars plus the twenty or so left from his prizefighting winnings meant that he was in the best financial shape since he had come back from the Klondyke. The first thing he could do was get his bicycle out of hock. That would make getting around the city easier. He would be able to pay off the grocer to whom he owed money and rent a typewriter. Life was good!

He had not forgotten his assignment though. He would be able to write with greater confidence after the offer from *The Black Cat,* but he was fiercely determined to pursue his investigations. He even had an acquaintanceship with the great Rudyard Kipling to drop into conversation—but only after this business was concluded, he reminded himself sternly.

At the public library, the librarian, Ina Coolbrith, was well known to Jack, as he had spent so many hours there after dropping out of university. She knew him to be interested in a wide variety of subjects, so when he came in asking for the section containing maps of California, she was not in the least surprised.

After almost an hour of fruitless searching though, even the resourceful Miss Coolbrith had to admit defeat.

"Are you sure it's in California?" She repeated the question and Jack said again he believed it was

"You're sure of the spelling?" she persisted.

"I heard it spoken, I haven't seen it written," said Jack, but he spelled out the name of Vermilion Bay.

"Well," said Miss Coolbrith, "it's not a name that's on any of our maps."

When Jack left, he had no idea of where it might be located or what the significance of the name might be. He went back to his rooms and began polishing and revising the Klondyke story.

*   *   *

The evening found Jack in the Midway Plaisance once again. The baskets of food on the bar offered some different delicacies tonight in the shape of slices of turkey and nuggets of roast pork. Andy, the barkeep, brought Jack a beer. Jack was about to order a whisky with it but cautioned himself not to spend money before he received it. He did not know how long it might be before he saw the forty dollars from *The Black Cat.*

"Is Flo in tonight?" Jack asked.

"No. Having a day off. Went down to Monterey, or so I hear."

It was still quiet. A group of men walked across the floor to the stairway at the end that Jack knew went up to the gambling rooms above. Only seven or eight tables were occupied with more or less well-behaved customers.

"How about Fritz?"

"In back, talking—about a show for next month."

Jack drank his beer and ordered another. A couple more tables were taken and a few more hopeful gamblers went upstairs. Across the floor, Jack saw Fritz approaching. With him was a chubby man with a fat, well-fed face who was waving his arms, smoking a big cigar and talking animatedly. Fritz caught sight of Jack and grabbed the other man, bringing him to the bar.

"This is Jack London," Fritz said, his Teutonic accent very evident. "He's a writer. Jack, meet Oscar Hammerstein, he's putting on a show for us next month."

"Oy, oy!" wailed Hammerstein, shaking Jack's hand, "next month, would you believe! I get three months in New York to put on a show—Fritz wants it next month."

"It's going to be a great show," said Fritz, rolling right over Hammerstein's finishing words. "Best we've ever put on. Oscar, did you know we have more theaters in San Francisco now than any other city in the whole United States?"

"Does New York know about this?" demanded Hammerstein.

"Sure they know. They're furious! And they'll be even more furious when they find out that you're going to put on a better show here than you ever did there!"

Hammerstein grunted noncommittally. "Next month!" he grumbled. "Next month already!" He turned to Jack. "A writer? Did Fritz say you're a writer? What do you write? Books?"

"I just sold another one today," Jack said, too pleased with his day's success to bother correcting the impresario.

Hammerstein took the cigar out of his mouth and regarded him with increased interest. "Is that right? You live here?"

"I sure do."

"Where do you sell?"

"New York," said Jack.

Fritz was looking from one to the other. "Hey, Oscar, maybe—"

"Sure, sure." Hammerstein waved him off. "I'm way ahead of you." To Jack, he said, "How about writing for me? A few sketches, funny—you know, girls and—"

Jack grinned. "I appreciate the invitation, Mr. Hammerstein, but I'm pretty tied up right now."

Hammerstein jerked an angry thumb at Fritz. "This knucklehead wants a show next month. He doesn't know how long it takes to put a show together. I need girls, I need comedy acts, I need music—and I need material. You don't want to write material for me?"

"I'd like to, really I would," Jack said, apologetically. "I just can't right now." Why couldn't this have come at some other time? he was thinking.

The impresario took another puff. "How much they pay you, those people in New York?"

"They pay me pretty well," Jack said. "In fact, they just doubled my price." He found no need to say that the increase had been accomplished by cutting the number of words in half.

"H'm," murmured Hammerstein, "they pay you double, eh? Maybe you and me should talk about this."

Fritz was leaning back against the bar, out of the line of Hammerstein's sight. He was frantically nodding and making expressions to Jack to agree.

"Sorry, Mr. Hammerstein. Some other time maybe but not just now."

"Look," Fritz said, "no need to decide on the spot. Let me get you two together again. I'm sure we can work out some deal."

"Sure, sure," agreed Hammerstein.

"Maybe," said Jack, thinking that despite his new-found wealth, it might be well to keep open such a promising opportunity as this. "Let me see what my publisher says."

"Great, great," Hammerstein said. "Now I gotta go. See you around."

They parted on good terms, all three convinced that they had won their point.

When Hammerstein had gone, Fritz insisted on buying Jack a whisky, happy in his conviction that the show would be able to open on time. The two talked about shows that Fritz had put on recently, with the saloon owner emphasizing how popular they had been so as to ensnare Jack more completely. This suited Jack, who wanted to maneuver the conversation in that direction.

"You having trouble getting girls?" Jack asked innocently.

"Not me," Fritz said emphatically. "I pay top dollar.

Get some of the best girls on the Coast." He winked. "When I say 'best,' you know what I mean."

"I thought it might be a problem, that's all."

"Problem? No, not for me." Fritz signaled for two more drinks. He frowned. "Why a problem?"

"After the murder of one of your girls, Jenny Morris."

Fritz sighed. "Poor Jenny. Tough business, that. She was a good dancer, learned fast. Made good money—for me and herself."

"Where had she worked before?" Jack asked as the barkeep brought them the drinks.

"She said she came to San Francisco from Laramie. She came for a job and I gave it to her. Before Laramie, I don't know."

Jack drank some beer. Flo had told him that Jenny came from Dawson, Alaska, after saying she was from Butte, Montana. Why these different stories? Perhaps it didn't matter, it could be a lapse of memory on the part of either of them, or perhaps Jenny had something to hide. Still, he had so little to go on that any point was worth examination.

"You knew her, didn't you, Jack?"

"A little," Jack admitted. "I didn't know she had been in Laramie though. I mentioned once that I had been through there and she didn't say anything. The police have talked to you about her, I suppose."

"Pooh!" Fritz's expression was enough without the words. "Police! They'll never find out anything."

"Then the murder of Lola Randolph over at the Cobweb," Jack went on. "Only a few days earlier. They don't seem to have found out about that either."

"They won't!" Fritz was vehement. "Saloon girls aren't important enough. Now if it was one of the Spreckels girls or one of Judge Hebard's daughters—then they'd be rousting out every man on the Coast!"

They talked a while longer, then Fritz banged his empty glass on the bar. "Getting near showtime. I have to get my whip out and see everybody's getting ready."

"I have to go too," said Jack, finishing his beer.

Fritz put a hand on his shoulder. "You think about that, eh? Writing sketches for Oscar? You'd be good at that."

"I'll think about it," Jack promised.

Chapter 13

What was the mystery involving the two girls? Whatever it was, it had got them killed. Jack suspected that Ted Townrow knew a whole lot more than he had told him. That might mean that the mayor was involved too.

He reached the end of speculation and took out his notes. Returning to the icy wilderness of the Alaskan mountains temporarily drove out all other thoughts and he wrote until well after midnight.

Perhaps his experience had left a deeper imprint on his mind than he thought, but the next morning when he read what he had written the night before, he was not happy with it at all. He crossed most of it out. Was his sudden success in selling a story to *The Black Cat* making him dissatisfied? Or were his standards rising? He hoped it was the latter, and the more he thought about it the more he decided that was the case. Now that he knew he could write at the quality level demanded by top magazines, he knew he had to write better—and better.

He spent most of the rest of the day rewriting and revising. When he stopped, he was more pleased with his day's work. He got dressed to go out and renew his investigation.

On Mason Street, Jack went into the Golden Slippers. This establishment had previously been located in Sydney-Town, the area along the waterfront and

running up the slopes of Telegraph Hill, so named
because it was the haunt of escaped convicts and
ticket-of-leave men from the British penal settlements
at Sydney in New South Wales. It had burned down
after one particularly destructive riot and its owner
had bought another place on Mason Street and given
it the same name, although it had now acquired the
popular nickname of the Golden Knickers.

The owner was Manassas Mike, who now lived in
a fine house in Carmel and spent little time in the
saloon. In his absence, the staff appropriated what
they considered an extra share of the intake. Mike
knew it and fired one periodically as a lesson to the
others, but he had made plenty of money in his time.
Now, he was one of the rare ones—he preferred to
live a life of ease in Carmel on less income rather
than endure the stress of being present in a saloon on
the Barbary Coast on much more.

Jack's acquaintances there were the manager, a
Chilean called Eduardo, and two of the pretty waiter
girls. The costume of these consisted of very short red
jackets, black stockings, fancy garters and red slippers.
Variations on this outfit could be found in many places
on the Barbary Coast but it had originated here and
had been a spectacular and immediate success.

The clientele was of a lower order than the Midway
or the Cobweb and consisted of more miners, dock-
workers and sailors. Jack ordered a beer, and a few
minutes later Tessie came over to slap him on the
back.

She was blonde and with a pretty face that had once
been ingenuous. It had led her into a life that had
included some time on the stage, where her lack of
any ability to sing or dance had been overcome by a
willingness to display her physical attributes without
the least reticence. A fall while drunk had broken her
ankle and ended her stage career. She had taken to

waiting on tables, and though one foot dragged she was nimble and hard-working.

"Jack, me boy, it's great to see you!"

"You too, Tessie. Prettier than ever."

She smiled. She never knew whether he meant such compliments or whether he was being kind but she loved to hear them and no longer wondered.

They talked about common acquaintances, who had gone where, some who had left the Barbary Coast altogether and a few who had died.

"Got another new stage manager," Tessie told Jack. He was not surprised. In Manassas Mike's absence, it was an unenviable job.

"Eduardo is still running everything else except the shows?"

Tessie nodded. "He keeps talking about quitting and opening his own place but he's still here."

"Business still good?" asked Jack casually.

"Sure. It's early, be crowded in a while."

"I just wondered if the deaths of Lola Randolph and Jenny Morris had made any difference."

Eduardo drifted over to them just as Jack made the comment. Swarthy and with a lean face and a trim black mustache, Eduardo looked like a Latin gang member but Jack had always found him to be friendly and more honest than most.

"Police find nothing about those two girls, huh?" asked Eduardo.

"What do you think?" said Jack contemptuously "They couldn't find their nose with both hands. I'd like to get hold of whoever killed them," he went on, taking the opportunity to establish support for his role in asking questions. "They'd never see the inside of a jail."

Jack had first owned a gun at the age of thirteen and all on the Coast who knew him did not doubt that he had used it and every other weapon he had owned since. He was also known for his boxing skills and he had done some fencing. His reputation was perhaps a little more fearsome than the reality but this was another chance to expand it.

Eduardo nodded approvingly. Tessie said, "Good for you, Jack. Somebody should do something."

"You knew Lola, didn't you, Tess?"

"She worked here for a short time."

"On the stage," added Eduardo.

"Any of the girls still here know her?"

"One of them seemed to know her," Tessie said. "It was when they found Lola—dead," she added with a shudder. "Can't remember who it was though."

"When's the show come on tonight?" Jack asked.

"About half an hour," Eduardo told him. "Going to wait?"

"I might," said Jack.

A raucous voice was demanding table service and Tessie left. Eduardo went to pour whisky for a group of college boys having a night out. Jack noticed that he overcharged them. Eduardo might be fairly honest but he was not above making a little extra, as did all of them in Mike's absence.

Tables were filling as showtime neared. The bar became crowded. Suddenly, shouting could be heard over the regular noise of the saloon. A young man with untidy hair and carrying a sandwich board advertising a show at one of the music halls burst in the door. At first, his cries were unintelligible, then as the nearby tables quieted the words dropped like ice cubes.

Eduardo stared at him in alarm and his gaze fell on Jack, farther down the bar. He waved urgently and Jack put down his mug and went to join him. The two pushed through the crowd toward the young man and his words stopped them in mid-stride.

"Down the street—the Yellow Canary—girl murdered!"

Jack was out of the door in a flash and running

down the street. It was as busy as usual with people seemingly oblivious to the disaster that had struck. Some of the small groups might have been talking about it, but death was a regular visitor to the Barbary Coast, and as Jack burst in the door of the Yellow Canary nothing appeared too different there either. No music could be heard but card games were continuing at most of the tables and smoke clouds billowed over each one.

"In here," came a call, and Jack went into a tiny dressing room behind the stage. It was crammed with clothes, but reflected in the dressing mirror was the body of a girl wearing only part of a white-feathered costume.

Jack turned to see her half lying across a chair. He took her wrist. Her flesh was warm but there was no pulse. Several slashes of a blade had left blood seeping from cuts, but the expression on the girl's face was surprise rather than terror.

A man forced his way into the room. He was big and fat with a mean-tempered face. "What's happening? What is—?" he started to shout. He stopped as he saw the body.

Girls were peering in curiously. Bolder ones were sidling in the doorway. Noises came from outside, where a few members of the audience were anxious to see the cause of all the commotion.

"Keep everybody out of here!" Jack said swiftly.

The man who had just entered started to bluster. "Who are you?" he asked. "Why are you giving orders?"

"Do as I say," snapped Jack.

"I'm stage manager here and I—"

"Keep—everybody—out!" Jack's voice cracked like a whip. The other gave one more frightened look at the body and went out. One of the girls standing in the doorway came in.

Jack turned the dead girl's head to one side.

"It's Hannah Green," the other said in hushed tones.

Hannah had been a pretty girl despite a hard cast to her features. She had a shapely body and long dancer's legs, as revealed by the partial costume.

"Is she dead?" The girl's question was understandable, for the cuts did not look serious, but Jack had knowledge that she did not. He turned her head slightly to the other side and saw what he was looking for—the same tiny incision that had killed Wes Montague and Lola and Jenny.

There was a rapping at the door.

"It's me, it's Tessie! I have something to tell you."

Jack went to the door and opened it just enough for Tessie to squeeze in. Beyond her, he could see faces and figures struggling to see into the dressing room.

Tessie's eyes widened as she stared at the corpse.

"They said it was Hannah." She stifled a sob. "That's what I came to tell you. I couldn't remember before who it was who had come to the Yellow Canary at the same time as Lola Randolph—it was Hannah."

Chapter 14

It was half an hour before the police arrived. Captain Patrick O'Donnell scowled when he saw Jack but Jack knew one of O'Donnell's men, Constable Neill. He greeted Jack as an old friend and immediately referred to their association when Jack had been a law officer with the Fish Patrol. That got him past O'Donnell's questions about Jack being the first to examine the body. Jack was forthright without being forthcoming. He volunteered nothing but answered all the captain's questions briefly. To his surprise, the police captain did not persist, nor did he seem too aggressive. Jack wondered if he had been briefed by the mayor's office on Jack's unofficial role but decided it was unlikely.

When Hannah Green's body had been taken away to the morgue, some measure of normalcy returned. It was obvious to Jack, as it must have been to the police, that the murderer had left the Yellow Canary as soon as he had committed the crime, certainly before Hannah's body was found and probably before the alarm went out.

Jack left even as the orchestra began to play and the music hall resumed its nightly routine. He had lost his taste for saloons and bars and went home to an unusually early bed.

He did not sleep well. Dreams of a disembodied hand with a knife woke him more than once. He rose early, drank some strong tea, dressed and went out.

His first destination was Washington Street in Oakland. At number 862 was Treager's Loan Office, always open early. Through the slot under the steel mesh window, he handed over his ticket, number 1037. He marveled at the array of musical instruments, toys, ornaments, rings, watches and many other objects, some of obvious personal value only. Still, Lou Treager loaned money on anything. Jack noticed a couple of typewriters. They looked old but he resolved to come back at a later date to look at them. He had a thrifty streak that rebelled against buying a new one if he could find a serviceable used machine.

"Rambler bicycle." Lou Treager read the ticket and looked at Jack. "I remember you. This'll cost you five dollars for the loan plus interest—that's a total of, let me see . . ."

"I have the money," Jack said and paid him.

"Bike's in the back. Takes up too much room in the shop. Come to the back door."

He rode proudly down Washington Street and turned on Eighth Avenue. At the ferry, he bought a ticket and wheeled his bike on board. From the ferry building in San Francisco, he rode to the *Examiner* building.

A receptionist did not want to let him in to see Bierce, a little alarmed at Jack's dark blue seaman's sweater and wrinkled pants, but his cheery smile and his confident declaration that he had a vital news item for Bierce got him through.

He was shown into an office with glass-paneled walls from chest height up. From it, Bierce could see every desk in the large outer office, where men pounded typewriters, smoke wreathed the air and young boys hurried with stacks of paper and folders.

"I don't like being disturbed at the office," Bierce rapped. His desk was tidy and racks of shelves were piled with books and newspapers.

"I know it," Jack rapped back, "and I don't like these girls being murdered."

Bierce gave him an irritated glare. "I don't know if it's you who has been stirring things up but a lot has been happening. Another girl murdered. . . ."

"I was there."

Jack's simple statement surprised him. "You were?"

"Shall I start at the beginning?" asked Jack. "When you told me to go talk to Kipling?"

Bierce nodded. "All right."

Jack gave him a review of the conversation in the farmhouse in San Sebastiano. At the end, Jack added, "He told me to keep in touch with you. So I'm here." At times, Bierce's irascible, constantly critical attitude annoyed him, but he forced himself to be calm.

Bierce must have realized it. He nodded, almost affably. "Ruddy told me he was expecting to be sent to South Africa but he didn't think it would be this soon." He grinned. "'The Great Game,' did he tell you that's what he calls it? Well, he's going to one great game in Africa but he's certainly leaving us with another great game right here."

Jack was still irritated, though he was getting it under control. "You say he's leaving 'us'—you mean me, don't you? You have a newspaper to run."

"Don't try to goad me, Jack," Bierce said equably. "I'm too good at goading, I can spot it easily in others. You're right, I do have a newspaper to run and I intend to keep running it. It's where I make my best contribution. You don't think I should spend my nights going from bar to bar, do you? That's your contribution."

"All right, Ambrose, I'll keep up the drinking if you really insist. But I hope you won't refer to this business as a 'game' in your column. These are girls' lives we're talking about."

Bierce nodded somberly. "You're right. I was forgetting that you know many of these girls." He switched the subject adroitly. "I suppose you thought you were going to have a partner in Wes Montague?"

"You know about him? Yes, of course you do, you're in the newspaper business. Was Montague working for you and Kipling?"

"He passed on some very useful information to Ruddy," said Bierce. "Who killed Montague?"

"I don't know," said Jack.

Bierce gave a short, sardonic laugh. "Put together what we both know and what do you have? Zero." He drummed fingers on his desk. "This girl last night, tell me about her."

"Hannah Green."

"Yes, well—"

"That is her name," said Jack, getting a little testy again at the memory of the previous night. "She was a human being—like Lola Randolph and Jenny Morris. They aren't just names in your newspaper. Hannah was killed—just like the others."

Bierce darted him a sharp look. "Was she? Just like the others?"

Jack realized his near mistake. He was not supposed to know how the others died and that it was by the same method. But did Bierce know that too? Jack felt guilty at the thought that while working with Bierce he was keeping information from him. Then he reflected that while he had not mentioned the murder method to Bierce, Bierce had not told him either. Did he know? Jack wondered. Jack consoled himself with the reminder that, after all, the mayor had sworn him to secrecy. He had to respect that.

He covered his error as best he could. "Yes, all three were killed and all were showgirls. It looks like some kind of a pattern."

"Seems probable. What's the link?"

"That's what I'm working on. I'm going to talk again to Wes Montague's widow. She may know something."

"You've talked to her already?"

"Yes."

"Good. That's fast work. When you follow up on this Hannah Green's murder, maybe you'll learn more." He threw an appraising look at the young man before him. "I wouldn't have believed it but you may uncover some of this business after all."

Jack grinned. "I appreciate your confidence in me, Ambrose. Tell me—haven't you and Kipling picked up any hint as to just what the intentions of the Big Three might be?"

"First, let me tell you this. Collis Huntington is the most dangerous man of them all. *The Arabian Nights* told of the forty thieves. Well, Huntington is thirty-six of them. He has one leg in the grave, one hand in the treasury and one eye on the police. When it was the original Big Four, Mark Hopkins was the yes-man, Leland Stanford was the greediest of the lot and Charles Crocker was the big fixer.

"But it was always Huntington who was—and still is—the dominator, the leader." Bierce went on with a distant look in his eye. "No more major railroads are being built. So the Big Three need other areas for their expansion."

"What areas could require the killing of saloon girls?"

"You should be ashamed," said Bierce solemnly. "A young, idealistic man like you, suggesting that one of our upright, honest, political leaders would stoop to unlawful perhaps even criminal endeavors."

They both laughed. A knock came at the door and it opened. A man came in. He had slick black hair, a broad smooth face. He looked from Jack to Bierce, and the editor greeted him with a handshake.

"We're just finishing up here—you're right on time for our appointment." To Jack, he said, "This is Carl Heindell, the deputy mayor. He's about to tell me the building plans of the city commission. Carl, this is Jack

London—you may have heard of him, one of our city's most promising young writers."

Heindell had a firm handgrip and he looked Jack in the eye. "A writer, eh? What do you write? Political comment for Ambrose here?"

Bierce let out a guffaw. "He'd better not—he's a socialist, Carl. Still, don't worry, I wouldn't print it anyway. No, he writes adventure stories about the Yukon."

"Really?" Heindell turned his attention back to Jack. "Been up there, have you?"

Jack gave him a brief account of his unsuccessful search for gold. Heindell looked sympathetic. "Have I read any of your stories?" he asked.

"They've been in *Black Cat, Overland Monthly* and *Atlantic.*"

"I probably have read some of them," Heindell said. "Tell me, do you make a living this way or do you have another job?"

Had the mayor told his deputy that he had unofficially hired Jack? Had the mayor or Townrow told anyone? Or was something else behind the question?

"I do a few jobs here and there when I have to," said Jack. "But I'm having more and more success in selling stories now."

They chatted for a while longer and again the same question crossed Jack's mind. Meanwhile, Bierce was drumming his fingers impatiently on his desk, although the deputy mayor ignored him.

Finally, Bierce said, "Well, Carl, I'm sure you want to tell me of the city plans for expansion and I certainly want to hear them."

Heindell smiled. "All right, Ambrose. Good luck with your writing, young man. This city has some fine writers already—you sound to me like you're soon going to join their number."

*   *   *

Enjoying being on his Rambler bicycle once again, Jack swerved nimbly through the traffic and left his steed in front of the Yellow Canary. Outwardly, there was no sign of the previous night's terrible occurrence. Even inside, only one constable was to be seen. He was interrogating the members of the orchestra, and as far as Jack could hear he was asking them if they had seen or heard anyone last night who might be involved in the murder. It appeared to be bringing no results but Jack was pleased to see that the police were making some efforts. Much criticism was heard of their apathy when the victim of a murder was "only" a dance hall girl.

As Jack had hoped, the showgirls were rehearsing new numbers. The audiences at the Yellow Canary, like other similar places, became rapidly dissatisfied when a show or even a number was repeated. They demanded fresh material continually and the places that brought in the most customers were often those that changed their show frequently.

While a line of girls practiced a dance, others sat at the tables by the stage, resting or waiting their turn. Jack scanned the faces of the girls, finally finding one he knew.

"Hello, Dinah," he said, joining her at her table. "Didn't know you were here. Got tired of the Eureka?"

Dinah was a Southern girl with dark hair and dark eyes. Her strong Georgia accent was unaffected by her time on the Coast and her musical voice was a further asset in addition to an attractive body that she could use to devastating effect.

"That's about it. Good to move around," she said. She looked sad. "Isn't this dreadful?—about Hannah, I mean."

She had saved Jack the task of bringing up the subject. He nodded. "Did you know her well?"

"We were good friends. Some of the girls didn't like her but I did."

Jack understood that. Dinah liked everybody. "Had she been here long?"

"Only a few weeks. I helped her find a place to live when she arrived. She really needed help—she was in a terrible state at first, she'd been seasick for days."

"Do you remember when that was exactly?"

He was surprised when she nodded. "She arrived on April first. It was my birthday," she added with a smile.

"Where did she work before?"

Dinah was an uncomplicated girl and not used to subterfuge. Jack saw her hesitate and knew she was concealing something. He took her hand. "Dinah, she was murdered. Now I don't want you to tell anyone this but I'm trying to find out about these murders."

She looked at him with wide, trusting eyes.

"You mean Lola Randolph and Jenny Morris too?"

"Yes."

"Are they all something to do with each other?"

"That's what I'm trying to find out. Do you know where Hannah came from? Can you tell me?"

She looked at him doubtfully but then made up her mind. "She told people she had worked in Amarillo but she once told me that she really came from—"

"Go on, Dinah."

"She really came from Dawson, Alaska."

Jack nodded. "Go on."

"She said she hit a man over the head with a bottle in Dawson. He died. She decided to say she was from Amarillo in case they tried to trace her."

Here was another girl hiding the fact that she had come from Alaska. "She have any special men friends here on the Coast?" Jack asked.

"Not that I know of," Dinah said. "She was—well, not easy to get along with."

Jack asked further questions but no more useful information came out. "Have the police talked to you girls?" he asked.

"Yes. None of the girls really had anything to tell them though."

"How about you?"

"No," said Dinah. "Oh, I suppose it couldn't matter now. I mean, what if she had accidentally killed a man in Alaska. It couldn't matter now she's dead, could it?" A tear began to well in the corner of one eye.

"No, it couldn't matter," said Jack softly. "But it's better you didn't tell them. Don't tell anyone."

She nodded and sniffed.

Jack had a feeling that some meaning was here. Perhaps it was merely a girl lying to protect herself from her past, which was quite understandable. Or was there more? He recalled talking to Meg Ballantine at the Cobweb Palace. He had been asking her about Lola Randolph. There had been some element in his conversation with Meg that had bothered him. What was it?

Meg had said that Lola had described herself as having come from Kansas City. Meg had gone on to add that another girl, also from Kansas City, had asked Lola about it and Lola had apparently not been familiar with it. Had Lola been lying too?

Perhaps he was missing something here, Jack thought. Such girls could live in a city and in their line of work not know the city well. Was that all it was? Or did they all have something to hide? As he had agreed with Ambrose Bierce, their sum total of knowledge in this whole affair was not much more than zero. Any possibility was worth tracking down.

He gave Dinah a kiss on the cheek and was rewarded with a ghost of a smile. He went to his bicycle and rode the short distance to the Cobweb Palace. He was fortunate there. They were not rehearsing a new show but they were getting rid of old costumes and making room for new ones. Meg Ballantine had another job besides a singer and dancer—she was the assistant wardrobe mistress, and so she was there, arguing with an older woman.

The usual few hard drinkers were present. Jack was glad he had reformed, for he had been close to being a drunk in earlier years. John Barleycorn still sat on his shoulders, he was inclined to say, but he had learned to ignore him. He still drank but rigidly limited his intake.

Jack waited until Meg was free, then he called her over and they sat at an empty table. He reminded her of their earlier conversation about Lola.

Meg nodded. "Of course I remember."

"Did you ever have a suspicion that Lola did not come here from Kansas City at all?"

Meg's pretty face did not change. "Why should I?"

Jack reminded her of what he had told her before—that he wanted to find Lola's killer. The police were doing nothing, he said. He was determined to try at least.

"Meg, do you recall any tiny thing that might tell us where she worked before she came here?"

Meg's soft eyes searched his. "How did you know?" she whispered.

Jack leaned forward. "What? What was it, Meg?"

She shook her head.

"I hate to say this, Meg, but these killings may not be over. You don't want to see any more girls murdered, do you?"

She looked away. Jack remembered the words from his conversation with Dinah at the Yellow Canary. "After all, whatever it is, it can't hurt Lola now—and it might save the life of another girl."

"I suppose so. . . . Well, when Lola first came here, I helped her sort out her clothes. She had thick, heavy things. I told her she didn't need clothes like that in San Francisco. She said without thinking, 'I needed these in—' I waited but she didn't go on. I said,

'Surely not in Kansas City!' She said, 'No, not in Kansas City'—but she didn't say where."

"Were they the kind of clothes she might have worn in Alaska?" asked Jack.

"Somewhere very cold," Meg agreed quietly.

"One other point. Do you recall when she arrived on the Coast?"

She wrinkled her brow. "Must have been early April, the beginning—"

"Could it have been the first?"

She thought. "I think so, yes."

Chapter 15

Jack received a surprise as he entered the Midway Plaisance. Little Egypt was in the middle of the stage talking to a priest.

Flo, as Jack knew her, was wearing a tight one-piece garment in a silvery gray color. It fit her beautifully proportioned body perfectly. Her legs were bare and she wore ballet slippers. Her silky black hair was swept back and fastened behind her head.

The man with her looked weary and disheveled. As he talked with a New York accent, he kept running a hand through his unruly hair. Each time, it promptly returned to its previous disordered state. He was a most unusual figure to be found on a dance hall stage in the Devil's Acre. He was clad in a Prince Albert coat, a black waistcoat with shiny buttons, ill-fitting baggy black trousers, pointed high-button shoes, a stand-up collar and a Stanley necktie. Jack thought he resembled an eccentric clergyman caught in some illicit activity.

As soon as Flo saw Jack, she waved excitedly for him to join them on the stage. He did so and the man examined him critically, not too happy at being interrupted.

"This is Jack London, the writer," said Flo. "Jack, meet David Belasco. David's bringing *Floradora* here from New York."

"It was a tremendous success in London. New York

loved it. Now I'm bringing it to the West Coast." Belasco's New York accent sounded even stronger now.

Jack had heard of Belasco, one of the greatest of the impresarios in the theater business. "The Bishop of Broadway" they called him, and Jack had to admit to himself that he could see why. The bizarre outfit would raise eyebrows anywhere—except perhaps in a cathedral.

"I was born here in San Francisco," Belasco was telling them both. "I've always wanted to bring a really great Broadway show to my hometown. Now I'm going to do it."

"Didn't you say you might get Lillian Russell?" asked Flo.

"She's interested, very interested," said Belasco. His features were rough-hewn and Jack supposed women found him romantic in a virile, coarse way. Jack remembered that he had played in *The Corsican Brothers* and that it had been an immense hit. Jack couldn't recall any of his other roles, but in any case, he knew that Belasco had given up acting in favor of producing.

A drunk had wandered in and was standing swaying in front of the stage. The strange figure up there seemed to fascinate him. He stared, hiccuping. Flo stood with her hands on her hips, a little annoyed at the interest the "Bishop" was getting, even if it was from a drunk. She was used to being the center of goggle-eyed attention when she was on the stage.

Jack went to the edge of the stage and spoke quietly to the drunk, who smiled vacantly and made his unsteady way to the bar.

Belasco took out a large gold watch from his waistcoat pocket and consulted it. "I have a lunch appointment at the Pacific Union Club. I hope you'll excuse me." To Flo, he said, "Perhaps we can continue later." Jack caught Flo's petulant nod. The Pacific Union Club was for men only. She had probably expected that Belasco would take her to one of San Francisco's best restaurants.

"You're going to do the choreography for him, I guess," Jack said to Flo after Belasco had gone. "Big job. That *Floradora* is a huge hit, they say."

Flo seldom remained upset for more than a few minutes, and Jack's words cheered her. "It's a great chance for me," she agreed and her lovely smile returned.

"Are you still investigating, Jack?"

He nodded. "Certainly am."

"Hannah Green now." Her words were heavy.

"Yes—and there may be more."

Flo's hand went to her mouth. "Oh, no, not more!"

"Can we sit down?" Jack asked. "I want to ask you a couple of questions."

They sat at a table far from the bar. A Chinese was mopping the floor. They watched him finish and leave.

"Jenny Morris," said Jack. "When she came to the Midway, was this her first job on the Coast?"

"Yes, it was."

"Didn't you say she arrived about two months ago?"

"About that. Might have been less."

"Could you be exact?"

Jack's question made her frown. "I'm not sure—wait a minute, Educated Edith will know. She's here, I saw her earlier working on the books."

Educated Edith was a tall girl with glasses and short straight hair. "Edith used to be a dancer," said Flo, bringing her from the backstage area and introducing her. Jack could see that she had the figure and, with makeup and without the glasses, would be quite pretty. "She had a good education though," Flo went on, "and decided she could make more money keeping books than dancing."

When Edith heard from Flo that Jack was a writer, she would have done anything to help him. "Have you read Spencer?" she asked eagerly. "I just love him. What about Huxley?"

"Two of my favorite writers," Jack said. "Then there's Darwin—"

"Aren't his theories marvelous? I think—"

Flo was observing all this with a smile of wry amusement. "Edith—could you hold your book-club meeting some other time? Jack has an important question to ask you."

When Edith heard that Jack was investigating the murders of the three girls, she immediately swore herself to secrecy. "What do you want to know?" she asked.

"Do you know the exact date that Jenny Morris started to work at the Midway?" Jack asked.

"Of course," Edith said without hesitation. "It was April first."

"Bull's-eye!" Jack said and slapped the table.

Flo was looking at Edith in undisguised admiration. "How do you remember the exact date?"

"I was going on a picnic with Harry, who I had just met. Jenny came in, said she had been hired. I had to help her get settled and it made me late getting away to meet Harry."

"But how do you remember the date?"

Edith pushed up her glasses primly. "Well, because it was the first time Harry and I—"

"I see," Flo said quickly.

"Poor Jenny, she was in a bad way."

"What do you mean?" Flo asked.

"She was still seasick. Apparently they had some very bad weather and she had come straight off the boat."

Jack leaned forward eagerly. "From where? Did she say?"

"Seattle."

Jack's enthusiasm cooled a little.

"But I don't think that was true," Edith said with the look of one who knows a secret.

"Why do you say that, Edith?" Flo asked.

"Because a few days later, I overheard one of the girls mention Seattle and ask Jenny if she knew it. She said she had seen it only from a ship sailing past."

"Thanks, Edith. You're a jewel," said Flo.

Edith gave Jack a warm smile and was walking away when Jack called out to her, "How about Ernst Haeckel? You must read him."

"I have," replied Edith over her shoulder. "Three times!"

When she had gone, Jack took Flo's hand. "You don't know what a great help you've been, Flo. This gives me a big step forward."

"Are you going to be able to catch this murderer?" Flo's big dark eyes were solemn.

"I'm doing everything I can," said Jack.

"Might there be still more murders? You said—"

"I know I did. I meant that until the killer is caught, there is that risk. I have to find him soon."

Flo stood. She looked alluring in the one-piece costume. "You said I've helped you. Now you can help me."

"Sure. What is it?"

She kept hold of his hand and led him backstage. They went into her dressing room.

"You've moved things around," Jack said. "Where's the love seat?"

"I got rid of it." Flo motioned. "I replaced it with this." It was a brass bedstead, polished and gleaming. The bed was high off the floor and piled with silk pillows.

"Is it better?" Jack asked.

"Let's find out," said Flo.

It was sometime later that Jack remounted his bicycle and started pedaling. He soon reached the Embarcadero with its twenty miles of berthing, enough space in the Bay around it to berth every vessel in the world at one time. Far off into the Bay on the left, Jack could see the island of Alcatraz, its only population being pelicans. But as more people came to San Francisco, the pelican population was declining, and the city council was frequently engaged in debates as to what use to make of the island.

Jack rode past Pier number 43. Yes, it was in, one of the most majestic sailing ships in the world. The *Balclutha* had been built in Scotland in 1886 and had sailed around the Horn more times than any other ship ever built. A two-hundred-and-sixty-foot-long, square-rigged four-master, she was a sight that many came down just to see and Jack never missed the opportunity.

Beyond it was his destination. . . .

Chapter 16

Two tall telephone masts made the Revenue Cutter Service site plainly visible from a distance. Small huts adjoined workshops where repairs were being carried out on the vessels. When the work was completed, the cutters could be taken outside and onto slips that led down to the Bay. A drop hammer thumped, making the ground shake. Smoke rose above the rooftops from what must be a foundry.

Jack made his way to a hut indicated to him by the uniformed guard at the gate. Lloyd Sickert was waiting for him and took him into a room with a desk, several filing cabinets and a large blackboard covered with names and numbers.

Sickert was tall and spindly, a little older than Jack. His reddish mustache and reddish hair looked to Jack as if they belonged on a Viking figure. They sat at the table and Sickert said, "It's really good to see you again. The last time was when you were speaking at one of the meetings at the Ruskin Club." He looked at Jack with undisguised admiration. The Ruskin Club included teachers from the University of California and would-be poets and writers. "Are you still writing, Jack?"

"I just sold one to *The Black Cat,* an Eastern magazine," Jack said.

"Did you just send it in to them? I mean, you didn't know them or anybody there or get introduced or—"

Jack described his earlier days and his many rejections. No, he had known no one in the magazine business, he emphasized, not an editor and no writers.

"You're writing too, I'm sure," said Jack.

Sickert shrugged. "I have written a few stories. Trouble is, I don't know what to do with them."

"Which writers do you read?" asked Jack.

"I like Richard Harding Davis, I thought his *Soldiers of Fortune* was great. Stanley Weyman too— *Under the Red Robe* was really good. Oh, and George Barr McCutcheon."

Jack knew that these were all serialized novels. He had a contempt for these writers, considering them as afraid of the physical world, preferring to write nice stories with no originality and using characters who existed without ever sweating or having fever or severe discomfort. He did not want to sound too critical of Sickert's opinions though, so his response was measured.

"Good writers, all of them," he said. "I write a different kind of story. I try for more vitality, more realism, characters who suffer, get hurt."

They discussed magazines, books, writing and editors for some time and Sickert was eagerly soaking up all that Jack could tell him. Jack, for his part, encouraged Sickert to be more adventurous, both in his writing and in his approach to magazines. "Send them in," was Jack's advice. "Don't worry if you get rejections. Keep sending them in."

"I appreciate all you have told me. It will be a big help. Perhaps I shouldn't have spent so much time talking like this," Sickert said finally. "You have something you want to ask me."

"Well, it's to do with writing too," said Jack, trying to minimize his request. "I'm trying to put together a story based on odd rumors I've heard in the waterfront bars. But first, let me ask this—is Skagway still the main port of exit from the Yukon Territory?"

"Absolutely," said Sickert, "and the main destination is San Francisco."

"What about Seattle?"

"Oh, it may become a major port one day, but today it lacks the facilities."

So much for Jenny's claim to have come from Seattle. But why should she lie? Jack looked at the blackboard. "You keep track of all vessels in and out of San Francisco, is that right?"

"Sure do."

"Do you have a record of a ship leaving Skagway and arriving in San Francisco on the first of April?"

Sickert climbed to his feet, walked over to the board. He ran a finger down. "Here—*The Jewel of the North* made that trip—docked at Pier 23 at eleven in the morning."

"What happened to her after that?" Jack asked.

Sickert went to the first filing cabinet and pulled out a bulging file. After a moment riffling through it, he said, "She sailed two days later for Surabaya in the Dutch Indies."

"That's an awfully fast turnaround, isn't it?" Jack asked.

"It is," Sickert agreed. "Do you know something about her?" he inquired cautiously.

"I'm not sure yet," Jack said. "Do you have a copy of its manifest there?"

Sickert went back to the file. " 'Cargo and passengers,' that's all it says." He frowned. "That's odd. Ah, no, it isn't, it's because she was privately chartered."

"Is that usual?"

"It's not unusual. Some big companies prefer to charter a vessel, put their own crew on board, arrange the loading and unloading. In effect, they are leasing the ship."

"So there's no chance of talking to any of the crew?" asked Jack, disappointed.

"None at all. Don't know who they are or where they are."

Jack drew a breath. Why did that have a ring of familiarity? It came to him—Kipling's question, 'Had he heard any gossip about a freighter docking under mysterious circumstances?' Could this be that vessel?

"Who was she chartered to?"

Sickert turned the papers in the file. "Must be in here somewhere. We'd have to know who to send the bill to. . . . Here we go, Western Holdings."

"Do you know them?"

"No—but wait a minute—the bill was mailed to the Bank of Southern Nevada for payment."

"Did they pay it?"

"Ah, let's see, yes, they did. Paid it in the form of a draft on the Crocker Bank."

Jack could not suppress his smile of satisfaction. Sickert saw it. "Means something, eh?"

"It might. Shame there's no manifest though."

Sickert looked up at the ceiling. Jack waited a moment then asked, "There is a manifest?"

"Not exactly," Sickert said, "but one has to be filed with the insurance company."

"By the people who charter it?"

"Yes, but—well, we have a copy—"

Jack leaned forward.

"It's private, of course. Strictly within the Revenue Cutter Service."

"I heard that Congress wants to change your name—call you the U.S. Coast Guard," said Jack conversationally.

"Yes and the Navy doesn't like it. We'd take over a lot of their responsibilities."

"Pity I couldn't get just a quick look at that manifest," Jack said. He managed a look of dejection. Sickert studied him with sympathy. Jack put on a little more pressure.

"You know how it is when you plan a story. All

you need is a few ideas. Then the rest is all imagination. That's how it would be in this case. No one
would recognize it as being the story of *The Jewel of
the North.*"

He glanced at Sickert and was delving into his mind
for a further convincing plea when the other rubbed
his gingery mustache and stood up. "Wait just a
minute."

Jack had not noticed, but in the ensuing silence the
drop hammer still thumped and shook the walls. He
waited in the empty office with nothing to look at but
the walls.

Sickert came back in, closing the door carefully. In
his hand was a thin red folder. He put it on the table
and turned it toward Jack. "You can look at it for
just a couple of minutes then I'll have to put it back."

Jack tried to conceal his elation as he opened the
folder. The first page was an official summary, full of
jargon, but the next page was a manifest and Jack
read it eagerly.

"One wagon-load of artifacts from the Ketchiwan
diggings, consisting of statuary, primitive tools, art
work, tombs and pottery. These objects confirm the
beliefs in an earlier Eskimo culture than has been previously supposed. . . ." Jack read on, puzzled but fascinated. Pages containing details of weights, sizes,
number of pieces, description, condition followed but
it was the next page that caught Jack's eye.

"Passenger list."

There were only four names—

Lola Randolph
Hannah Green
Jennifer Morris
Beth Garland

So four girls had come to San Francisco on the same
boat! Three of them had been murdered by the same

method. They must have been in fear of their lives too, for they had lied about where they had come from.

Jack read quickly through the rest of the file. It contained recordings from the ship's log regarding course, daily location, wind speeds and directions, depth readings and other nautical information. He looked at the dates—eleven days from Skagway to San Francisco. It was a voyage that should not take more than eight days, nine at the most. He read the log through again. So why had it taken eleven days?

He passed over the weather log, then had a sense of something wrong. He went back. It showed calm conditions every day. Calm? But Jenny had told Edith of suffering from seasickness and Hannah had complained to Dinah of being seasick for days. One girl might be particularly susceptible to motion, but two?

The last document was a certificate of clearance from the United States Customs Service. There were no comments attached so no queries had been raised.

He looked once more at the names on the passenger list, then closed the folder and handed it back to Sickert.

"I hope you'll let me know when the story comes out," said Sickert.

"I will," said Jack. "I won't be able to complete it right away. I have a story on the Klondyke nearly finished and I want to get that out and published."

He knew that the "published" part of his statement was premature, but he wanted to maintain his status as an accomplished writer in Sickert's eyes.

"What's it called?" the other wanted to know earnestly.

Jack had been mulling over possibilities for a title for some time. Various candidates had passed through his mind. "I'm thinking of calling it 'Northland Incident.'"

"Intriguing title!" Sickert beamed.

They left on the best of terms, Jack slightly concerned at misleading the other but reminding himself sternly that this was a matter of multiple murders. He had no intention of compromising Sickert's position, nor was he being patronizing about Sickert's writing. He was willing to encourage him and help him however he could.

Jack was elated as he rode his bike from Alameda back to Oakland then toward the ferry to San Francisco. At last, he had made some real progress! There was a link between Lola Randolph, Jenny Morris and Hannah Green. They had all been passengers on *The Jewel of the North* on its passage from Skagway to San Francisco.

Had they known each other before then? Probably not, and that meant that the ship itself was the link. Then there were these mysterious artifacts of an ancient civilization in Alaska. Where were they now? Presumably they were valuable. Valuable to whom?

The most vital and urgent piece of information, however, was the name of a fourth girl. Besides Lola, Jenny and Hannah, a girl named Beth Garland had been on board. Where was she now? Was she destined for the same fate as her fellow passengers?

Jack was a practical soul. There was no point in wrangling over the ship and its cargo now. That would have to come later—now he had to concentrate on finding this fourth girl and warning her. That should hardly be necessary, surely. If she read newspapers, she would know of the deaths of the other girls. Still, as Jack knew, many girls in San Francisco were illiterate. She might not know of the danger stalking her.

Some of the saloons and dance halls would be open already, catering to early drinkers eager to administer the hair of the dog. From his extensive knowledge of the Barbary Coast, Jack picked out those places first.

Dancers, singers, pretty waiter girls, barkeeps, saloon owners, managers, musicians, floorsweepers, bouncers—anyone who was on their feet was subjected to Jack's questions. He interrogated everyone he knew and many he did not know. In order not to put a spotlight on Beth Garland, he invented names of other girls and used names of girls he knew had left the Coast. His inquiries tossed in Beth Garland among the others.

When the evening came, he was going from place to place, his vitality undiminished. After all, he had carried loads of a hundred and fifty pounds a day over the six-mile Chilkoot Pass in temperatures below freezing, every day for ninety days in a row. He had the strength of a bull and little could tire him. The thought of a knife poised behind Beth Garland's neck was enough to keep him going even if he had felt like resting.

At nine o'clock, he was in Canterbury Hall, a popular saloon that was always crowded. He had just come from Every Man Welcome, where his inquiry had met with blank looks and head shakes. It had been the same in every establishment he had been in before it. Jack had assumed that Beth Garland was on the stage like Lola, Jenny and Hannah, but maybe that was wrong. She did not have to be an entertainer.

In Canterbury Hall, he got another head shake from the barkeep and from two of the girls. Both had worked in several saloons and knew a lot of entertainers, but even they could not help. He was at the bar and about to move on when he found someone shaking his arm. A tiny man, wizened and mishapen, probably from excessive labor and rheumatism, stood there. He spoke in a voice not much above a whisper.

"Did I hear yer asking for Beth Garland?"

Jack nodded, not wanting to show too much interest.

"I know where she is."

Jack nodded again.

The man looked at him expectantly.

Jack had bought and sold boats, weapons, sleds, tools and dozens of other commodities. He knew how to bargain. The man wanted two dollars. Jack offered a glass of whisky. Eventually, they settled at a bottle— but only after the man had said enough to satisfy Jack. The man's story was that Beth was afraid of something—or someone—and was hiding out, working in a store in Chinatown.

Jack was honest but he was not gullible. This had a partial ring of credibility. Certainly, from what Jack knew, Beth Garland had every reason to fear for her life. It might be a false lead but Jack was ready to take a risk. He went out onto Montgomery Street and then to its corner with Columbus Avenue.

The Chinese invasion of America's west coast had begun with the discovery of gold at Sutter's Fort in 1848. Soon, forty thousand Chinese were in San Francisco. They were not popular. It was said of them that they worked more cheaply than the white man, they lived more cheaply, they sent all their spare money back to China, they did not adopt American manners and they lived under the laws of their own tribunals rather than American law.

Almost all of these forty thousand lived in squalid and crowded conditions in Chinatown, a small enclave adjoining the Barbary Coast and, in ironic contrast, a mere six blocks from Nob Hill with its splendid mansions. There, flimsy wooden shacks were erected in sections shipped from China. These shacks lined narrow, dirty streets, and below ground level were known to be cellars and chambers that housed many more Chinese than above ground. White San Franciscans knew nothing but rumors about this subterranean city. Many knew little more about the city above ground, other than the fact that they took their dirty clothes to the two thousand Chinese laundries there.

Occasional adventurous seamen ventured into Chinatown and seldom suffered any loss other than their money, but most San Franciscans avoided it. Jack had been there a few times only. One of his earlier friends had been a Chinese cook on a boat and Jack had visited the place with him. Now, entering the "hidden city," as some called it, was a risk he decided he had to take.

The address he was given was a large store on Columbus Avenue. He observed it from across the street. It looked harmless enough. Customers hurried in and out with arms full of groceries, vegetables and fruit. Some dragged sacks of rice to carts outside.

Jack walked in.

He was the biggest man in the store. Most Chinese were barely up to his shoulder. All wore shapeless garments with baggy pants, and some had the flat coned coolie hats. This was another complaint of white San Franciscans, that the Chinese did not make any attempt to look like Americans but maintained their native costumes. None of them paid any attention to Jack, even though white men were not often seen.

He went to a spectacled older man who seemed to have some authority. "I'm looking for Kow Toy," Jack said, as he had been told. The other looked blankly at him and shook his head. Jack was looking for some one else to ask when a Chinese even shorter than the rest came up to him.

"You look for Kow Toy? I take you to him."

He instantly pushed his way through the people without a look back to see if Jack was following. Jack had barely had a chance to see his face and knew he would not recognize him again. He lost him two or three times but found him, due to the other's diminutive size, just as they reached a wooden door. The man pulled it open, went in and down a flight of wooden stairs that descended at a precipitous angle. He seemed still to be oblivious whether Jack was following. At the bottom, he hurried across the dirt floor of a large chamber. It was unlit but some light was filtering in from another smaller chamber.

Suddenly, Jack found the Chinese had disappeared. He peered into the shadows of the chamber but could not see the man. A rustling sound came from the small chamber and Jack approached it cautiously.

His first impression was that shelves covered all the walls, but he realized that these were the bunk beds on which the Chinese slept in this buried city. They were crammed closer together even than the bunks he had been used to at sea. As his eyes became adjusted to the dim light, he saw that the only other feature of the bare room was a cot on the floor. A girl sat on it.

She had big eyes and a face that would have been pretty if it had not been for the bones that showed beneath the skin and a sallow complexion. The former was the result of not enough to eat, and the latter came from not enough sunlight. She wore only a plain white cotton shift and her pose was seductive but quite without artifice.

"You wanted to talk to me?" Her voice was feeble.

"What's your name?" Jack asked carefully.

"Beth Garland."

Jack moved closer. She began to slip off the thin garment.

"Don't," Jack said harshly. "You're wasting my time. You're not Beth Garland."

"I am, I—"

"You're too pale. You've spent months below ground. Beth has only been here a few weeks after a long sea voyage."

The girl looked away, confused. Abruptly, she rose and ran across the chamber. In a dark corner, Jack saw an Army blanket hanging over a doorway. The girl jerked it aside and disappeared. Jack was about to follow but the blanket moved, pulled from the other side.

Two figures appeared. One had a pistol and looked

familiar. The other carried a large cutlass, and it was this man who claimed Jack's full attention. He wore a military-style jacket, but with the epaulets and pockets removed, the buttons replaced. The brimmed hat was military style too, of the pattern popularized by Teddy Roosevelt's Rough Riders.

He was the man who had been with General Walter Williams at the prizefight. He was the man who called himself Captain Cutlass—and whom Bierce had described as a cold-blooded killer.

Chapter 17

The man with the pistol was Spike Odlum. He grinned mirthlessly at Jack as if eager to pull the trigger of the big six-shooter.

Jack took in those details in a swift glance, for despite the gun, it was Captain Cutlass whose grim expression was a death threat in itself as the faint light in the chamber glittered on the shiny blade of the cutlass that he waved slowly.

"I said that wouldn't work with the girl. I'm glad it didn't. I'm going to have the satisfaction of getting you to tell us what you know and who you're working for."

It was the voice of a man who was utterly without mercy and would enjoy torture for its own sake as much as for the information extorted.

Jack edged back slowly. The only way out was the wooden staircase. If he could reach that, he might have a chance. Spike had not used his pistol, so they did intend to keep him alive temporarily.

Captain Cutlass started to circle, his eyes never leaving Jack's face. As he did, Spike came slowly forward. These two knew each other's intention and had performed such maneuvers before. Jack knew he was in desperate trouble. His only hope lay in doing something thoroughly unexpected.

He stopped and pulled off his seaman's jacket. He made a pretense of wrapping it around his arm as if to defend himself against the captain's cutlass. The two of them stopped, momentarily perplexed. It was all the time Jack needed. Instead of wrapping the jacket around his arm, he gave it one more twirl and flung it in the captain's face. A muffled curse came as the captain tried to pull it loose with his free hand. Jack feinted toward the staircase then raced instead for the blanketed doorway.

He hurried through into a short tunnel, then pounded through a chamber, empty except for piles of wooden packing cases with Chinese lettering. He could hear the two behind him as he raced on. A wooden door ahead of him was not locked. He pulled it open, dashed through—and found himself looking at dozens of men.

They were all Chinese and sitting at tables, four or five at a table. A few glanced up at him but most of them were too engrossed in their game of fan-tan. The room was quiet but fuzzy. Gray and blue smoke rose in clouds, diffusing into the darkness above the gamblers.

Jack had no time to see more. He raced between tables, colliding now and then with the corner of a table, brushing into a seated Chinese, once tripping over an outstretched leg but recovering to race on.

A door in the far wall opened readily just as he heard the commotion from behind as Captain Cutlass and Spike Odlum burst into the fan-tan chamber. A few growls could be heard from the players, not pleased at being disturbed.

Jack knew that underground Chinatown was far more extensive than it was on the surface. Rumor had it that in places it went six stories deep, and legend said that no man—not even the Chinese who spent their lives down here—knew all the ramifications. Jack had no idea of where he was going. All he knew was that he must get away from the murderous captain and his henchman with the pistol.

The next chamber was larger and well lit compared to the others. It was filled with long lines of tables and about a dozen Chinese moved to and fro among them. Jack's priority was escape but he could not miss seeing the stacks of pieces of colored paper covering the tables. They had a familiar look, and as he ran past he recognized them as lottery tickets. The Chinese were inveterate gamblers and the Chinatown lottery was renowned for the large amounts of money disbursed. The Chinese bought most of the tickets, but many shops in the rest of San Francisco sold them too and many whites took chances and occasionally even won.

Jack heard the door crash behind him and he did not need to look back to know that the captain and his pistol-toting companion were close in pursuit. The Chinese looked up curiously at the sight of two white men chasing a third but their curiosity ceased there.

The spaces between the tables were narrow. Jack spotted a door in a corner. He sprinted for it. His breath was coming in gulps as he pulled at the handle. The door was locked on the other side.

His two pursuers had separated to come down parallel passages. Spike had gained his second wind, it seemed, and he reached Jack first. He gave Jack a nasty grin then swung at him with the pistol. Jack took the blow on his forearm and groaned as the pain flowed to his shoulder. Captain Cutlass arrived, panting, and stood, blocking Jack's only exit. His slit of a mouth widened slightly in ghoulish anticipation.

"You're causing us a lot of unnecessary trouble, lad." His voice was cold with anger. "Now tell us who you're working for and maybe I won't let you suffer too much."

Jack tried to force his way past Odlum but he was faster than he looked and stepped back, ready to strike again with the heavy gun.

The cutlass flickered in the light of the naphtha

lamps, a silvery blur, and Jack flinched instinctively. He looked at his left shoulder where the tip of the blade had brushed him. The cloth of his shirt was ripped and he stared in disbelief at the blood that was oozing out.

The shock had stunned him momentarily, and in the second before he could recover the blade flashed again and he was gaping in bewilderment at the blood coming from his right shoulder.

"Now you wouldn't want me to mark up your face that way, would you?" came the captain's mocking tone. "I could open up your mouth, shorten your nose and—if you still wanted to be obstinate—go to work on your eyes. Would that make writing difficult, I wonder?" He paused to let his jibe sink in. "Yes, I suppose it would. You would have to get a tray and sell matches at the depot," he sneered.

Jack had no doubt whatever that he could and would do as he threatened. He had tortured war prisoners this way and was clearly a master of his weapon, able to inflict any level of pain or disfigurement.

One of the Chinese came closer, calling out words in the sing-song intonation. Spike turned his pistol in that direction and waved it threateningly. The Chinese backed away quickly but called out again, louder this time. Spike turned angrily and Captain Cutlass glanced over his shoulder involuntarily.

It was only a slim chance but Jack took it without hesitation. He threw himself into the nearest of the tables. It tumbled over and Jack rolled as he fell, deliberately knocking over another table.

That was enough to get the full attention of all the Chinese as they saw colored lottery tickets flying in all directions. They had presumably been sorting them and all were shouting and jabbering, their arms waving and gesticulating.

The air was still thick with fluttering tickets as Jack

leaped out from beneath the table and dashed away—
anywhere as long as it was away.

Spike let out a cry and the two came after him. Not
for the first time Jack wondered that Spike did not use
his pistol. They must really want him alive and talking.

The next door opened to reveal a long tunnel. At
the end, he could not hear his pursuers but he did not
look back. The tunnel turned in both directions. Jack
turned left. He faced a wooden-barred gate but again
the tunnel gave him a choice. He turned left again,
feeling a temporary exultation.

A small room was open on Jack's right. He could
hear nothing behind him. The room contained only a
wooden staircase with rickety steps. Some were badly
broken and gave way, others creaked but held. A trapdoor at the top resisted at first but Jack's desperation
lent him strength.

He heaved mightily, and with a screech it flew open.

Chapter 18

He was in a storage room piled with crates. The powerful smell of food told him that this was a restaurant. A few paces and he was in a kitchen.

It was thick with steam and clinging odors and it was a madhouse of motion. White-clad Chinese scurried to and fro with bubbling pots and foaming pans. A hot plate sizzled, crowded with cuts of meat and vegetables.

Behind Jack, something moved. He turned—and his breath caught in his throat. It was Spike, entering behind him.

The pistol was not in evidence but Jack saw a hand dive out of sight. A waiter came near Jack with a loaded tray. Jack grabbed the nearest thing on it—a pot of hot soup—and flung it over his shoulder, not waiting to see the result. He heard a yell from a Chinese and a curse from Spike but he was already dodging between the startled cooks.

One of them, short and fat, was slow to move and Jack crashed into him. The Chinese, dripping hot soup, ran out, shouting. Spike, clutching a burned face, immediately came rushing at Jack.

He was lucky that Spike was so furious that he had not stopped to pull out his gun. He grabbed for it now but Jack saw the move and clamped on to his wrist. For long seconds, they glared into each other's face, only inches apart. Jack saw the blazing eyes, one of

them severely bloodshot, and the reddened skin. He
jerked hard and suddenly. The big six-shooter came
loose and clattered onto the floor.

Spike was no amateur. He did not go for the gun
but swung his left arm in a blow that jolted Jack's
kidneys. He tried to follow up with another but Jack
suddenly let go of his wrist, backed away to get clearance then jabbed a punishing straight left into his opponent's face.

A gasp of pain was all Spike had time for as Jack
closed in. He had learned boxing by the rules but also
knew all the dirty tricks of the alleys and the ships
and the dockyards. He thrust a right into the other's
stomach, aiming as low as he could, and was rewarded
with a whoosh of expelled air, but Spike was not finished by any means. Before Jack could move back,
Spike grabbed him with both arms and pulled him
close in a bear hug, their faces almost touching.

It was Jack's turn to gasp for breath. He struggled
to free himself but Spike was strong, and though he
was wheezing he held on tight. Jack's arms were
pinned to his sides and breathing was getting difficult.
He shifted his weight to his left foot and kicked hard
with his right.

His seaman's boot had a hard toe-cap and Spike's
grip loosened abruptly as the kick connected with his
shinbone. Jack kicked again in the same spot and si-
multaneously jabbed out his elbows to free himself.
Spike staggered back and Jack hit him with a flurry
of blows with both fists. The last knocked Spike to
the floor and he writhed, clutching his stomach, then
without warning he reached out a long arm, gripped
Jack's leg and pulled.

Jack went down, trying to roll away out of reach.
Both men, spluttering for breath, wanted to be first
on his feet. They glared at each other. Around them,
startled Chinese faces watched intently.

Spike was flicking glances at the floor, looking for the pistol. Jack saw it first, reached for it—

"That's enough of this brutality. Spike, pick up your gun and take better care of it in future."

It was the voice Jack had least wanted to hear. The cold, almost inhuman tones of Captain Cutlass.

"So—you're back with us!" the voice went on. "I hoped we hadn't lost you. We have some unfinished business, you and me!"

Any intention Jack had of escape was cut off by the appearance over his shoulder of a cutlass blade. It was ready to strike at any such move. Jack turned slowly as a couple of Chinese gasped at the sight of the cutlass.

The captain stood there with the baleful stare of a serpent. "You can, of course, use the pistol now if it should be necessary," the captain said to Spike. To Jack, he said, "It wasn't safe before. Ceilings could collapse in these rattraps."

Jack had not thought of that but there was scant consolation in the knowledge now. Spike picked up the six-shooter and his vicious look caused the captain to say, "Control yourself, Spike. This is not the time to use it. Not just yet anyway."

He turned to Jack.

"The first question is the same," purred the captain. "You are not doing all this on your own. Someone has hired you. Who is it?"

Jack let his shoulders slump. He tried to portray dejection and despair as well as exhaustion from the fight. "I don't know his name—" The captain raised his edged weapon and Jack went on quickly, "—but I followed him once and he went to the Huntington mansion on Nob Hill."

He lowered his head. Duplicity did not come easy to him but if there was ever a time to portray it, this was it. He did not want the other to see the gleam in his eyes at his own satisfaction with this answer. It had an ingenuity to it, for the captain would be fully aware of Huntington's crafty methods, and it was not at all unreasonable that he might employ the captain and then hire someone else to keep an eye on him.

Jack did not want to look up but he judged from the momentary silence that Captain Cutlass was at least contemplating the idea.

"I don't believe you," said the captain harshly.

Jack told himself that was what the captain should say whether he believed it or not. The other rapped out a different question.

"What have you found out about those dance hall girls?"

"They didn't know each other before they came to the Coast. . . ."

"What else?"

"Spike beat up one of them. That's why I went looking for him."

"Which one?"

Jack knew that the captain already had the answer to that so it was best to tell the truth. "Jenny Morris, at the Midway Plaisance."

"Who told you?'

"Oh, several of the girls," said Jack. "They all seemed to know." He hoped that the other did not know of his close acquaintance with Little Egypt.

"What did you learn from Bierce?"

"Nothing about the girls. I sent in an article and hoped he would print it, an article on socialism." It was a little weak but it was the best he could do.

"You must have asked him about the girls—you're so concerned about them."

Jack shook his head firmly. "I didn't. Anyway, it wouldn't do any good. He never gives anything away. He keeps it all for his column."

He wondered if the captain knew of his meeting with Kipling and was concocting a story about a fellow writer, but the question did not come. Meanwhile, as he talked, he was edging toward the ring of Chinese, who were still watching the cutlass and the gun in fascination. The sharp-eyed captain was too experienced a hand not to divine Jack's purpose. He moved to intercept him, that deadly cutlass weaving through the air in front of him.

Jack's options were reducing fast and the pistol-carrying Spike was still between him and the door.

"Tell me about Wesley Montague," Captain Cutlass invited.

"I didn't know him," Jack said, as convincingly as he could.

"Are you sure you haven't been meeting with him?"

"I have never met him. I don't know him."

The cold eyes searched his, and for a second Jack thought the weapon was going to strike at him like an angry snake, but the captain apparently accepted Jack's denial.

Jack's relief was short-lived. "What about Montague's wife?" came the captain's next question. Jack was at a loss for a ready answer, but at that moment a Chinese waiter came in carrying a massive pewter bowl.

The door had not closed behind him when in came another Chinese, this one with a large metal tray. Behind him came yet a third, then a fourth and a fifth. All carried large metal vessels and they crowded the little space remaining as Spike and the captain regarded them with baffled amazement.

"Go quickly," hissed one of them in English to Jack, who immediately dived for the exit. Spike must have swung his weapon in that direction for Jack had a glimpse of a pewter tureen moving through the air and knocking the pistol to the floor. A spatter of the Chinese language was followed by a clang as the captain's sword struck the large tray that one of them held. Then Jack was in the kitchen. A hand fell on his arm.

He was looking at the short, fat Chinese whose face was still blotchy from a drenching of hot soup. He suddenly realized that the man looked familiar.

"Sun Ling!"

He had been the cook on the *Sophia Sutherland,* the three-masted sealing schooner on which Jack had signed on at the age of seventeen. Big Red John, a burly Swede and the ship's bully, had badgered the Chinese unmercifully. Finally, Jack had stepped in and defended Sun Ling, almost choking the Swede to death.

The ship's cook, now chef, beamed. "My friend Jack! Go quickly. I keep them busy, help my friends."

Jack clasped his hand briefly and raced into the restaurant and out into the street.

Chapter 19

His exertions of the night before had brought night-
mares of flashing swords and dark endless tunnels.
Jack awoke sweating to find that it was later than he
usually slept. He had only just thrown on a sweater
and some pants when a knock came at the door.

He was instantly on the alert. Had Captain Cutlass
found out already where he lived and come after him?
Jack had a number of friends who came around to
chat and drink but they all knew when he was trying
to write and were staying away from interrupting him.
Who else could it be? Not Ted Townrow again?

The knock was repeated. He was able to study it
this time. It was gentle and timorous. Well, he could
not hide forever. He opened the door a few inches.
A woman stood there.

"Could I talk to you for a few minutes?"

He peered past her but there was no one else in
sight. He was about to ask her what she wanted when
her face reminded him of—it was Nancy Prescott, the
widow of Wes Montague.

She looked very different. As well she might, he
reminded himself. The last time he had seen her, she
had been wearing only flimsy pieces of blue material.
Now she was wearing a light brown cotton dress and
a wool jacket. She had no makeup on her face at all
and looked, well, not ordinary. Vulnerable, he
thought. He opened the door.

She came in, noticing the typewriter and the pages beside it. "Yes, you said you were a writer." She had a cloth bag in one hand. She set it on the table. "I wanted to show you this."

"Sit down," Jack invited, and she sat in his chair before the typewriter. He pulled another chair over and sat opposite her.

"The police brought me Wes's belongings," she said. "This was among them." She reached into the cloth bag, fumbled for a minute, then her hand came out with a strange-looking key.

It was half flat and half tubular shaped. Jack picked it up and examined it. He read the stamped inscription. "WF 142." He looked at her. "Was this your husband's?"

"I suppose so but I've never seen it before."

Jack looked at it again. "It looks as if it is important. These aren't his initials, are they?"

"No, he was just WM."

"Do you know anyone with the initials WF?"

"No, but it started me thinking. In his profession, he wouldn't keep any important evidence on a case he was working on in his rooms, would he?"

"I suppose not," said Jack.

"So what would he do with it?" She fixed Jack with a knowing look.

He looked back. "What *would* he do with it?"

She was trying not to appear too pleased with herself.

"Don't banks have safes where people can put valuables? Jewels, private papers, things like that?"

"Safe deposits, I think they call them," said Jack. "I've never seen one though. Have you?"

"No," she said triumphantly. "But they have to have keys to them, don't they?"

Jack looked at the key. "You think that's what this is?" He was noticing that she was lovely with that smooth soft complexion that was not common among

dance hall girls, most of whose faces showed the ravages of disease. He hurried on. "Was your husband
the kind of man who would trust valuables to a safe
deposit?"

"Only if he felt it was really safe, and where would
that be? The only one that I can think of is the one
owned by the company he worked for—Wells Fargo!"

"Wells Fargo—WF." Jack turned the key over in
his fingers. "You may be right. Wells Fargo has a bank
right here in San Francisco."

Her eyes danced. "I'll bet it has safe deposits!"

"So what are you going to do?" Jack asked flatly.

She looked disappointed, perhaps because he had
not showed more enthusiasm, but she went on. "Open
the safe deposit with this key, of course. There might
be some reports of his—there might be notes on what
he was doing and that might point to who killed him."

Jack had not forgotten that it had been this same
lovely face that had smiled the smile luring him upstairs to look into the muzzle of a gun. She seemed
honest and yet . . .

She must have seen his hesitation—it was not well
concealed. "The problem is that they must have this
safe deposit listed as belonging to a Wesley Montague.
Well, I can go in and say that I'm his wife but they
probably won't give it to me."

"Probably not."

"But a man could do that." Her level gaze met his
over the typewriter.

"You mean me."

"Yes," she replied decisively.

Jack was seeing her for the first time as a woman.
Previously she had been an entertainer, a symbol of
sexual desire. He felt himself being pushed toward
helping her. He was able to tell himself that in the
course of doing so he could also be helping his own
investigation. The common factor of the same weapon
and murder method used on her husband as on Lola

Randolph, Jenny Morris and Hannah Green was inescapable.

"They may want proof of my identity."

She reached into the cloth bag and came out with a leather wallet. She dropped it on the tabletop in front of Jack. He flipped it open. On one side was a silver starred badge, imprinted "Wells Fargo Investigator." On the opposite side, metal letters embroidered into the leather said "Wesley Montague."

Jack was almost out of arguments but he tried one more.

"They may know your husband. After all, he worked for Wells Fargo."

She was ready for that too. "He worked for Wells Fargo Investigations. It's not likely the bank staff would know him."

Jack said nothing.

"Anyway, it's a risk we have to take," she said.

"*We* do?" His emphasis on the first word was heavy.

Her mouth, even without the bright lip rouge, was very attractive, Jack thought. It did tighten up very slightly now though. "You do want to find out—"

"Yes," Jack said. "When do you want to do this?"

"Now."

He was about to argue but she jutted out her chin obstinately. "Yes, now."

"The Wall Street of the West" was what San Francisco proudly called it. The comparison was extravagant but the area did house several prominent banks. The Nevada National Bank, the London and San Francisco Bank, the German American Savings Bank, the California Bank, the Canadian Bank of Commerce and the Union Trust were all on Sansome Street. Among those on the adjoining Montgomery Street were the National Savings Bank, Western Union—and the one that Nancy and Jack headed toward, number 114, near the end.

A billiard hall had been next door to the Wells Fargo Bank, and the disreputable nature of its clientele had caused an amount of complaints from the Wells Fargo Bank's customers. Still, it had taken a few years to buy out the lease and set the customers' minds at ease.

The two of them walked in together. Jack had put on his best jacket. It was worn but was made of expensive Mexican leather. He had won it in a poker game in the Yukon. They went past the guard on the imposing iron grille gate at the front door after watching from across the street for a short time, waiting until a number of people had entered and the staff would be busy.

They passed the row of tellers' cages and walked by several small desks, all occupied with customers.

"Over there," murmured Nancy without moving her head, and Jack saw a steel-barred door with a uniformed guard in front of it. Jack took out the key and the wallet. The guard glanced briefly at the key, longer at the wallet while Jack held his breath. The guard unlocked the door and they entered a room lined with steel panels, all painted with white numbers. Nancy quickly assessed the numbers and led the way, stopping in front of number 142.

Jack inserted the key. It turned readily and he pulled out a steel drawer. He looked around for somewhere to put it, and Nancy nudged him and said, "Over there." A smaller room opened off of the one they were in. It had wide tables against each of the walls. They went in and Jack fumbled with the lid of the box.

"You're sweating," Nancy said. Jack brushed an arm across his forehead. The two of them peered into the box. All it contained was a notebook. Two minutes later, they were out on Montgomery Street.

Mindful of being followed, as Captain Cutlass's words had indicated, Jack took Nancy down the street

and into the Western Union office. They sat for ten
minutes, then Jack went across the street and Nancy
watched. When Jack returned, she shook her head.
They went to the National Savings Bank and repeated
the maneuver, but this time Nancy crossed the street
and Jack watched. Satisfied they were not being followed, they walked down to Front Street on the edge
of the Produce District. Breezes off the Bay brought
mingled smells of salt and fish.

Fruit and vegetables, live chickens, fresh-baked
bread, eggs, meat, fish, fresh milk—all the yield of the
farms, the Pacific Ocean and the countryside were on
sale to the city dwellers of San Francisco. Behind the
open stalls were small cafés, and Jack knew the couple
who owned one of these. It served simple fish meals
and Jack had become acquainted with it during his
days on the Fish Patrol.

The old woman looked approvingly at Nancy but
Jack headed off any probing questions, asking about
the day's catch. They were the only customers and
took a table that was tucked away in the corner.

Nancy reached into her bag and took out the
sharkskin-covered notebook. She glanced through it
and handed it to Jack. At first, he supposed it was
an abbreviated version of the Irishman John Gregg's
shorthand, which he knew some writers used. Then he
admitted, "Can't make out a word. You must know
his handwriting." He handed it to her.

She studied it. "It's his own personalized code. It's
not shorthand, just letters left out and so on. I know
he used it a lot."

"So what does it say?"

She was silent but her lips moved now and then.
Jack watched her, becoming entranced, but was glad
when the fish arrived so that he could deliberately
concentrate on it and avoid being spellbound by those
moving lips.

"Something about a general here. . . ."

"Read it," Jack said. "You never know what's important."

"Wes got a deposition from a man in Humboldt Wells saying that he recognized one of the gang that robbed it. Said he was a general." She frowned dubiously. "Does that make sense?"

"It might," Jack said, applying his concentration to the fish. He did not show his jubilation, reminding himself that it may have been knowledge of General Walter Williams and his activities that got Wes Montague killed. "What else?"

"Several numbers of documents belonging to the Pacific Coast Shipping Lines. They seem to have been passed on to Wes by the Wells Fargo agent in Skagway. That's in Alaska, isn't it?"

Jack nodded impatiently. "Yes. Go on."

"Oh, the documents were shipping manifests—what's a manifest?"

He was about to tell her to stop asking questions but she had her head raised to him, her eyes were wide and her mouth partly open. She looked particularly young. He softened his tone as he said, "It's a list giving details of a ship's cargo."

She went back to the notebook. "He writes about the jewel—what does he mean by that? He has a note here about going to the Natural History Museum—is that in San Francisco, I wonder? He doesn't say. Anyway, he wrote—it's not easy to . . . oh, yes, I see, he goes on to say 'No knowledge of early Eskimo civilizations. Cannot understand why—something—considered of value.' "

She looked at Jack again and took up her fork to the fish. "What does all that mean? Eskimos? A museum?"

"I'm not altogether sure what it means," Jack said. He was a fast eater and had already finished his fish. "What else?"

She took a second forkful of fish before going back

to the book. "I don't know what this is all about. . . .
I think it says, 'Where was the second wagon?' "

"Are you sure it says 'wagon'?"

She looked again. "Yes. It's wagon. Does it make
sense?"

"It may make a lot of sense. We need a few more
items of information. Go through the rest of the
book."

Nancy did so, alternating mouthfuls of fish with
comments on each page, from which Jack judged if he
wanted her to read the remainder.

"There's a certificate number—it says Western National Insurance Company." She went on but nothing
that had any meaning emerged until Nancy said, "This
must be important. It's the last entry Wes made before
he—before he was killed."

"Read it."

"It's longer than the others. It starts, 'WW seems
to know my—' I can't quite make out the next word,
oh, it might be 'moves.' "

"Go on," said Jack, barely controlling his
impatience.

" 'Sent report on HG—' "

"That's Hannah Green," said Jack. "Keep going."

"She's the girl who was killed at the Yellow Canary,
isn't she?"

"Yes," said Jack through his teeth. "Go on!"

"All right. 'Sent report on HG to WF'—we know
that's Wells Fargo—'through D4 office and she's dead
next day.' Then Wes goes on, 'Must change route
next report.' "

"Yes?" Jack urged.

"That's all," Nancy said. "What's a D4 office?"

"I have no idea. Are you sure that's what it says?"

She read it again. "I'm not certain but it looks
like it."

Jack was frustrated but not dissatisfied. Without
knowing all that the book signified, he was sure that

the data they had gathered was part of a pattern. A few more pieces of the puzzle might clarify everything.

They finished the meal. "What shall we do with the book?" Nancy asked.

"Let's put it back in the safe deposit," suggested Jack.

She agreed and they left the café. The market was still a hive of bargaining and good-natured banter. They walked among the stalls and Jack stopped at one. It was a knife and scissors grinder.

"Let me have the key," said Jack.

Nancy looked at him questioningly but did so. Jack handed it to the gray-haired man intently sharpening a carving knife. He handed the knife back to the next stall, where the owner was waiting to slice his hams and pork loins. Jack said a few words to the knife sharpener. He put it in his vise and Nancy watched, still baffled, then she smiled as Jack handed the key back to her. The man had ground off the number.

"It won't help anyone now even if they should get it," Jack said.

"I'll have to be sure to memorize that number," said Nancy.

They returned the book to the safe-deposit box and walked on. "Are you coming to the Duke of York tonight?" she asked without looking at him.

"I had a gun pointed at me the last time," Jack said, waving to yet another acquaintance who was unloading mussels.

"It couldn't happen again," she told him.

They laughed together and she took his arm. At the cable-car stop on Powell Street, she said, "I can ride back from here. Thanks for your help." Her eyes danced for a second then the conductor clanged his bell, yelled, "Watch out for the curve!" and she was gone.

Chapter 20

Jack returned to his writing. He went over "The White Silence" yet again. Finally, he was satisfied with it. He decided to send it to *Godey's* magazine, which sometimes used outdoor action stories. He packaged it ready to send then commenced organizing his notes for another story. He needed some names and he jotted down some possibilities. . . .

When evening came it took him by surprise. He often got carried away when he wrote. He arranged everything carefully so that he was prepared when next he sat down to write. He changed clothes and went down to the ferry.

The weather was uncertain, a balmy breeze one minute then a damp chill the next. He cut across the Embarcadero and on to Drumm Street. A few blocks and he turned on Green Street and walked into the Devil's Acre.

A group of drunken sailors went past, singing and waving to everyone they saw. Some self-conscious Easterners stood outside a particularly vicious looking bar debating going in, afraid of what they might encounter in there. A couple of cowboys in fringed jackets, chaps, knee-high boots and Stetson hats swaggered down the street with the bowlegged motion that came from a lifetime in the saddle. They made no secret of the six-shooters in holsters on their belts that appeared ready for instant action.

Jack was still trying to locate the elusive Beth Garland. He had no doubt that she was in mortal danger and she must know it, which was why she was so hard to find. It was possible that she had left the Coast but Jack did not think so. He felt that she was still here where it was not that hard to get lost among a third of a million people, a large number of whom were fugitives of one kind or another.

The Strassburg Music Hall was the first place he tried. Run by Belle Branson, it provided liquor, dancing and bawdy shows. Several tables offered fifteen-ball pool, and this mild form of entertainment provided a relatively harmless ambience, in strong contrast to most of the other places on the Barbary Coast. No one responded to the name of Beth Garland at all, and Jack found he was raising no sympathy for his plight as heartbroken and searching for "the only girl for him."

On Davis Street was Miss Piggott's boardinghouse and saloon. It was a possible hiding place for a young woman as the redoubtable six-foot, two-hundred-pound Miss Piggott had a soft spot for people in trouble. This was in direct contrast to her role as her own bouncer and chief bartender. She had a punch that many a man envied—and that had felled many a man.

She was well known to locals as a crimp. She engaged in this activity only when the saloon and bar business was slow, but then she would supply as many unwilling crew members as the ships in the Bay cared to order. Her technique was common knowledge to her regular customers. Any unsuspecting prospect entering the saloon would be served with a "Miss Piggott Special" at an enticingly low price. This consisted of equal parts of rum, whisky and gin, heavily laced with opium. She would nudge the future sailor along the bar until he stood on a trapdoor. The lever controlling this was under Miss Piggott's hand and after a couple of minutes for the opium to take effect, the lever was pulled. Mindful of the need to furnish only able-bodied seamen so as to keep her reputation as a reliable supplier, a mattress was carefully placed in position in the cellar below.

When the unfortunate regained consciousness, he was at sea, bound for some exotic foreign port. The regular customers of Miss Piggott's Saloon knew the location of the trapdoor and carefully stayed away from it. There was a tacit understanding that even regulars could be "crimped" in this way if they were unwary, forgetful or drunk enough concerning the location of the danger spot. Sometimes, the regulars watched this profitable means of recruitment for the merchant vessels with a mild interest, but it was a regular enough occurrence that it did not attract a great deal of attention.

Jack was careful to use the other end of the bar as he talked to Miss Piggott and to the other bartenders. They convinced him that Beth Garland was not there in any capacity nor did they know anything of her. He went on to Madame Gabrielle's Lively Flea with the same result and then to the Richelieu Bar, which was slightly less depraved but equally unhelpful.

The first show was just starting at the House of Blazes, just outside what was considered the limits of the Devil's Acre at the corner of Mason and Powell Streets. It was a large three-story building and had the reputation of having been visited by the police only once. This was because on that occasion their handcuffs, whistles, pistols and blackjacks were stolen before they were allowed to escape.

He visited three more places, including the Coliseum, known as the Big Dive, and drank only half of his beer at each before leaving. He did not intend to fall back into the rapacious arms of John Barleycorn, and although he was well known on the Coast and relatively safe from the local toughs, some newcomer to town might consider him a mark and club him for his money. The next place he went to was the White Whale.

It might have been named after Herman Melville's popular novel, though it was doubtful that any of the staff or customers had read or even heard of the book. The whaling theme was evident with nets, oars, gutting hooks, machetes and carved wooden prows from boats on display on the walls. The air was thick with smoke and the noise level was rising. It rose even further as the girls came on stage in theatrical versions of sailors' uniforms that clearly were not going to survive the next five minutes.

Jack was sipping a beer when a voice called to him.

"Heard you were back from the icy mountains, Jack! Glad you remembered to come see your old friends!"

He turned to see a redheaded girl with a wide smile.

"Hello, Olive," he greeted her warmly. "Didn't know you were here. Last time I saw you, you were at—"

He was momentarily at a loss. Many of the waiter girls and entertainers in the saloons and music halls moved from place to place at frequent intervals.

Olive saw his hesitation. "The Louisiana. Yes, I used to be but the tips are better here." She winked at him. She had bold features, a little hard from her enthusiastic approach to the earning of what she referred to as tips, which Jack knew to be prostitution. She wore a short purple jacket with silver buttons and black stockings. It was a variant on the revealing costume that the Golden Slipper had originated. Olive's long legs were amply demonstrated and the short jacket that was the only garment lured the roving hands of potential customers. She had the body of a dancer but lacked the will to practice and rehearse.

"You won't get into trouble if you stay and chat with me for a few minutes?" asked Jack.

She shook her head, amused. "Ned Noonan won't

give me any trouble. He knows what will happen to him if he does," she said scornfully.

Jack knew that Olive protected her job in the safest way she knew—by sleeping with the boss. For a few minutes they exchanged gossip on who was where. They had a lot of friends in common and some of them were still customers here. Then Jack said, making it sound like a random remark, "I haven't seen Beth Garland around for some time, have you?"

Olive's reply was unexpected. "Not since she left."

"Left?" Jack had not known that she worked here. "Where did she go, do you know?"

She eyed him. "I didn't know you two were—"

"No, no, we weren't," said Jack. "I didn't know her that well. She wasn't here very long, was she?" he asked conversationally.

"Only a few weeks."

"When did she leave?" Jack asked.

"Just last week. It was sudden. Seems she did a show and was talking to one of the other girls after it when she decided to go. Nobody has seen her since."

"What kind of a conversation was that," Jack asked, keeping his tone light, "that it made her decide to leave so suddenly?"

"You'll have to ask the girl she was with at the time."

"Which girl was it?"

"It was Rosella." Olive was getting curious. "Why are you so interested in Beth if you didn't know her that well?"

Jack could see that he was not going to learn much more unless he confided in Olive to some extent. "A conversation I heard," he said carefully. "Beth may be in danger."

Olive was not educated but she was shrewd. An unusually loud roar from the crowd died down. A hush followed as further clothing dropped to the stage. During that hush, Olive asked, "Is it to do with those other girls? Lola at the Cobweb Palace, Jenny at the Midway and—"

"It may be." Jack nodded.

"But why—?"

"I'm not permitted to answer any questions," said Jack, using what he had learned in his days with the California Fish and Harbor Patrol about how to make pompous statements like that.

Olive nodded. If anything, his ring of officialdom made her more cooperative. "Do you want to talk to Rosella?"

"Yes," said Jack.

Olive pointed to the stage, where the girls were taking a bow. "That's her," said Olive, "second from the left."

In the wardrobe room beneath the stage, Rosella listened to Jack with her big eyes wide and her sultry mouth slightly open. She was of Mexican origin but had been born in El Centro in Southern California. Rather than work in the fields picking fruit, she had chosen to come to San Francisco, "where I can make enough money to buy nice clothes," she said. She was not wearing any now; she was almost naked after the finale of the girl-sailors number, and although she tossed a robe over her shoulders, she was completely natural about the exposure of her shapely legs. She was young, probably seventeen, but her body was voluptuous and she moved with a lazy ease that helped her to be a natural dancer.

She had accepted Jack as someone to be trusted upon Olive's introduction, and his bright blue eyes, his honest and straightforward manner and curly brown hair quickly reinforced that acceptance. She spoke without an accent and like Olive and many other girls on the Barbary Coast had a streetwise intelligence.

"I suppose I was Beth's closest friend," she told

him in a light voice. "We didn't see each other much outside of the Whale, but we spend a lot of our time here—shows, rehearsals, costume fittings and things. So we knew each other well."

"Tell me about your conversation with her after that show—the one where she disappeared right after it." Jack kept his tone friendly and chatty.

Rosella frowned prettily. "Well," she said, collecting her memory of the occasion, "I guess it began with that newspaper. One of the girls brought it in. Most of us don't read them much," she said with an apologetic smile, "but that one terrified Beth."

"Did you see what it was that scared her so much?"

"Sure. It was near the bottom of the front page— I remember the headline, 'Dancer Found Murdered' it said."

Jack was about to prompt her but reminded himself to let her go on and tell it in her own words.

"One of the other girls and I took the paper from her and read. It said that Hannah Green, over at the Yellow Canary, had been killed. During a performance, I think it was."

"It's understandable that Beth should be frightened," Jack said. "Another girl, also a dancer—"

"No, no," said Rosella fervently. "It wasn't just that. I asked her if she knew Hannah and she nodded. 'We came here together,' she said."

"Oh, I see," Jack said. "They were friends before coming to the Coast. Well, that makes a difference. She would be upset, having a friend murdered—"

"It was more than that," Rosella cried, her voice becoming anguished. "Beth said, 'I've got to get out of here, right now.' I asked her why. She just pointed to the last part in the paper. I read it. It said something about 'This follows the deaths of two other dance hall girls, Lola Randolph at the Cobweb Palace and Jenny Morris at the Midway.' One of the girls said, 'Didn't you hear about them?' sort of sarcastic like, and Beth said, 'No. I haven't seen a newspaper.'"

"Then she left?" asked Jack. "Right away?"

Rosella nodded. The significance of the three girls' deaths coupled with Beth's abrupt departure was only now coming home to her. "She started to pack right there and then. She left and none of us have seen her since."

"Do you think she left town?" asked Jack.

Rosella shook her head. "I doubt it. I heard that she didn't even pick up her pay, so she wouldn't have had enough money even if she'd wanted."

"Do you have any idea what all this means?"

Rosella's big eyes were round as she shook her head again. "Nobody knows why those other girls were killed, do they?"

Jack rose. "Listen, Rosella. Don't mention a word of this to anybody. You don't have to worry. You're not in any danger."

"What about Beth?" Her tone was almost pleading. "She'll be all right, won't she?"

"I have to find her," said Jack. "Do you have any idea at all where she might be?"

"No."

"What does she look like?" Jack asked. He caught Rosella's surprised look and realized that Olive may have passed on to her what Jack had told Olive, namely that he didn't know Beth "that well." Rosella expected him to know at least the color of her hair. He covered up quickly. "She changed her hair color a few times. Is she still a blond or has she changed again?"

"It's still that same yellow color," Rosella said, satisfied. "Corn-colored, she called it."

"She can't have put on much weight if she was still dancing a week ago?"

"No, she's still about the same as me." A thought came to her. "There was somebody else asking."

"Oh?" Jack was instantly alert. "Who?"

"A man. He was asking Jim, one of the bartenders."

Jack gave her a pat on the cheek and she smiled wanly. The loss of her friend had been brought back to her all over again and, Jack realized, with a greater fear of the danger that Beth must be in.

Jack went out and into the barroom, where he sought out Jim. "A mean-looking cuss with black hair that he must cut himself," was Jim's description, and it was all that Jack needed to identify Spike Odlum. No, Jim said in response to Jack's further questions, he had just asked if anybody knew where Beth had gone.

When Jack arrived home, there was a letter waiting. He opened it eagerly, hoping it was from an editor, but it was on the stationery of the Office of the Mayor of San Francisco and it invited him to a "Literary Evening" at the mayor's mansion. The date of the event was tomorrow. Many famous writers would be there and attendance was by invitation only, it added.

Jack felt a thrill of acknowledgment that he was accepted as a writer by his community, but then he noticed a hand-written note in the same envelope. It was from Ted Townrow.

"Sorry you didn't get one of these when they were sent out, Jack," it read. "Hope you can be here though. It ought to be very helpful—in more ways than one."

Chapter 21

It was not a rewarding day. Jack spent a few hours on the beginning of a new story set in the Yukon but it lacked the intensity he wanted. It did not convey the sense of desolation and impending doom that the vast frozen wilderness really possessed and that Jack wanted to express. Still he had learned enough about writing not to throw anything away. Some, at least, of what he had written could be salvaged, rewritten and revised.

The bars and saloons he visited in search of the elusive Beth Garland had no knowledge of her and he had the feeling that his approach needed a new direction.

During the day while he was pursuing these two endeavors, his thoughts had strayed more than once to the evening ahead. It was a great opportunity for him to move up in the literary world, and he had been looking forward to being at the mayor's mansion.

Now there, he tried not to stare like a country bumpkin as he entered the brown and white marble tiled hall. A colored servant in a dark blue livery with gold trim glanced at his invitation and waved him into the main hall. Magnificent oil paintings in mahogany frames hung on the tiled walls and sculptures of male and female figures stood like frozen sentinels. Large cabinets held ceramics in a range of blues from dazzling cobalts to muted azures.

As Jack walked in, he was greeted by Mayor Hiram
T. Nelson. They exchanged a handshake and it was
purely routine, with no hint of the secret commission
between them. The deputy mayor, Carl Heindell, was
next to him.

"We have met," said Heindell with a wide smile.
"How are you, young man? Keeping up the writing?"

"Yes, indeed," Jack told him. "I write every day."

The mayor then introduced two aides. Jack did not
know the first but Ted Townrow was the second.

"Hope you'll enjoy the evening," said Townrow
with a political smile. "Look forward to talking to you
later," he added.

The large buffet table was under an enormous crystal chandelier. The well-dressed crowd was being
served drinks by waiters moving smoothly among
them. Jack accepted a whisky and tried to spot a familiar face. He saw Frank Harris deep in conversation
with a group, though judging from Harris's vehement
gestures it was more of a lecture. David Belasco, the
Bishop of Broadway, was holding forth to another
group and his motions suggested that he was acting
out a scene from a new production. William Kellaway,
the head of the English literature department at the
University of California at Berkeley was in the center
of a further agglomeration that appeared to be in serious debate.

A large crowd farther away was hanging on every
word of someone who was outside Jack's vision. A
hand took his arm and he turned to see an attractive
matron with an elaborate coiffure. "Excuse me, aren't
you Joaquin Miller?"

"No, I'm not," Jack said. "He is probably here
somewhere though." He looked around the room.
"Ah, there he is."

The famous poet was not difficult to find among the
well-dressed crowd. His soft shirt in blue with red
stripes and Western pants tucked into high cowboy

boots made him an outstanding figure. "At least he's not wearing his ten-gallon Stetson hat," said Jack.

The lady looked at him enquiringly. "Does he usually?" she asked in some doubt.

"He lived with an Indian tribe in California after running away from home at the age of fifteen. He married the chief's daughter, but when she was killed in an accident he went back to his native Oregon and became a lawyer."

"A lawyer!" The lady sounded disappointed.

"Yes, but he wanted only to write and spent a number of years in England, where they loved the Western motif. He got into the habit of wearing a Stetson at that time."

The lady was looking increasingly dismayed and Jack felt a need to reassure her. "His love of the West and his romantic approach to it made him very popular and now that he's back here, he seems to have returned to the poetic image."

The lady had lost interest. "Well, maybe I'll look him up later. . . . Who else is here?"

"I'd be surprised if Oscar Wilde isn't among those present," Jack said. "And if he is, he's most likely to be in the middle of a crowd such as that one over there."

He nodded and the lady followed his direction. "I think you're right. I'd love to go and talk to him. Do you think I could?"

"I doubt it," Jack told her, "but you could certainly go and listen to him."

A young man of about Jack's own age was standing looking nervous and ill at ease. Sympathizing with him as he felt the same, Jack introduced himself.

"My name's Sinclair," said the other, pleased to have someone to talk to, "Upton Sinclair."

"Are you a writer?" asked Jack, and the other looked embarrassed.

"Not yet. I want to be though." He was regarding

Jack with a look akin to hero-worship. "I know your name—it really is a pleasure to meet you. I've read all your writings on socialism."

"Well, thanks," said Jack. "You are a socialist?"

"I certainly am. I want to be a muckraker."

A passing waiter had a tray full of drinks. Jack put down his empty glass and took a full one. Sinclair took a cocktail in a fluted glass.

Jack knew the term—it was becoming increasingly popular. Muckrakers were writers whose goal was to expose political and social evils. Many were socialists, like Jack, but many others had the same aim and yet had different political views, like Ambrose Bierce.

"I'm only here in San Francisco for a few days," said Sinclair. "Will I be able to hear you speak?"

"I don't have any engagements coming up," Jack said. He felt impelled to explain further. "I have some writing contracts to fulfill and I'm trying to meet the deadlines."

The exaggeration impressed Sinclair. "That's great. I wish you luck. I'm planning a book myself but it's probably going to take me some time, a few years even."

"On socialism?"

"Not directly. It's going to be an exposure of the terrible conditions in the meat-packing industry in Chicago, where I live."

"That's interesting," said Jack. "I spent some time in the tuna canneries north of here. Conditions are awful there too. I'm sure you have a lot of material. How are you going to treat it?"

"I was going to do it as a journalistic effort but now I'm wondering if I shouldn't learn from Harriet Beecher Stowe."

Jack nodded. "She wasn't very successful in her anti-slavery campaign until she put it all into a novel, was she? It might be a good idea."

They talked on, about writing, about socialism, Sinclair being enthusiastic about Chicago and Jack being equally enthusiastic about San Francisco. A loud voice from close by was attracting a gathering and drowning their conversation. "Who is that?" asked Upton Sinclair.

"He owns banks," said Jack dryly, "lots of them. His name is Fred Crocker. His father was Charles Crocker, one of the Big Four."

"Oh, of course," Sinclair said. "Everybody knows who he is. Should we go hear what he has to say?"

Colonel Charles Frederick Crocker was still in middle age but his portly build and well-fed face made him look older. His voice was strong and assertive. He was clearly not discussing but lecturing. As one of the most influential men in the United States, however, whenever he spoke, everyone else listened. He was apparently reaching the end of his preamble and embarking on his main theme.

"My fellow bankers and I are firmly committed to upholding standards in San Francisco. We intend to improve the way of life and raise the quality of living. We want to raise prosperity and increase employment. We intend to encourage construction of houses and stimulate business expansion." He paused to survey his audience, awaiting the mild spatter of applause before continuing.

"We want to see all our banking customers, business and domestic, and all our shareholders share in the highly promising future of our fair city." This statement, pleasing to all, elicited stronger applause. Crocker beamed and continued. "We are determined to support the fight against crime and corruption and we intend to do all we can to stop money flowing down the rat-holes of charity and good works."

"Oh, brother!" breathed Upton Sinclair as he and Jack exchanged astonished looks.

"His wife sends all her laundry to Paris," commented Jack. They shook their heads despairingly, their socialist and humanitarian opinions in rebellion against Crocker's words. Both were inclined to speak out accordingly yet both were aware that they did not want a confrontation of any kind.

Their indecision was settled as Ted Townrow made his way through to join them and Jack introduced the two. Townrow looked pleased at being described as "my old college chum" and Sinclair was proud at meeting an aide of the mayor.

"There's a fellow Chicagoan of yours over there," said Townrow to Sinclair. "I just left him—Frank Norris. Do you know him?"

"I've heard his name," admitted Sinclair, "but I don't know him."

"He's been out here on the coast for a couple of years," said Jack, "as assistant editor on the *Wave*. He's a good reporter."

"That's right," Townrow said. "He was in South America before that, writing assignments for the *Wave* and for the *San Francisco Chronicle*." He smiled wryly. "Not very popular with some of our city fathers, I regret to say."

"He's writing a novel right now about how the railroads have taken control of California wheat farming," Jack explained for Sinclair's sake, seeing that Townrow did not feel comfortable criticizing any of the Big Three. His own knowledge of Norris came from Ambrose Bierce, who used his column to champion any knight of the pen who tilted at the windmills of the Central Pacific and the Southern Pacific Railroads.

"I'll take you over and introduce you," Townrow said easily to Sinclair. He took him by the arm. To Jack, he said, "We must have a chat—got a lot to talk about." He led Sinclair away.

Jack saw that Oscar Wilde was still the center of a worshiping cluster of admirers. Another familiar figure was moving in his direction though, and Jack had the thought that his investigation was certainly giving him the opportunity to meet a lot of well-known people. This one was Oscar Hammerstein, who turned toward Jack.

The impresario was wearing a light gray cutaway coat and trousers with a waistcoat that sported a gold chain. He was smoking another large, fat cigar. "Ah, Jack, isn't it? The young writer. You're going to tell me that you've changed your mind and you're going to write for me—isn't that right?"

"I'd like to," Jack said, "but I just can't at the present."

Hammerstein smote his forehead. "Oy, oy, I can't believe this! You don't want to write for me? Why, I could make you a big name on Broadway!"

"I don't think so," Jack said and grinned. "I don't believe I could ever live in New York."

Hammerstein shrugged philosophically. He waved the burning cigar in circles over his head and his volatile mind took an abrupt change. "I was thinking of bringing Offenbach's *Orpheus in the Underworld* here—then I saw some of the dances the girls here on the Barbary Coast put on! I thought the crowds would go crazy for the cancan but this town is years ahead! Have you seen the hoochy coochy?"

Jack nodded.

"Isn't that some dance! Still, it's not easy to know what the people here would like. Victor Herbert's *The Fortune Teller* is in its second year in New York. When it closes there, I thought maybe I'd bring it to San Francisco, but now I don't know. Maybe it's not wild enough for the folks here. What do you think?"

Jack was relieved that he did not have to make an immediate decision about becoming a big Broadway writer. It was a giant step when he was barely recovering from the excitement of getting forty dollars from *The Black Cat.* They discussed theater and the taste of the San Francisco patrons, Jack doing his best to conceal his slight knowledge of the subject. A man and woman approached and greeted Hammerstein by name. The three of them entered a lively conversation and Jack was excusing himself when a hand fell on his arm. He turned to see Carl Heindell, the deputy mayor.

"Having a good time?"

"Very much so," Jack told him. "I've already seen Frank Norris, Oscar Wilde and Joaquin Miller."

"Fine, fine." Heindell beamed. "Let's you and I have a few words, shall we?"

They moved into a space between two of the full-size sculptures. "Tell me about the state of your investigation," invited the deputy mayor.

Jack was taken aback at first. Then he realized that the mayor must confide in his deputy. Nevertheless, Jack's talks with Bierce and with Kipling about the far-reaching tentacles of the Big Three made him wary. He decided to tell most of what he had learned but not necessarily all of it. His own life had to be considered.

"The three girls who have been murdered all came from Alaska. They came together on the same boat. It was called *The Jewel of the North*. I think something must have happened on that boat but I don't know what it was. I think they were all killed because of that knowledge."

Jack paused to get the deputy mayor's reaction to that. His smooth face showed interest in Jack's words. He nodded slightly. "You've done well. What do you know about this vessel?"

"It was only in San Francisco a couple of days, then it sailed to the Dutch East Indies. The crew was disbanded immediately and there is no tracing any of them."

"Three girls dead." Heindell's voice was thoughtful. "Then the only bright spot in all of this is that we won't be having any more murders."

His eyes were on Jack's face. Jack kept his features composed, said nothing.

"Is that right?" asked Heindell. His voice was soft, presumably because he did not want to be overheard.

"I hope we won't be having any more," said Jack in measured tones. Before the other could pursue the point, he continued, "I need to ask you something. Who in the city government has the responsibility for the museums?"

Heindell frowned. "Does this have some connection?"

"I'm not sure," said Jack truthfully.

Heindell digested the answer, looked around the room. "That would be Jim Jefferson. He's over there. Shall we ask him?" Without waiting for an answer, he waved over a tall, elderly man with a surprisingly full head of wavy hair.

After introducing them, Heindell said, "Jim, this young man wants to ask you a couple of questions."

Jefferson waved a hand. "By all means."

Was Heindell merely being helpful? Jack wondered. Or was it a clever way of finding out what Jack's questions were and making sure that he was present when the answers were given? Once again, he was in a tricky position. Investigation for the Fish Patrol had not required this much subtlety, thought Jack. Still, if he considered himself a writer, he needed to be able to face any predicament with imagination.

"A vessel named *The Jewel of the North* made a voyage from Skagway to San Francisco recently," Jack said to Jefferson. "Was it commissioned by any of your museums?"

Jefferson looked mildly puzzled but he answered. "No," he said with authority.

"Was it carrying goods for your department of museums?"

Jefferson looked mildly amused. "No, it was not."

Jack persisted. "Have there been any major archaeological discoveries in Alaska recently?"

Jefferson shook his head. "Not to my knowledge. I
think I would have heard had there been any."

Jack looked rueful. "I must have been given some
wrong information. Thank you for your help."

Jefferson left them and Heindell turned to Jack.
"Have you tried to find out about this vessel?"

"Yes," said Jack. He put on a look of disappointment. "I can't find out a thing. Still—" he replaced
the look with one of brave resolve—"so many leads
do result in dead ends. I just have to keep trying."

Heindell nodded sympathetically. "I'm glad we got
to talk. I'll pass along your comments to His Honor."
He excused himself and merged into the throng.

The number of guests had increased considerably
by now. A band of musicians was trying to make itself
heard and was playing tunes from Gilbert and Sullivan, probably in deference to Oscar Hammerstein,
who had first brought their operettas to San Francisco.

Ted Townrow made his way through. "I just talked
to Stephen Crane," he told Jack. "Do you know him?"

"I know his works," Jack said. "He's a great writer.
I've never met him though."

"Probably better you don't," said Townrow. "He
has tuberculosis, looks and sounds terrible. Doesn't
seem likely to live the year out."

"I'll talk to him anyway," said Jack, "if I can find
him. By the way, I just had a talk with Carl Heindell.
He knows all about my mission for you and the mayor."

Townrow waved a deprecating hand. "Of course.
He's the mayor's deputy, he has to know everything."

"That's all right then," Jack said in relief.

"His Honor may not get a chance to talk to you
this evening," Townrow said. "All these people. Is
there anything to report?" He listened attentively as
Jack told him what he had told Heindell. Jack also
repeated the conversation with Jim Jefferson.

Townrow looked baffled. "Museums? What do museums have to do with anything?"

"Possibly nothing," said Jack. He said nothing about Beth Garland. He intended to find her himself and saw no reason to say anything until he did so.

Townrow moved away. The gatherings of guests were changing their composition and Jack found Oscar Wilde leaving one adoring group and starting another. The playwright waved cheerily to Jack. He looked as if he were in his element, with a continual replenishment of acolytes.

"Hello, there, young man."

Guests within earshot looked curiously at Jack, wondering who this was to be hailed by the great man. One of Wilde's newest entourage was evidently asking a question and the playwright replied, "Yes, the world is a stage—it's such a pity that it is so badly cast." Jack could not hear the precise query about marriage but he caught the reply.

"Women should always marry. Men, never."

Laughter rewarded all of Wilde's witty epigrams and maxims and Jack found himself in awe of the ease with which they flowed from his lips. He himself had a hard time forcing out the words and putting them together. Wilde seemed to do it so effortlessly, and although he undoubtedly had an ample stock of ready-made answers, so many of his clever ripostes had to be impromptu.

His eye fell on Jack again. He hailed him jovially. "Jack, my friend, I shall always regard you as the best critic of my plays!"

The attention of the assembly swiveled in Jack's direction. Jack was uncertain how to respond to this accolade, for he had learned to become suspicious of Wilde's satirical humor.

He felt he had to reply though. He said uncertainly, "I have never criticized any of your plays, Oscar."

"That, my young friend, is precisely why!"

Chapter 22

Jack's life had made him something of a night owl. He did not sleep late in the morning, but the irregularity of his routine when at sea had resulted in his mind and body becoming accustomed to sleeping at varying times and for varying periods. His time in the Yukon had trained him to get by on fewer and fewer hours of sleep. As a result of the intense cold and howling blizzards that made uninterrupted sleep impossible, he now slept five hours a night at the most.

As he left the mayor's literary party with a dozen thoughts revolving in his head, he did not feel tired. Maybe it was the stimulation too, he thought. Regardless of the reason, he headed for the Midway Plaisance. It was only a little after midnight and the action there would still be approaching its zenith.

A new motif was on the walls. The Alpine terrain had gone and was replaced by Roman chariots, gladiators and enticing slave girls. The air was thick as ever with tobacco smoke, and the angry buzz of conversation ebbed and flowed in the interval between shows. The pretty waiter girls hurried among the tables, trying to satisfy the seemingly endless thirsts, and the bar was four or five deep.

Owner Fritz Danner left a table conversation and came to Jack. "Think any more about Oscar's offer?" he wanted to know. "He liked you—you could make some real money writing for him."

"I just left Oscar," said Jack nonchalantly. "We talked about it some more. He has some good ideas."

Fritz's face lit up. "That's great! What are we gonna call the show?"

"We didn't get to that yet," said Jack. "The way these things work, the name of the show sometimes comes last."

"Sure, I understand." Fritz was delighted. "What are you drinking, Jack?"

Jack accepted a beer. An old acquaintance from seafaring days came to chat with Jack while Fritz went off to quell a potential fight at a poker table, arriving before firearms were produced as an easy solution. From the bar, Jack's pal Andy beckoned. "Flo's backstage, getting the girls ready for their next number."

"Something from ancient Rome, I gather," Jack said, pointing to the newly painted walls.

Andy leered. "And the whips aren't for the horses, either. Want to see Flo?" he asked. "She'll be coming out as soon as the girls are all dressed—which won't take long," he added with another leer.

Jack nodded. He surveyed the crowd and drank some of his beer. In a short time, the orchestra struck up an unbalanced musical number, the lack of balance being due to the inebriated trombone player, who was having trouble recovering his slide from a mischievous customer.

Flo appeared, eyes sparkling and looking spectacularly attractive in a dark purple dress that fitted her body to perfection. A small table had magically appeared at the same time despite the place being crowded and was set up in a niche with a view of the stage.

"Girls all rehearsed?" Jack asked. "I hear you have some new numbers."

"Not fully rehearsed," she answered with a smile, "we're trying them out tonight. Tell me, will the hoochy-coochy look like it belongs in ancient Rome?"

"Probably not," Jack said and grinned. "But I doubt if you'll get any complaints."

"How is the investigation going?" she asked quietly. "I want to see the killer of those three girls punished."

Jack knew that she had a strong bond with the girls she trained and was genuinely concerned. He made sure that the noise was sufficient that he could not be overheard before he told her that there was a fourth girl whose life was in danger.

"Beth Garland?" Flo shook her head. "I've never heard the name. You think she's in danger of being killed like the other girls?"

"I think so."

"But you don't know where she is?"

"She's hiding out and I think it's somewhere in this city," Jack told Flo. "I have no idea where. I've tried bars and dance halls and saloons." He did not want to upset Flo unduly so he did not tell her of the false lead he had followed.

She had one fingertip to her lips in a particularly lovely gesture but Jack knew she was concentrating. "If you have any ideas," he said, "tell me. I'm running out of them myself."

The trombone player had recovered as much of his sobriety as he needed and the playful customer had tired of the game and given him back his slide. The powerful instrument blew a blast of sound that made a few heads turn and Jack grinned.

"I was thinking . . ." Flo said.

"I could see that," Jack told her.

"Don't interrupt. I was thinking of that old saying, 'Can't see the woods for the trees.' "

"Go on," Jack invited.

"Well, there's another one like it. The question is, 'Where is the best place to hide a tree?' "

An inkling of where this was leading was coming to Jack. "And the answer is—?"

" 'In a forest,' of course."

Jack leaned forward, nodding. "Good, Flo. You're saying that the best place for Beth Garland to hide herself in San Francisco is—"

"Well, it's not in the dance halls where she could be seen on the stage. It's not in the saloons or the bars where she'd be on display waiting on tables."

"But the best place is—where?"

"Battle Row."

This was the area east of Kearney Street and down toward the waterfront, which comprised the red-light district and contained three main types of brothel— the parlor house, the crib and the cow-yard. The parlor house girls were the aristocracy of the profession, the prettiest and the youngest and charging as much as twenty dollars an hour. The crib was a room with one girl, while the cow-yard was a group of cribs under one roof—often several hundred cribs with a girl in each. The girls in the cribs charged as little as twenty-five cents.

"The Nymphia is the biggest place," Flo went on, "there are five hundred girls in there. Can you think of a better place to hide?"

Jack did not frequent such places but he knew of their existence and probably knew more about them than anyone not an habitué. He had a great respect for Flo's mind and knew that she was a sharp, clear thinker. He had to admit that her notion was sound.

The slave girls came out onto the stage amid tremendous applause. As slaves, they owned little or nothing and their poverty was reflected in their clothing, although Jack reflected that their bodies showed no signs of malnutrition.

"I'm trying out some new movements tonight," Flo said into Jack's ear. She was obliged to speak loudly as the applause continued unabated. "This one is called the Cifitelli."

"I like it," Jack called back. It consisted of slow, sensual convolutions of the body that started with the head and continued to express itself at continuing levels through the neck, then the shoulders, the breasts, the waist and the hips. It was all performed in a wriggling dance with motion like the contortions of a snake. The girls seemed boneless and their skimpy costumes swirled as if they would fly off. The trombone slide tilted into the smoke-filled air with flashes of brass and blaring sound.

"Now it gets faster," Flo shouted. "This is called the Karsilama." Jack knew that as Little Egypt, Flo claimed to have learned the hoochy coochy in Egypt, where it was said to have been performed in the time of the pharaoh. She certainly knew a lot about it and said that paintings on the insides of the pyramids depicted the dance.

It was much faster now, with rapid twirlings, more joyful than the earlier, lazily passionate gyrations. The audience was being encouraged to clap and the girls moved in time to their clapping. The dance increased in tempo and it soon was a contest to see who could outpace the other. The dance became a frenzy with the audience rising to its feet in excitement. This reached its peak as the costumes failed to stay in place and flew all over the stage like small fluttering birds.

The girls raced offstage, pretending to be embarrassed at their nudity. A few stopped to pick up the tiny garments, only to engage in arguments as to which belonged to which girl. The audience enjoyed this almost as much as the dance.

Finally, the stage was cleared and the orchestra played some highly inappropriate Strauss waltzes. The noise of the crowd settled down to its normal loud buzz.

"What about Nietzsche?" asked a voice. It was a question rarely heard in the Midway Plaisance. Jack turned to see, as he had expected, Educated Edith.

"Good question," Jack said. "When I was in the

Yukon, I spent hours reading him and many more hours thinking about his ideas."

"I liked *Beyond Good and Evil*," Edith said. "I think there's a lot in the way he shows how the words *good* and *evil* mean different things at different periods in history."

Jack nodded. "I like Nietzsche's theory of the superman—able to conquer all obstacles and overcome all difficulties. That's the kind of men we want as leaders and rulers. We want them to teach us and direct us."

Flo was looking from one to the other with an amused smile. Edith was warming to her theme. "At one time, good and evil meant 'us' and 'them.' At other times, it meant 'strong' and 'weak.' We can probably find lots of other meanings."

"Nietzsche found the world cruel and wicked," said Jack. "Doesn't that make it harder to find opposites?"

"He must have spent time here in the Devil's Acre," said Edith with a sly smile.

"I liked reading Nietzsche because he faced the realities of life—by being able to write about death," said Jack. He did, in fact, admire him for that reason, as he himself had faced death dozens of times, at sea, in the Yukon, on the Barbary Coast.

"I would have thought you were too much of an optimist to accept Nietzsche's attitude of futility and despair," said Edith, and Jack again found himself surprised at her range of understanding.

"It must be the superman notion," Jack said. "The superman has to be an optimist, to believe in himself and in his ultimate triumph."

"Are you two trying to change the world?" Flo asked gaily. "What about those of us who like it the way it is?"

"You couldn't like it the way it is here on the Coast," protested Edith.

"There are other places," Flo said archly.

Edith regarded her with dismay. "You wouldn't leave, would you, Flo?"

"Maybe," said Flo. "It depends."

She was looking at Edith as she said it, and Edith stole a glance at Jack. His expression did not change.

"I have to go," said Edith. "Start listing tonight's receipts."

"Let's talk about Nietzsche some more another time," Jack called out. "We should discuss Herbert Spencer too."

Flo watched Edith leave. "What a girl!" she said admiringly. "Not many like her on the Coast."

"There certainly are not," Jack said emphatically. He turned to Flo. "Tell me, is it safe for me at the Nymphia?" he asked.

Flo shook her head. "No, but you'll probably go anyway. I should have asked though—what do you mean by safe?"

"Well, I don't want to get hit on the head or even stabbed."

"I thought you meant safe from the girls," Flo said with a wicked smile.

"No," Jack said, "I'm safe from them here so I should be safe there too."

"You're safe here, are you?" Flo moved her chair closer.

Jack turned and matched her smile. "I thought I was."

Flo put her hand over his. "Not thinking of going there to Battle Row tonight, surely?"

"I was, yes. No time like the present. Why, don't you think this is a good time to go?"

"It'll be busy now. Might make it harder to find this Beth Garland. If she's popular, she might be taken all night." She patted his hand. "Besides, I've been getting a new show ready."

"Another?"

"Fritz wants another new one next week. I wanted to show you the set."

She led him by the hand. They went backstage and deep into the maze of rooms. Finally, Flo went into a room decorated to represent a Turkish harem. Lush curtains in scarlet and gold hung on the walls and Jack found himself ankle-deep in the purple, blue and yellow carpets. Bronze, copper and gold samovars rested on dark wood tables. Incense burners as tall as a man stood here and there. Huge mirrors in magnificently carved frames adorned the walls, and Jack paused in front of a large tree, where gaily plumaged birds on every branch regarded him with glassy eyes.

He was about to turn away when Flo came alongside him and reached for a button on the wall. As she touched it, the birds began to move and burst into song. Jack almost jumped out of his skin and Flo laughed merrily. Jack watched in amazement as the birds flapped their wings and pecked at imaginary food. She touched the button again and the birds reverted to frozen silence.

"This came from Gump's," Flo said.

Jack nodded. "I might have known." The fabulous treasure house on Post Street, half a block off Union Square, contained art and artifacts from all parts of the world. It had been owned and operated by Solomon Gump for fifty years, and all of the great mansions on Nob Hill relied on it for their most expensive jewels, baubles and decorations. Its collection of jade was said to be the finest in the world.

Jack was looking around him in wonder. "If you're looking for the bed," Flo said softly, "there isn't one."

"There isn't, you're right," he agreed.

"But there is this." Flo pointed to a heap of dazzling silks, spread out to make a divan. She walked over and dropped languorously onto it. She lay there, her head propped on one elbow and one shapely hip curved provocatively.

"Can't the Nymphia wait till tomorrow night?" she asked huskily.

"No, but it can wait," Jack said and dropped alongside her.

Chapter 23

By six o'clock the following evening, Jack had snatched a few hours of sleep and managed a few hours of writing. He walked along Stockton Street toward Pacific. Despite the early hour, the streets were filled with people. Some were leaving their day work, others were going to their night work. Tinkers were selling pots and pans, strident-voiced boys were selling the evening newspapers, knife grinders were pushing their converted bicycles, cabs were out on all the street corners, prostitutes were out in their finery while men and women carried boards advertising cafés, restaurants, dance halls. Even the Turkish and Russian baths had a steady flow of customers.

The Nymphia was a flimsy, U-shaped building, three stories in height. It had only just been erected but already it looked old. As Jack neared it, he wondered if it would withstand even one of the earth tremors that had been rocking the city over recent years. He was optimistic about this part of the search for Beth Garland though, as the Marsicania, the Nymphia's only real rival, had just been closed down through the efforts of the Reverend Terence Caraher, pastor of the Church of St. Francis and chairman of the Committee on Morals of the North Beach Promotion Association.

The Reverend Caraher waged incessant warfare against the brothels, raising a veritable army of volunteers to act as pickets and closing the streets for blocks in every direction for days at a time. Every newspaper published at least one of his letters a week in protest and his sermons named names of public officials who either owned or patronized brothels. In his zeal, the reverend also condemned dancing of all kinds, especially public dancing. He demanded the abolition of San Francisco's trolley cars as "dance halls on wheels" and vehemently attacked the roller-skating rinks that were becoming popular as "dangerous to both body and soul."

In front of the Nymphia, two uniformed policemen stood on guard. Even one policeman was a rare sight in the Devil's Acre. Jack stood across the street and backed into a doorway. He was still apprehensive of being followed and waited in the doorway, watching passers-by and looking for any suspicious dawdlers. Finally, satisfied, he crossed and approached the two policemen. He nodded to one of them as he entered and received a nod in return. The police were not there to interfere with the operation but to restore order should a fracas occur outside.

Inside, it was depressingly squalid and dim. Jack started on the ground floor. Long corridors were lined with wooden doors, each door with a viewing slot that could be opened from the outside by putting in a dime. Jack found the first three occupied and was not enough of a voyeur to stop and watch. Nor could he ask about the subject of his search, as it was clear that the occupants were too far along in their coupling to be willing to stop and answer questions.

At the fourth crib, a girl with a sad, pale face gave him an inviting smile and began telling him of the delights she was prepared to share. He cut her off quickly. "I'm looking for Beth Garland. If you can tell me where she is, I'll give you fifty cents." The girls accepted as little as twenty-five cents for their normal services so this was an offer that should be tempting.

"Come in first," the girl suggested. "We can—"

"No," said Jack firmly.

"I think I know her," the girl said. "Come in and—"

Jack moved on. The next room also brought a girl to the door. She was older, harder. She immediately began a bargaining session, wanting a dollar for the information.

"What does she look like?" asked Jack quickly. Her hesitation gave her away and Jack went on. Another room was occupied and the next two contained girls who were too transparent to be able to lie convincingly. At the end of the corridor, Jack was about to turn and try further when a man confronted him.

He was older but had a tough, mean look. He would be a difficult proposition in a fight, was Jack's assessment, even as he determined to avoid one.

"Having trouble finding a girl you like?" asked the other in a grating voice.

He was evidently one of the men employed to maintain order inside the Nymphia, for the policemen at the door would not enter no matter how serious events might become.

Jack put on his best smile and tried to sound like a lovesick swain. "I'm looking for one girl. I was here last week and she was wonderful. I'm trying to find her again but she's not in the same room."

"What's her name?"

"Beth Garland." Jack watched the other carefully but saw no flicker of recognition at the name.

"She's not on this floor," the man said harshly.

"I'd pay double if I could find her." Jack reached into a pocket. "Maybe you—"

The man shook his head. "I told you she's not on this floor. Try the next one."

He stood watching as Jack went to the rough wooden staircase. Jack was already considering that if Beth was in hiding, she might very well be using a

different name, but that was a dead end. He could
only pursue the name he knew.

On the next floor, he resumed his inquiries. The
results were the same. Most girls tried to inveigle Jack
inside but he had dealt with all kinds of riffraff on the
Barbary Coast and most of them were expert liars. He
could spot a lie easily and the girls in the Nymphia
were not convincing in their stories. One girl claimed
that she was Beth Garland but was unable to say how
she had come to San Francisco. Another claimed to
know her but that soon proved to be an obvious
untruth.

Jack was about to raise another sliding panel when
an enormous Negro came along the corridor. He out-
weighed Jack by at least one hundred pounds and was
built like a wrestler. His eyes gleamed red outside the
white and he had hands like giant hams.

"Choosy, ain't you?" His voice was deep and
booming.

Jack repeated his story. The small eyes studied him
suspiciously but Jack's ingenuous appearance and his
frank approach seemed to satisfy him.

"She's not on this floor. Try the top one."

Jack went up another flight of creaking stairs, relieved to have passed that hurdle. At the top, he
turned into another of the identical corridors. As he
did so, he heard a movement behind him. He stopped
and glanced back.

All he could see was a hand that was holding a knife
aimed steadily at his right side and only a foot away.

He moved his hands slowly away from his body,
opening the fingers to show that his hands were empty.
He turned very slowly. The grin that greeted him gave
him an icy feeling, for it was without humor and the
kind seen on a man who killed for the sheer enjoy-
ment of it.

Then the grin changed, became more human. The
face looked familiar too . . . a nose broken at least

twice, a swollen cheek where another bone had been broken and not healed properly, a heavy, chunky body that was all muscle.

"Looking for girls, Jack? That's not like you! They usually flock around you, don't they? What's so special about this one?" The words came out as if with difficulty and probably indicated further damage inside the mouth.

Jack knew that was the case and a grin broke out on his own face as he said delightedly, "Dutch Schultz! Ugly as ever! Boy, am I glad to see a friendly face—even such an ugly puss as yours! It means you're going to put that knife away!"

The knife disappeared and the two clapped one another on the back. They had been shipmates on the freighter *Santa Anita*. Jack had been about eighteen at the time, and though a veteran of a few years at sea, still young enough to attract the unwanted attentions of older sailors who found the absence of females on board intolerable. Dutch had a strong Puritan upbringing and intervened on Jack's behalf more than once.

"They told me to watch out for a shady character prowling about looking for some girl!" Dutch told him after they had exchanged stories of experiences in places and ports that both had frequented since they had last drunk together in a Barbary Coast bar where they had had such a riotous time that neither could remember its name. "That's why I was ready. Didn't know it was going to be you though!"

"So you're the security man on this floor," said Jack. "Don't tell me they trust you with all these girls!"

"I'm like a father to 'em," Dutch said and grinned.

"Then you know them all," said Jack, and the grin vanished.

"Who's this one you're looking for?" Dutch asked, but his question was curious, not suspicious.

"All I can say," Jack said quietly, "is that this girl's life is in danger. I have to find her before someone else does, otherwise she'll be killed."

"Don't read no newspapers," Dutch growled, "but I heard about those dance hall girls being killed. Is it something to do with them?"

"It could be," Jack said. "This girl's name is Beth Garland. Do you know her?"

Dutch shook his head. "Naw. What does she look like?"

"Corn-yellow hair, nice build, was a dancer, still looks like one."

Dutch shook his head again. Jack tried a different approach. "Any new girls come in recently?"

"Get new ones all the time."

"About a week ago? Any new ones arrive then?"

Dutch screwed up his face into an excruciating expression as he concentrated. It turned into delight as he said, "Yeah, there was one. Could have been a dancer, nice looking, clever sort of girl—cleverer than most of the ones we get here." He gave Jack a look of disappointment. "Doesn't have yellow hair though. It's black."

"What's her name?"

Dutch thought a few seconds. "Betsy something . . . I got it—Betsy Gannon."

Jack felt a momentary exultation. The same initials, Betsy Gannon, Beth Garland, it was understandable she should change her name. The change in hair color was a natural precaution too.

"Is she still here?"

"Sure. Wanna see her?"

Jack followed him to a room a few doors along. He put in his dime and opened the viewing slot. A girl lay on a bed. She sat up and smiled. She rose and walked slowly to the door. She had dark hair and the carriage of a dancer.

Jack saw that she was pretty and not yet showing

the ravages of working in a place like the Nymphia. Jack waited until she was at the door, close to the viewing slot.

"Beth Garland," he said. There was no query in his words.

She caught her breath and he saw the flash of alarm in her eyes. "No, my name is Betsy—"

Jack gave her no chance to say more. "Beth, I know who you are," he rapped. "Lola, Jenny and Hannah have all been killed. You are next. The men who killed your friends are looking for you. They'll kill you when they find you. I've come to help you."

She gaped at him, eyes still full of shock. "I don't believe you—who—"

"My name is Jack London. You don't know me but I know you and what I'm telling you is the truth. Your life is in immediate danger."

He leaned back so she could see him clearly through the slot, hopeful that his appearance would convince her. Beside him, Dutch had been listening to the exchange with amazement. He stepped forward, saying to Beth, "You know me, Betsy. Jack's a good guy. If he says it, it's true."

Her lips quivered. She reached for the bolt to open the door. Jack was looking through the slot when, out of the corner of his eye, he saw Dutch turn suddenly. Looking past him, Jack saw two figures hurrying along the corridor toward them.

They were Captain Cutlass and Spike Odlum.

Chapter 24

Jack's first thought was for the girl. "Keep it locked!" he shouted. "Don't open it till I tell you!" He had a glimpse of her terrified expression as he turned to meet the captain and his henchman.

Dutch stood staring at them uncertainly. Jack's words had alerted him that the two newcomers were dangerous, and even though Dutch's brain was not the swiftest on the Barbary Coast, he had heard Jack tell Beth that men were looking for her to kill her.

The corridor was narrow and barely had enough space for two men abreast. Captain Cutlass snapped out an order to Spike Odlum but Jack could not hear it. Nor did he wait to find out—he saw the captain's hand grasp the handle of his cutlass and start to pull it out of its scabbard.

During Jack's years of seafaring, he had been involved in dozens of fights, on ships and in ports. He had learned several invaluable lessons, many of which had helped him to stay alive. One of the most important was to make the first move.

That deadly cutlass was part of the way out of the scabbard already but Jack did not hesitate. He leaped at the other, concentrating on clamping one hand tightly onto the hand withdrawing the cutlass. For a few seconds, the two glared at each other, face to face, only inches apart. The cold eyes of the captain were implacable, the lack of emotion more chilling than hatred. His breath was hot as it escaped through the thin lips.

Jack could hear scuffling behind him where Dutch and Spike Odlum were grappling. He hoped Dutch had had time to pull the knife that Jack had seen earlier. There had been no time to see what weapon Spike was carrying.

The captain tried to jab his fist into Jack's ribs, hoping to cause him to loosen his grip, but Jack held on, determined not to let that weapon emerge from the scabbard. Jack blocked the blow with his elbow. They both fell off balance and crashed against the wall. Jack took the opportunity to throw a punch at the captain's throat. The blow was only partly effective but it clipped the captain's Adam's apple and Jack had the satisfaction of seeing tears trickle down the other's cheeks.

They swayed together, both straining over the cutlass and both seeking a chance to use their other fist. The captain was first, drilling a punch into Jack's midriff, but Jack had time to tighten his stomach muscles. In retaliation, he swung another blow at the captain's face, aiming for the eye. It missed and searing pain raced through Jack's hand as his knuckles connected with the cheekbone.

As the two of them rocked against the wall, Jack had a fleeting glimpse of the other contest. Dutch and Spike Odlum each had a knife and were within lethal distance of each other. They wove from side to side in the narrow corridor, eyes fixed, waiting for the chance to strike.

Blood was running down the captain's face from the laceration below his eye. It was only torn skin but Jack knew he must be aware of it. In a burst of anger, Jack punched again at the same target. Skin ripped further, and this time Jack connected with the eye. As he rolled back after the punch, he had the satisfaction of seeing the one eye closed. He tried to punch again but the captain pushed him back with his free hand and then dropped that hand on top of the other, using the power of both arms to pull his cutlass loose.

Jack tightened his grip but it was too late. The cutlass scraped as it came free. Jack tried to squeeze his body closer to the captain so as to give him no room to swing but the other raised his knee and rammed Jack in the testicles. Jack fell back, moaning with pain, and the captain swept his cutlass up to shoulder height and thrust forward with all his body weight behind it.

Jack was aware of movement directly at his back. He could hear Dutch's heavy breathing further away, so the man behind him must be Spike. Jack saw the shining blade coming at his throat. He was suffering too much agony to move, but as the blade came he swayed to avoid it penetrating his chest.

He felt the knife-sharp edge slice into the flesh below his armpit but the point went on past him and from behind him came an anguished yell from Spike.

The captain had thrown himself with his weapon and was well within Jack's reach. Jack swung a wild left hook that smashed into the side of the captain's nose.

The ex–Rough Rider was in a tough predicament but he had survived many a battle by his ruthlessness as much as by his skill. He held on to his cutlass, trying to pull it out of Spike, and Jack risked a glance over his shoulder. The weapon had penetrated Spike's back and he stood almost petrified with pain. It was the chance Dutch had been looking for. Without hesitation, he plunged his dagger into Spike's chest. There was a choking gurgle and Spike crumbled to the floor, the cutlass coming loose with a sucking sound.

Jack turned his attention back to the captain. He was a hideous sight. His cheek was bleeding freely and the eye above it was closed. His nose spouted blood and he was trying not to choke on the flow.

He looked more dangerous than ever.

His cutlass dripped blood as he came at Jack. For the first time, some emotion showed. His eyes glittered with fury and he was muttering through the blood in his mouth.

Jack pulled away, getting the captain between him and Dutch. He saw that Dutch had pulled his knife out of Spike as the other had fallen. The captain's bloody face turned this way and that as he assessed his chances in both directions. Jack guessed that he would spring at him, as he was unarmed, and he prepared himself as the captain swiveled in his direction.

It was a feint and the captain reversed and dashed at Dutch with a fiendish yell. He waved the bloody cutlass over his head and Dutch wisely shrank against the wall, holding his knife at the ready as the captain rushed by, his intent being escape rather than further conflict.

Jack went to Dutch after the noise of the captain's hasty descent down the rickety stairs had died away.

"Any damage?" he asked anxiously. "I was tied up with the captain," he explained. "I didn't see much of your fight."

"I'm fine." Dutch grinned. "Haven't had so much fun since I had to throw out three big Swedes last week." He pointed to Jack's shirt where the blood from his cut was seeping through. "Looks like he got you."

"The best part of his cutter took care of Spike here," Jack said.

Dutch looked contemptuously at the inert body. "Now how in the hell am I gonna get rid of that?" he wanted to know.

They both heard the thumping at the door at the same time. "Forgotten about her," muttered Dutch. "She must be the frail everybody wants." He gave Jack a mischievous glance. "What is she anyway? Some kind of virgin?"

The cover over the slot was up and Jack looked into a pair of blue eyes that gazed past him at the still-bleeding body. "Is he dead?" Beth asked. Strangely enough, she had composed herself and Jack felt relief that he did not have to deal with a hysterical girl.

"I have to get you away from here," he told her.

She nodded and opened the door.

"It's against the rules," Dutch reminded him, then grinned. "But seeing as it's you—"

"Can I help you with him?" Jack pointed to Spike's inert body.

Dutch shook his head. "I can handle him. You got to get out of here." He dragged the body into Beth's crib. Jack followed.

The crib was small with double casement windows on one side. It was divided into two even small chambers. In one were a built-in window seat and a couch. The other chamber had an iron framed bed, a washstand with a marble top and a kerosene stove with a kettle on it. There was a chest presumably containing clothes but Jack shook his head as Beth moved to it. "We'll try and come back for it later," he told her. "We have to go fast." To Dutch he said, "What about the guards on the other floors?"

Dutch propped the body by a wall so that it could not be seen through the viewing slot. "It'll be a while before I find him there!" He winked. "Come on." He scouted the staircase then beckoned them down. He had them wait until the ground floor was clear, then they hurried to the main entrance. The policemen on duty gave them only a glance as they went out.

In a small bar several blocks away, Jack watched Beth drink a brandy. She relaxed visibly when she was halfway through a second. The composure he had been surprised to find in her had obviously been part of the self-control she had had to exercise when entertaining men in the Nymphia. Both the tension and the composure were gone now and she was nearer to being a normal girl.

"How did you find me?" was her first question.

"A friend of mine had a good idea. Where do you hide a tree? In a forest."

She gave a tiny smile. It disappeared quickly. "Why are you looking for me?"

"I think you know, Beth. There were four of you on *The Jewel of the North*. Lola, Jenny and Hannah have all been murdered. I suspected that you might be next."

She shivered and looked at her brandy glass.

"Were there any other passengers?" asked Jack.

"I don't think so. We never saw any." She went on, "We were kept in one cabin, all four of us." She saw Jack's look of doubt. "You've been at sea, I can tell. Yes, it was crowded, very crowded. All of our meals were brought in to us." She grimaced at the memory. "It was very rough."

"Rough weather?" Jack recalled the ship's log. It had said that the weather was good.

"The ship rolled something awful. We were sick—all of us."

"Didn't they let you out at all?" Jack had suffered from seasickness himself during his earlier days and remembered the utter misery, not caring whether he lived or died.

"We complained," said Beth, "to the sailor who brought our food to the cabin. He felt sorry for us—the cabin smelled terrible even though he brought us a jar of Lysol. He must have talked to somebody, and after that they let us on deck every evening after dark. We never saw anyone except that one sailor. Our cabin had the porthole boarded over"—Beth smiled slyly—"but we managed to get one of the boards loose. It was the sixth or seventh day." Her smile vanished and she looked about to cry. "It must have been what happened then that got Lola, Jenny and Hannah killed."

"Go on, Beth," Jack urged. "What did you see?"

"We were near land. It was sunset. Another ship came out to us. They tied the two ships together and then we saw a wagon that must have been lashed on deck rolled down a ramp and on to the other ship."

"A wagon," Jack repeated. He was thinking of the manifest that Lloyd Sickert had let him see, the one that had listed a wagon loaded with Eskimo artifacts. He was mindful too of Nancy's words as she read from her husband's sharkskin notebook. "Did you see a second wagon?" Jack asked intently.

"No, just the one. We had a scare though when we thought someone on deck might have seen us. We put the board back so we couldn't see what happened next but we could hear. There was a lot of scraping and the ship rocked. There was shouting and yelling. It was some time before we left."

"Could you hear anything at all? Make out any words?"

"A man was giving orders and I thought one of the others called him 'General,' but I must have been wrong. They don't have generals on boats, do they?"

Jack did not reply to her question but he was sure that Beth was not wrong. It had been General Walter Williams on board *The Jewel of the North*.

"Did you see anything on deck when you got on in Skagway?" he asked.

"It was night. There was a big shape on the deck but we couldn't see what it was."

"What about when you arrived in San Francisco?"

"It was night again. That big shape was still there on deck but they hurried us off the boat before dawn."

"After that encounter with the other ship?" asked Jack. "Did you see or hear anything the rest of the voyage?"

"The ocean was smooth the rest of the way here. We took the board off two or three times but we couldn't see anything but water."

Jack sighed with frustration. It did not make sense.

A wagonload of antiquities from prehistoric times? Could it have been unloaded in that episode? Why? And if so, why was it still there when the ship docked in San Francisco?

"That was the sixth or seventh day, you said? When all that happened?"

"Yes," said Beth. "At least we knew where we were then."

"What?" Jack snapped. "Where were you? How did you know?" He noticed her empty glass despite this startling announcement. Maybe more brandy would bring more revelations. He waved for another.

"I said it was sunset," said Beth, as if that explained all. She caught Jack's expression and hurried on. "You see, Lola lived near there when she was a kid. Her parents often took her to see the sunsets—it's famous for them. That's why they call it Vermilion Bay."

"Vermilion Bay," Jack echoed the name.

"Oh, have you heard of it?" Beth sounded surprised. "Most people haven't. It's not a real name—it's really called Half Moon Bay."

Jack knew it. It was near Skeleton Point, a promontory north of San Francisco with particularly dangerous rocks that jutted out into the Pacific.

A waiter brought another brandy. Beth looked at it for a moment. "That might have been what got the girls killed," she said, almost to herself. She sighed and looked up at Jack. Her blue eyes were wistful. "As we were leaving the ship, Lola said, 'It was great to see Vermilion Bay again.' One of the crewmen getting us off the ship gave her a strange look. I think he heard her. After we had left the ship, he might have told somebody, but I don't know what harm there could be in that. Still, just in case, I told the girls not to say they were from Alaska but from some other place."

That clarified the point of the girls' conflicting stories, but it may have been the cause of their deaths.

Something had been unloaded from *The Jewel of the North* at Vermilion Bay. It had to be on to another, smaller ship, for the bay was shallow. The unloaded cargo sounded as if it must have been the mysterious archaeological remains on the wagon—but Jim Jefferson, the man who supervised the museums, knew nothing of it and even doubted that Alaska had any such remains of value. Or had Jefferson been covering up? Did he really know what this was all about? Was it a secret that was precious enough that three girls' lives had already been sacrificed to it as well as the Wells Fargo agent, Wes Montague?

"Drink your brandy," Jack ordered. "We've got to get you somewhere safe. You may not know what all this means but your life is at stake."

She gulped her brandy. "Where are we going?"

Jack had been trying to decide that while Beth was talking but the remarkable story she told had interrupted his thoughts. He could not take her to his room. There could be a man watching the ferry. He knew a lot of people on the Barbary Coast with whom she could stay but that would mean exposing them to extreme danger too. He had a sudden idea.

"I know. Come on."

They stood inside the doorway of the bar while Jack watched the street. He could see nothing suspicious. Still he waited.

"There's a church not far away, St. Bridget's. There's a nunnery attached to it. They often take care of women—when they get pregnant and there's no father, when they're young and abandoned. . . . They'll look after you until we get this cleared up."

He gave her his best determined look and she nodded. "All right. When do you think I can get my clothes?"

He smiled. If she was concerned about her clothes while her life was being threatened, she was handling the situation well. "Very soon. We'll take a cab over there. It will be safer."

"There comes one now," she said and started out the door. Jack pulled her back. "Wait."

They watched as it went by. Another came and a third one appeared around the corner. "Should be okay now," Jack said.

As the second cab came level with the bar, the two of them ran out and scrambled into the cab before it had even stopped. The driver looked at them curiously but he saw a lot of strange sights. "St. Bridget's Church," Jack called out. The cabby nodded and flicked his whip. The horse trotted off and Jack settled back with a sigh of relief.

Beth peered curiously out the window. "I haven't been out of that place in a long time," she explained.

The cab jerked to a halt. The cabby swore and cracked his whip and there was a loud clatter of the horse's hooves. Jack leaned out the window. The cab in front of them had stopped and they had almost rammed into it.

The cabby was yelling for the other driver to move his vehicle when there was further noise from behind. The third cab, the one that had been turning the corner, had pulled up directly behind them. Their own cab was trapped and it all happened so fast that Jack had no time to react sooner.

"Out! Fast!" he shouted to Beth and kicked the door open.

As he did so, a man in seaman's clothes and a prison haircut ran out of the cab behind and grabbed Beth as she set foot on the cab step. He was strong and brute-faced. He clamped one hand over her mouth and half dragged, half carried her to the cab behind. As Jack jumped out in pursuit, another man materialized. Jack felt a heavy weight crash on the back of his head. The world and all in it swam away down a dark river.

Chapter 25

A gray mist was all Jack could see when he opened his eyes. It separated into different shades of gray and one of the gray shapes crystallized into a face. Jack found he was flat on his back, and when he tried to sit up an excruciating pain hit him in the back of the head. He groaned and closed his eyes but opened them again when the face said, "I've got questions to ask you."

It belonged to Police Captain Patrick O'Donnell, and he was in a raw mood. Jack's mood was even worse, intensified by the pain that felt as if the back of his head was being torn away, slowly, agonizingly.

"You probably don't feel well," O'Donnell said in a tone that made it clear he did not care whether Jack felt well or not. He was still going to question him.

A wet cloth was behind Jack's head. As he struggled to a sitting position, the minuscule comfort of the damp cloth was gone. He reached for it and pressed it against his neck.

He was on a cot in a damp, cold room with iron bars. It was not a cell but probably an examination room. Moisture trickled down one wall. A dim kerosene lamp burned. No one else was present but Jack could hear movement and voices.

"You're going to ask me what happened," O'Donnell's gritty, uncompromising tones went on, and the individual words jabbed like needles into Jack's tender skull. "You were in a cab with a girl. A shopkeeper saw a man come from another cab, drag the girl away. He saw you hit on the head. Our man on the beat was called and he had you sent here. You're in the Taylor Street Police Station."

Jack heard and understood all of this despite his pain. He tried to rub the back of his head but the torment made him gasp. O'Donnell paid no attention. "You're probably wondering why I'm here. Well, it's because of these dance hall girls. The last time I saw you was when Hannah Green was murdered at the Yellow Canary. The time before that was that Jenny Morris. And now here you are again. What have you got to say for yourself?"

A uniformed policeman came in and signaled to O'Donnell, who waved him over. He leaned back to hear what the policeman had to say to him in a low voice, too low for Jack to hear. He nodded and motioned the policeman to leave.

The insistent hiss of the kerosene lamp was the only sound. The voices from elsewhere in the station seemed to recede. O'Donnell pushed his stony countenance to within inches of Jack's face. "Well?"

The pain was subsiding but Jack contorted his face in pain to gain time. It was not difficult, his head still throbbed and his neck was on fire, but the agony was lessening.

"That message was to say that her body has been found," O'Donnell said without emotion. "She's dead. What's her name?"

Jack's pain intensified. He wanted to vomit but choked it back. A fourth girl murdered—and for what? He felt a fury rising in him that was overcoming the pain. He would double his efforts to track down those responsible and he sensed he was now very close.

O'Donnell watched the reactions flickering across

Jack's face. He gave him a moment to recover. He repeated his question.

Jack thought of giving him the name of Betsy Gannon but decided against it. "Beth Garland," he said, watching for some glitter of recognition, but there was none.

"Who killed her?" O'Donnell asked harshly.

Jack winced again as he moved his head.

"I would have thought you did if you hadn't been here unconscious the last few hours." The police captain sounded regretful that his prime suspect had such a perfect alibi.

He sat back and his position suggested an easing of his attitude. Jack resolved to show some cooperation in return. He told his story of sympathy for the dance hall girls being murdered, exaggerating his friendship with them but tossing in a dissatisfaction with the police for not making any progress.

"So you decided to play detective," grunted O'Donnell.

"I know a lot of people here on the Coast," said Jack. "I thought I might find out something."

"And when you did?"

Jack tried to shake his head but winced and thought better of it. "I hadn't got that far," he admitted. He pulled himself into a better sitting position. "How was she killed?" he asked.

"With a knife." O'Donnell did not elaborate and Jack did not press him. "Why were you with her?"

"I had a tip that she had danced in the same show as one of the other girls. I thought Beth might know something."

"Who was the girl who had been in the same show?"

So the police knew even less than he had suspected. "Hannah Green."

"Where were you going in that cab?"

"We were going to St. Bridget's Church."

O'Donnell's face was too grim to show disbelief but he came close.

"It's true," said Jack. "Ask the cab driver where he was taking us."

The police captain asked more questions and Jack handled them adroitly. Finally, a police doctor was called in and pronounced Jack fit enough to be released. O'Donnell did not offer him a handshake as he left, but instead said, "Be careful with the amateur police work. It can be dangerous."

Jack gave him a nod and hurried out.

In his room, he bathed the back of his head with cold water, made a sandwich with two slices of stale bread and some pork, brewed a cup of mild tea and was soon asleep.

Next morning, he had only a slight headache as he rose at six o'clock, packed a cloth bag and went down to the ferry. At the central railroad depot, he bought a ticket for Mira Loma. The train left on time at eight fifteen and puffed its way north through green countryside, every once in a while climbing just enough to give glimpses of the blue Pacific Ocean. Before eleven o'clock it was turning to the coast, and ten minutes later it stopped in the small depot at Mira Loma.

Jack was the only passenger to get off the train and he looked at the rolling hills and the narrow brown strip of road. The only transport visible at the depot was a farm wagon with a boy unloading crates of plums. Jack walked over to him.

"Live around here?" he asked.

The boy was about fourteen, with fair hair and freckles. He glanced at Jack, kept on lifting crates but said, "Sure do. All m'life."

"Know how I can get to Half Moon Bay?"

The boy stopped, wiped his nose on his sleeve. He gazed at Jack in amusement. "What you want to go there for?"

Jack smiled and retaliated with another question—
a technique he had learned when he had been on the
debating team at Berkeley.

"Why shouldn't I?"

"Ain't nothing there."

"You know Half Moon Bay?" asked Jack.

"Sure do."

"Ever been there?"

"Sure I have."

"Did folk ask you why you wanted to go?"

The boy burst out laughing. "Guess not."

Jack joined in his amusement. "I'm an artist," he
explained. "Going to do some sketching there. Heard
it's really beautiful."

He had thought of saying he was a writer but he
was still wary of being followed, and the thinner trail
he left the better. He had made sure that no one followed him onto the ferry or the train but he was taking no chances.

"It sure is. Ain't nothing there though and that's
the God's truth."

"How do I get there?" Jack asked.

The boy regarded him slyly. "It's a fair walk."

"Any other way to get there?"

"Got a few horses back at the farm. Pa might rent
you one."

"You going back to the farm?"

"Soon as I unload these here crates."

"I'll help you," said Jack.

An hour later he was riding a good-tempered palomino named Rosebud. He loved horses and enjoyed
riding them but living in a city made the chances few.
On one of the occasions when he had been seen by
an old seafaring mate, the other had called out, "Hey!
Lookee there! A sailor on horseback!"

The trail was little used but Jack had no problem
heading west by the falling sun. The palomino wanted

to stop and nibble the alfalfa but Jack kept it moving. The old Spanish-style saddle was comfortable and helped him to think. He had done plenty of that during the train journey, but without reaching any conclusions as to what he was going to do when he reached Half Moon Bay.

All he knew was that *The Jewel of the North* had anchored there and transshipped the wagon that was on her deck to another smaller ship. Wes Montague's notes referred to a second wagon but what did that mean? The subterfuge enveloping the whole affair must mean that there was a lot to hide.

The afternoon had been sunny and warm. Now it was cooling rapidly as the sun neared the horizon. Insects buzzed around the palomino but its long tail deterred them. Finally, Jack topped a small rise and below him lay a bay with a perfect half moon shape.

He dismounted, leaving the horse to graze. He sat and opened his cloth bag. He took from it a brass telescope, no more than a foot long but with powerful magnification, another memento of seagoing days. He spent some time studying the panorama before him.

The rocks came right out of the water. Only a shallow-draft vessel could get in close. He could not see any habitations as he went over every foot of the land, beach and rocks. The boy's father had accepted Jack's story of being an artist and told him that no one lived in or near Half Moon Bay. It looked as if he were right.

Far out at sea, a shape near the horizon caught his eye. It was the only vessel in sight at the moment, though coastal freighters must sometimes be visible. Jack steadied the instrument and focused. It looked like a Revenue Cutter and was headed south. Farther up the coast, some patchy fog was gathering.

Jack took the palomino to the edge of the cliffs. They were not steep and offered several ways down. Jack picked the easiest and led the horse, stopping frequently to examine the terrain. A couple of sea-birds swooped overhead, calling out harshly. Soon he was able to hear the gentle swish of the lazy waves on a tiny beach. He remounted and rode along the beach, getting the horse accustomed to the smell and sound of the sea.

The sun was setting and Jack could see why it was called Vermilion Bay in earlier years. The rocks were being splashed with reddish orange light—a color that Jack had always thought of as Chinese red. The color was turning deeper by the minute as the sun slid down into the sea.

He reached the end of the strip of beach. To the north the rocks receded in low curves and he could see some distance, though the fog was thickening by the minute. The coastline was much the same—with one exception.

He dismounted and took out his telescope again. It was a lighthouse. It sat on a low promontory that jutted into what looked like deep water. Jack knew that there were over fifteen hundred lighthouses around the American coastline. Sailors could identify their location at night by the specific number of short and long flashes of the light. During the day, sailors went by the day marker pattern, and this one had horizontal circles of red and white painted around it, now badly faded.

This was Skeleton Point, closed for some years since the building of a larger, stronger light farther north at Point Perez. He examined it minutely. The wind, the rain and the spray had almost removed the paint. The rail on the platform at the bottom was broken in one place and hung at a forlorn angle. The structure, once vital to North Pacific coastal shipping, now had a desolate look to it.

Jack had once taken a trip out to Point Reyes light-house in Marin County just outside San Francisco. It had been sunny and clear when he arrived, yet within minutes, while he was still walking toward it, a fog had swept over it and visibility was reduced to a few feet. All sense of direction was lost and it had been dangerous to move for fear of falling off the cliff. He did not intend to repeat that experience here.

In the lee of a large rock, the wind had removed much of the sand and created a natural shelter. Jack put his thick army blanket in there and tossed his thirty-two-caliber Colt short-barreled revolver on it. The weapon was old but serviceable. He thought back to his first gun, a twenty-two-caliber pistol he had gotten when he was thirteen years old.

He unpacked his meal. It was a frugal one—a few slices of bread, a can of bully beef, a leather sack of water and some plums the farmer had given him.

He removed the horse's rein and tethered it near some brush that it was already eating contentedly. He gave it some of his water then ate his own meal. The moist, leprous-white fog had completely enveloped him and his surroundings by now. It was early for sleep but too dangerous for exploration. He tucked himself as far under the shelf as he could to give him protection from ocean spray and settled down. His neck was sore but soon forgotten.

He awoke to find he was being nudged in the ribs.

Chapter 26

Four-hour watches while at sea had trained Jack's mind to be awake instantly. He slid one hand onto his pistol, grasped it firmly then turned. It was the nose of the palomino nudging him awake. She evidently had a morning thirst after munching plenty of alfalfa.

He shared what was left in the leather sack then ate the rest of the bully beef with two slices of bread. Two plums were left and he ate those.

Spiky fingers of light were creeping up into the eastern sky but it was not fully dawn for about fifteen minutes. The fog had thinned but hung close to the ground in wispy puffs, swirling in an occasional breeze. After making sure that nothing moved during a thorough scan with the telescope, he remounted the palomino and rode along the beach. When it ended in sand dunes and rocks, he rode through the lapping water for a considerable distance. No other beach was apparent in Half Moon Bay so he went back and rode north, past his sleeping hollow and toward the old Skeleton Point lighthouse.

It looked just as desolate as it had the day before. It was prominent though with its faded red and white stripes. A light, overnight mist had moved out to sea and seabirds screeched raucously as they began their search for food.

Half Moon Bay was mostly to the south of him, Jack realized. The rocks and sand dunes ahead and to the north showed no beach. The beach that he was on must be the only accessible part of the coastline here. He trotted the palomino into the water. Even thirty or forty yards out, the water was only up to his boots. It would allow a shallow-draft vessel to unload. He rode up and down the beach. The tides would have obliterated any traces of activity long ago, and the sand dunes above the high water mark were undisturbed.

He dismounted, led Rosebud to a bowl-shaped depression between dunes, sat down and took out his telescope.

He examined the lighthouse in detail, covering every foot of the outside. He had cautiously led the farmer to tell him how remote his farm was, and Jack was sure that if any other strangers had been seen recently, the farmer would have mentioned it.

The telescope grated metallically as he closed it. An air of finality seemed to Jack to accompany the sound. It was the deciding point. The lighthouse was the only structure visible. Maybe it had nothing to tell him but he had to go and find out. Beth's murder had been the ultimate deed that had hardened his resolve to take any risk to end this string of horrors.

He led the palomino through the dunes and among the rocks. As he neared the lighthouse, he noticed something that had not been obvious before. A fairly wide path led up from the beach to the lighthouse and at only a moderate rate of incline. It sloped through the dunes and Jack went to examine it. A light breeze was blowing off the ocean now and ruffling the sand. If it had been used for any transport purposes, no traces remained.

Up close, the lighthouse looked even more decrepit. The rail around the lower platform was rusted through in numerous places and ready to fall into the ocean. The concrete slabs of the platform itself were cracked and pitted. Only a storm could hurl the water that high, but there must have been several of those. The paint of the red and white stripes was peeling and would soon be gone completely.

The top of the lighthouse looked to be the only part that was still in good shape. The glass with steel mesh set into it was intact. Jack took the palomino to a patch of good grazing higher up and used its reins as a hobble. He took the pistol out of his bag and stuck it into his belt. He half buried the bag near the horse and began to scramble down the cliff.

As he reached the lighthouse, he noticed a feature he had not seen before. A single-storied house was close to it.

Tending the light was a lonely life and appealed to some who, for a variety of reasons, did not seek human companionship. Most of these were bachelors and lived in the lighthouse, but to staff all of the fifteen hundred lighthouses around the American coastline, it had been necessary to admit married men to the service. Recruitment was made easier when a house could be provided. This had been one of those. It was a simple rectangular shape and Jack guessed that it had one large room that could be subdivided.

Wind-blown sand had piled against the house on the ocean side. The only windows were on the landward side. They were crusted with dirt and sand. Iron bars added protection. Jack scraped one pane clear but wooden slats nailed on the inside blocked the view. A door was firmly locked.

He went to the lighthouse and climbed to the cracked concrete platform that ran around the base. A rusty iron door was set into the building and an iron chain hung over the handle. To Jack's surprise, the chain did not fasten the door. He took a grip on the handle. . . .

There was a fleeting doubt as to the wisdom of entering. It was soon gone. Jack had sporadic moments of recklessness when he assessed the danger and then plunged in without further regard for the risk. He had such a moment when he bought his first boat, the *Razzle Dazzle,* and promptly took it out into a raging gale. He had another when he was in the Klondyke and first looked up at the forbidding white hell that was the Chilcoot Pass. He knew that a score of miners had died there in recent months and he could see the blizzard sweeping down it. No other man dared to climb it that day. Jack had done so and survived.

These thoughts and memories flashed through his mind now. He liked to think that his inner brain worked faster than his consciousness—it was a part of the "superman" theory that he had briefly discussed with Educated Edith. The hazards carefully calculated, the decision was "go ahead."

He turned the handle. The door opened and he went in.

The rough walls had been painted once but most of the paint had long since peeled off. A smell of age and disuse pervaded the place. A large steel plate was set into the floor but dirt filled the crack around the rim. It looked not to have been lifted for a long time. An iron staircase went up, turning and turning. He took it, one hand near the pistol in his belt, peering up as far as he could see.

The staircase spiraled then came out on another floor. It looked exactly like the one below. There was a third level and it was the same. The fourth level had a door that went out onto an open balcony. It ran all the way around. It was wide, with an iron rail. On the fifth floor, more steps went to the level that had contained the light.

It was gone, detached from its concrete base. Other gouges in the walls looked like places where other useful equipment had been torn out and taken elsewhere. The wall came up to waist height and above it was the wire-reinforced glass.

Jack looked out at the vista. The glass was dirty and

stained but the view of the Pacific Ocean stretched way out to the horizon. A few patches of the morning fog remained, misty white blurs on the shimmering blue surface. Beyond the fog, the sea was devoid of vessels except for a speck near the horizon. Without his telescope, Jack could not make out its shape.

The sandy beach was below. Jack tried to spot the palomino, but it must have been among the dunes, for he could not see it. He walked around the full three hundred and sixty degrees. To the east, the land was empty of movement, and also to the west. He stood, pensive. Something bothered him about the air. He sniffed. Rank, musty—but there was more.

What was it? Some other odor that blended in yet should not be there. He sniffed again . . . tobacco! Someone had been smoking in here.

A hobo? Skeleton Point was surely too far off the beaten track for that. Besides, it was not the raw, offensive smell of the cheap tobacco that a hobo might smoke. It was a better grade, perhaps a cheroot.

He patted the pistol in his belt for reassurance and walked all the way around again. He could see nothing unusual or different. What was that . . . ?

Two moving contours were coming through the sand dunes from an inland direction. Where exactly had he left Rosebud? If she was in the path of the approaching figures, he was in trouble. These grew larger now and were distinguishable as two men on horseback, heading directly for the lighthouse. They showed no sign of having heard or seen Rosebud. Jack sighed with relief.

He thought of hurrying down the steps so that he could not be caught up here but the riders would probably reach the foot of the lighthouse before he could get out. Besides, he thought, why would they come in? There was nothing here so he was probably safe from discovery. Best to wait and watch.

They rode into sight. It was hard to tell much about

them. They might be farm workers. Both looked sturdy. They dismounted and went to the house. Jack could just see the far end of the structure and he saw one of the men unlock the door. The other joined him and together they pulled.

As the door moved, the entire end wall of the house swung open. The men went inside. Jack hesitated again. Should he make a dash for outside? He was still aware of the danger of being trapped up here. It was too late. The men came into view. They were straining to pull something outside. Jack watched it appear little by little. It was a large, high-sided enclosed vehicle.

"The second wagon," Jack murmured to himself.

The two men dragged the wagon well clear of the door. They went back inside and emerged with what looked like a section of floorboard, then another, then yet a third. Jack knew that many houses attached to the beacon lights had cellars. The men must have removed the flooring of the inside of the house so as to access the cellar. One of the men was unbolting the rear door of the wagon and hinging it down. The other disappeared inside and came out with something over his shoulder. It looked like a large brick, but surely the man was too strong to have to carry it like that. . . .

It must be made of a very heavy material. Jack knew of only one material that could be that heavy. He had spent an unforgettably agonizing portion of his recent life in seeking it.

Gold.

The first man finished his task and looked as if he were going to help the other. For a second, the other man paused, looking directly up at the top of the lighthouse. Jack ducked back. Had he been seen? He had been so mesmerized by what he was watching below that he may have been too slow in moving out of sight. He waited. Time passed. Jack began to feel relief.

A clanking sound from below told him that the iron door was opening. Heavy footsteps thumped on the metal staircase. Jack's heart beat faster. There was nowhere to go. He was trapped on the top floor. He pulled out the revolver and checked the chambers. They were all loaded. He flicked the safety catch off and pushed the gun back into his belt, making sure his jacket covered it.

The footsteps continued. Jack measured the floors by the pauses in between. Two, three, four, five . . . Jack tensed as the head came in sight.

The man stopped, staring at Jack. He came up the remaining steps to the top. "What are you doing here? This is government property!"

He was tall and strongly built. His eyes were hard and the rest of his features were sharp and angular. He wore a light jacket with several pockets. It was reminiscent of another similar garment. . . .

Two characteristics came together in Jack's mind at the same instant. The man had a rolling gait, like a cowboy, or at least one who had spent a lot of time in the saddle. Then there was the jacket. It was similar to the one that Captain Cutlass wore. It had been cut down from a part of the uniform of the First U.S. Cavalry Volunteers, the Rough Riders.

Jack smiled pleasantly. His right hand eased up slowly against his thigh. "I didn't know this was government property anymore," he said in a steady voice. "I thought this place had been decommissioned."

"It's government property," the other repeated.

"That's not what they told me in Alameda," Jack said. "At the Revenue Cutter Service," he added. He thought it unlikely that the man would know any different. He was right.

"It's going to be decommissioned," the man blustered.

"In three to five years," Jack said.

"What are you doing here?" the other asked sharply, abandoning that line of argument.

"I'm an artist," Jack said and smiled. "Painting a series of lighthouses."

"There's nothing inside here."

"I see that." Jack nodded. "It's a nice view though."

It was a standoff. Jack did not move and the other stayed at the top of the steps.

The iron door below creaked and groaned again. Someone else was coming in. Jack thought about running down the steps but he would be trapped between the two of them that way. He waited. Footsteps sounded on the stairs.

A floppy black hat came in sight, then a long black coat, and Jack did not need to see the face to know that it was General Walter Williams.

Chapter 27

His cold impassive expression showed no change as he came onto the top step and saw Jack. The other man moved aside to allow Williams to join him. "Says he's painting lighthouses," he grunted.

"Surely you haven't given up writing," Williams said, as if they were having a perfectly normal, friendly conversation.

"I do both," Jack said, equally normal.

"Pay better than prizefighting, do they?"

Jack said nothing.

"You've been interfering in my affairs too much lately," Williams said. He shook his head sadly. "I'm going to have to do something about you. I've been tolerant up to now."

"Your tolerance included murdering dance hall girls," Jack told him, feeling a flush of anger rising. "That's why I've been—as you call it—interfering."

Williams flicked a black-gloved hand. "That's all over."

"Because they're all dead."

The other man growled and took a step forward but Williams moved a hand. The advice that had served Jack so well before came to his mind and he acted on it without a second's delay. He pulled the revolver out of his belt and aimed it steadily between the two.

"Well, well," said Williams in a foppish voice. "I wasn't expecting that. We haven't seen you armed before. You writers are supposed to be thinkers, not doers. What do you intend to do with that weapon?"

"Step aside," Jack ordered. Neither moved.

"I can shoot you and your man can move your body," Jack offered amiably. Slowly, they moved away from the top of the stairs. Jack would have liked to search them for weapons but it was too risky. In this confined space, one could easily jump him while he was searching the other. He had nothing to tie them with, and anyway, that carried the same risk.

"Turn around." They did so reluctantly, both tense and waiting for the slightest chance. Swiftly, Jack twisted his wrist and cracked Williams on the back of the skull with the side of his pistol. He knew the spot, the nerve center that caused immediate unconsciousness but broke no bones.

Williams crumpled into an untidy heap, but even before he fell Jack stepped back, anticipating the other man's quick reaction. There was a look of hate but Jack waved the pistol and the other turned away slowly, then joined Williams on the floor as Jack repeated the blow.

He hurried down the steps. At the bottom, he eased open the iron door. He could see a figure coming out of the house with another gold brick over his shoulder. He heaved it into the wagon and went back for another.

As the man entered the house, the whinny of a horse sounded clearly across the dunes. It was Rosebud. Jack tightened. Had the man heard it? If they found the palomino, it would give him away. But when the man came out, he had another gold brick on his shoulder and Jack sighed with relief.

It was Jack's first opportunity to review his findings. The story about archaeological remains in Alaska had been a blind. The cargo that Williams had been bringing from Skagway on *The Jewel of the North* had been gold from the Yukon deposits, melted into bricks. It had been stored in a wagon and carried on deck. Little wonder it had made the ship unstable, causing sea-sickness among the girls and having to move slowly, causing arrival in San Francisco to be two days late.

The ship that had come alongside in Vermilion Bay—as Lola Randolph had known it—had taken off the wagon with the gold and replaced it with a second wagon. The substitution would not be noticed until unloading after arrival in San Francisco.

Meanwhile the gold was hidden in the cellar of the house at Skeleton Point and the wagon above it. Presumably, they were now taking it away. Perhaps the vessel out at sea that Jack had seen was coming to load it.

He had to get away and prevent that happening. He opened the door. The man seemed to be oblivious to the failure of his mate to return but he might soon get suspicious. There was no time to lose. Jack waited until the man was back in the house then he put the pistol back in his belt and went outside, heading for the sand dunes.

Something jabbed into his back. He felt it break the skin and there was a twinge of pain. The voice of Captain Cutlass said, "Not so fast. You and me—we've got some unfinished business."

Jack stood motionless. The captain had only to apply one sudden pressure to his weapon and that deadly sharp point would penetrate his body and come out of his chest, dripping blood.

"Where's the general? Where's Vince?"

"They're in there—"

"Did you kill them?"

Jack braced himself for a desperate lunge forward if he felt the cutlass move, but he was able to gasp, "No, I didn't. They're alive. You can see for yourself."

The captain called out to the man still carrying gold bricks. He came over. He had a callous look to him and a bristle haircut that had not had much chance to grow in the short time he had been out of prison or an army jail. "Go look in the lighthouse," the captain ordered.

Jack stood frozen for what seemed like an eternity. He knew that the cutlass had only to move another few inches and it would be in his heart.

The man came back. "They're out but they're alive, both of 'em."

"Search him."

The man did so, taking Jack's pistol.

"Watch him," the captain ordered. "Shoot him if he makes a move. I'm going to look to the general."

The cutlass point pulled out of his back and there was another spasm of pain but the wound was not deep. Jack ignored the pistol—his own—that the other was holding on him and gently exercised his shoulder. He heard the captain clang the iron door and mentally counted the levels until he figured that the captain had reached the top.

"I never keep a round in the breech," Jack said conversationally. "Only in the chambers." The man stared at him blankly for a second, then the words began to register. "Too dangerous," said Jack and launched himself through the air.

The hammer clicked. It was confirmation of Jack's statement but it didn't matter now. His body crashed into the other and they went down together, Jack's full weight thumping down on his adversary. The revolver fell to the sand and the air whooshed out of the other's lungs. Jack punched him once in the throat and again on the chin. The man slumped and Jack grabbed his gun and raced into the dunes.

He was soon panting. The sand was fine and soft. His boots sank into it and the dunes rose to several feet in height, making a zigzag route unavoidable. He heard noises and shouts but raced on. His head began to buzz and his chest felt as if a steel band encircled it and was tightening.

A cloud of sandflies rose and Jack plunged through it. He stumbled over the root of some plant but recovered. The cries behind were getting louder as his pursuers were catching up. He resisted the urge to look back. He raced on, keeping a tight grip on the revolver. The sounds behind him became a thundering tattoo on the sand. The nearest of those chasing him was on a horse.

He was staggering now and his breath came in deep, wrenching gulps. The horse was right behind him when Jack saw what he was looking for.

A large sand dune had piled so that the near face was almost vertical. Jack flung himself at it, rolled to turn and aimed the pistol.

The horse galloping toward him instinctively turned to avoid the sand dune. Jack had a perfect target. He fired promptly.

He had a fleeting glimpse of a face as the body flipped over. It was the man he had just left, the one who had searched him and taken his pistol. Jack was less interested in him than in the horse. He reached up to grab the reins but, startled by the gunshot, the animal reared, front feet prancing, nostrils flaring. Jack backed away from the flailing hoofs—and the motion saved his life.

A bullet sizzled past his face so close that he felt the heat and it thudded into the sand. It was Vince, the man who had first accosted him and who now without doubt had a sore head from Jack knocking him out. He was on a horse too and angrily pulling at the reins so that he could get a clear shot at Jack.

The riderless horse near Jack saved his life again. It tossed its head and stamped, staying in the line of fire. Jack had a fleeting glimpse of a long-barreled Navy Colt pistol in Vince's hand. The man was waving it and cursing both horses. Jack flung himself to the ground and took quick aim and fired underneath the belly of the nearer horse.

Vince let out a muffled cry and slumped in the saddle. At the shot, the riderless horse promptly galloped off, and Jack got off another shot with just enough time to aim this one more accurately.

Vince's horse raced off after the other. Vince slid out of the saddle and lay inert on the sand. Jack paused to get his breath, not taking his eyes off the body. Then he walked up to it, kicked the Navy Colt out of reach and picked it up.

He examined the body. His first shot had entered the thigh and blood was still spurting. The second shot had hit him in the heart.

He looked for the first body, taking no chances. He felt a grim satisfaction on finding it—his one shot had hit the man squarely in the chest and killed him instantly.

He looked for the man's weapon. When he found it in the sand, he saw that it was another Navy Colt. Jack noted that both men wore the blue flannel shirt and the brown trousers with leather boots and leggings that had been the standard uniform of Teddy Roosevelt's Rough Riders. Captain Cutlass had evidently recruited the worst element from that unit when it had been disbanded, and they had brought their clothing and their weapons with them.

Captain Cutlass! He had sent his men ahead and obviously thought that they could take care of Jack. If the horses had returned to the lighthouse with empty saddles, he would know that he was wrong, but perhaps the horses were grazing instead, grazing on the rich alfalfa. Jack sat so as not to be visible over the sand dunes and waited. He had one Navy Colt and his own thirty-two in his belt, and the other Navy Colt, not fired and with all six chambers full, in his hand.

He did not have to wait as long as he thought. A questioning call echoed through the dunes. It was faint, but when it came again, it was much closer. It was Captain Cutlass.

Jack saw him. He came riding a pinto with a skew-bald pattern, perhaps another trophy from the Cuban campaign. He had wondered how the captain and the general had got here. It must have been on horseback, and they must have tethered theirs at the other side of the house.

The captain approached at a canter, riding carefully, waving his cutlass as if chopping at invisible enemies. He must have been following hoofmarks in the sand, for he kept looking at the ground. He had not yet seen Jack but he was heading in the right direction. Jack tensed and raised the Colt.

Captain Cutlass saw him precisely at that same moment. He waved his sword triumphantly and clapped his heels to the horse. It came bounding through the dunes. This was going to be easy, thought Jack, but even as he raised the revolver to take steady aim, he had a pang of doubt. Was the captain that reckless? His cutlass was almost a part of his body, but to come charging a man with a pistol . . .

To Jack's astonishment, he tossed the cutlass onto the sand. A rifle appeared in his hands that must have been sitting across his saddle. It had a distinctive shape and Jack recognized it for a Krag-Jorgensen, the deadly carbine that had been rushed into production just in time to equip the Rough Riders and become the most feared weapon in the campaign.

A bullet whistled past Jack's head and another whacked into the ground at his feet. Jack threw himself full-length on the sand, aimed at the rider and pulled the trigger. The bullet went wide. Another from the captain's carbine kicked up a spurt of sand and Jack fired again and then again.

The horse gave a pitiful neigh, its front legs buckled and it fell dead. One of Jack's bullets had gone low and hit it in the head. The captain was almost trapped by its falling body but squirmed loose, the carbine in his hand. Still on the sand, he fired one-handed but the shot blazed over Jack's head. Jack sighted and emptied the chambers, firing as fast as the gun would cock. He pulled the trigger again but on an empty chamber.

The carbine fell out of the captain's hand. He tried to scramble to his knees, looking wildly for his beloved cutlass. He saw it and crawled toward it. He dropped his fingers onto the handle and desperately tried to lift it.

Jack was on his feet and walking to him. As he went, he tossed aside the empty Colt. The captain saw it and some hidden energy reserve sent a surge of strength through him. He rose to his feet and raised the cutlass.

For the first time, Jack saw his face show extreme emotion. He was transformed into a wild, raging fury of a human being. His eyes blazed and his mouth opened and closed. With a supreme effort, he swung the cutlass.

Jack pulled out the other Navy Colt and carefully shot him in the middle of the chest.

Chapter 28

Jack rode Rosebud back to the lighthouse at Skeleton Point. He had turned the other horse loose, retrieved Captain Cutlass's carbine and his cutlass. In the process of searching the body, he had found a knife in a sheath under the arm. It had a very thin and very narrow blade. There was no doubt that it was the weapon that had killed the four dance hall girls and Wes Montague.

Jack knew he should feel exhausted but survival against heavy odds had given him a feeling of exhilaration. The theme of survival was one he had used before but its range was limitless. There were the germs here of several stories, he thought. That had to come later though. For the moment, he had to forget writing and concentrate on the present.

Only one man was left now. General Walter Williams. He reined in Rosebud as he came close, frowning in amazement. On the platform at the base of the lighthouse stood a solitary figure, all in black. As Jack dismounted and walked onto the platform, General Walter Williams turned to face him.

"I did not realize that you were such a resourceful character, Jack London," he said, and there was genuine recognition in the words. "I suppose there is no need for me to ask about the captain, about Vince and Ike?"

Jack shook his head, uncertain.

"If you write as well as you fight, you will be very successful," the general continued. "Now, let me ask you something. How did you know?"

Jack was not clear about the drift of the question so he shrugged and said, "I figured it out."

"I mean, how did you know it was today? How did you know we were taking the gold out today?"

Jack tried not to smile. It was the one thing he had not known. He had only just learned that a shipload of gold was at the heart of all this. But how were they taking it out? He thought of the ships he had seen a couple of times. Now as he recalled the occasions, it had probably been the same ship, waiting to come in and unload the gold.

That meant that sufficient men would be there to overwhelm him. No wonder the general was calm and possessed.

He looked past the general, out to sea. Was the ship dropping anchor already? He could not see a vessel close in. No ships were visible at all—but wait . . . one mast was out there. It was the same one he had seen before. Even without his telescope, he could make it out as a Revenue Cutter.

The general saw the direction of his gaze. "Yes, the cutter's out there again. It's only a routine patrol but it has forced me to abandon my intention to get the gold out by sea. That's why we had to store it here until we could find a way to ship it overland. I have a special train coming in to Vacaville Depot tonight. But now, you have me in a quandary. Vince and Ike have only been able to load a few of the seven hundred bricks."

Jack felt a wave of relief that he did not have to fight a dozen sailors. He wondered what Williams was leading up to though.

"I can see that you're giving it some thought. There is ten tons of gold there. The bricks must be worth— oh, about ten thousand dollars each. Help me load the wagon and drive it to Vacaville Depot and you can keep five of them."

The sheer audacity of the proposal stopped Jack in mid-breath. Williams took it for greed. "I had heavy expenses with that voyage, leasing the boat, raising a crew, paying them off and getting them onto other ships immediately on arrival in San Francisco, storing the gold here."

"There was more," said Jack, his voice not steady. "You had to have the captain kill four girls who knew more than you intended. They didn't understand it all but if they told others, someone might have been able to put it together."

"Like Wes Montague," said Williams. "He was putting it together. He was on the verge of complete discovery. If I hadn't had an informant in the mayor's office, I wouldn't have known about him. Yes," he went on, "very heavy expenses. So my offer to you is a generous one. You'll have the gold in your hands at once. No waiting to be paid off. You don't even have to wait until I'm president. When I am, you can be my personal biographer. You might want to write the story of the Canal."

His voice took on a more persuasive tone. It sounded uncharacteristic after the authority of the military man.

"It's a lot more money than you'll ever make writing, even if you become as well known as Mark Twain. What do you say?"

His left arm hung by his side, the hand open. The right was hidden among the folds of the long black coat that Williams affected.

Playing for time, Jack pretended to consider. "I think ten bricks would be more appropriate, don't you? After all, a general alone doesn't load nine tons of anything into a wagon—not even gold."

A brief flame flickered behind the normally fathomless gray eyes. Perhaps Williams had already decided that his offer was not likely to be accepted. Regardless, Jack had no doubt whatever that killing him and disposing of his body near the Vacaville Railroad Depot was a far more probable method of payment than giving him any number of gold bricks.

Jack put a hand to his shoulder, slowly, not wanting to provoke the other too soon. "Your ungallant captain jabbed his cutlass into me. I can feel the blood still running," he exaggerated.

"Yes, the captain was frequently over-exuberant when he had that cutlass in his hand," sighed Williams. "It infuriated me when I found out that he was slashing those girls just as he had his prisoners in Cuba. My instructions were to kill the girls and I expected him to accomplish that with his knife only, leaving little trace."

Jack suppressed his anger with difficulty at the callous manner with which Williams said the words. But he wanted to keep him talking, especially with that right hand still hidden.

"You're saying you're not physically well enough for such strenuous work," Williams murmured. "That's a shame. In that case, you're not much use to me, are you?"

"I had one job where I stoked boilers for fifteen hours a day," said Jack. "I like writing better."

Williams nodded, as if in understanding, but his words were icy. "I have a twenty-five-caliber Derringer in my hand under this coat. I would hate to blow a hole in it but I can see you are not a reasonable man. Too bad, you could—"

An indistinct noise and a movement distracted him and he looked over his shoulder. Rosebud had wandered to the edge of the sand dunes and stood some feet from the stone platform. She had tossed her head and whinnied, probably wanting to return to the alfalfa pasture.

Williams spat out a curse, recovered and fired the

Derringer. Jack was only a split second later, jerking
his own short-barreled thirty-two out of his belt and
pulling the trigger.

The bullet from Williams's gun burned Jack's left ear
as it sped by. Jack's shot hit Williams in the arm and
the Derringer fell to the concrete platform with a clatter.
Then Jack was at grips with the general, scratching to
get at his throat. Williams was small but strong and
wiry. His arms came up between Jack's and he
smashed them aside. Jack was ready with a left jab
into Williams's ribs and there came a gasp of pain.

Williams was struggling to get a hand under his
cloak, where Jack supposed he had another weapon.
Jack clamped on to his wrist and dragged it away.
Williams punched with the other hand but there was
no weight behind it. Jack swung a right underarm jab
into Williams's midriff and then hooked his left
around in a blur of motion. It connected with the side
of Williams's face and he fell away.

That freedom gave the general the chance to reach
under his cloak again and Jack had to spring at him
to keep the hand from coming out. They strained together with Jack's superior weight and strength gain-
ing rapid ascendance. Jack rammed Williams back
against the iron rail.

A crunching, grinding sound came as the whole section of rail, rusted in the concrete, began to tear loose
from the impact. Williams yelled and tried to snatch
at the rail for support but it was falling away. He
gripped it too late. Jack pushed him, partly to push
him off the edge and partly to push himself back so
that he did not follow.

As Jack fell on his knees, he saw the black-clad
figure spin away, down and down, to disappear in the
spray and spume among the rocks below.

It seemed as if it had been the longest day of Jack's
life, but then he recalled long hours at the wheel of

the *Sophia Sutherland* while whaling off Yokohama battling through a North Pacific gale. That brought memories of his first day in the jute mill, fourteen hours of almost continuous labor, but even that paled by comparison with slogging up the endless slope of the Chilcoot Pass in a howling Alaskan blizzard with a hundred-pound pack on his back.

Enough of the memories, thought Jack. They were just reactions to the stress. He looked out of the window as the train rolled along the coast south toward San Francisco. He had put back the gold bricks that had been loaded into the wagon, replaced the floorboards, and with Rosebud's help pushed the wagon back inside the building. He had used some steel chain from the lighthouse to fasten the door securely. Then he had put the three dead bodies onto Rosebud, one at a time, and taken them to the cliff edge. He felt little compunction about dropping them out of sight.

Returning the faithful Rosebud had been a wrench. He wished he could tell the farmer that she had saved his life. Instead, he made him a present of the other two horses. They had scented Rosebud and insisted on tagging along, so Jack had removed their saddles and reins and buried them in the sand. The farmer thought it unusual to have stray horses "in these parts" but accepted them gratefully.

The train puffed into San Francisco on time and Jack hurried from the depot on Third Street, across Market Street and to city hall. A white-haired man at a desk at the entrance eyed the young fellow with unshaven cheeks and carrying a cloth bag. He was skeptical about any chance existing of this young man being able to see the mayor.

"Might get you in to see Mr. Carl Heindell, the deputy mayor," he said. "He's in his office—or perhaps Mr. Edward Townrow—"

Jack's dogged insistence on seeing only the mayor resulted in the dispatch of a message boy, instructed

to give Jack's name and say the words, "Extremely
Urgent."

Minutes later, Jack was being ushered into the may-
or's office despite three official-looking gentlemen
waiting outside.

"Jack, my boy!" The smile was slightly strained but
the even white teeth glinted and the smooth face
shone with practiced honesty. "I wish you had chosen
another way of seeing me. I can only spare you a few
minutes—I have this delegation waiting. Still, I'm glad
you're here and—"

"Mr. Mayor, you lied to me."

Many of the citizens of San Francisco felt this way
about the mayor but none had said it to his face in
his own office. A slight flush suffused the smooth
countenance. "Come now, Jack, there's no need—"

"I see you don't deny it." Jack was angry but controlled. "Anyway, we'll come to that in a minute. The
urgent thing I have to tell you is this. I've found your
gold—all ten tons of it."

The mayor sat back, his eyes wide. For once, words
did not spring to his lips.

"You have to get a detachment of the army to take
possession of it immediately. It's safe at the moment
but there isn't a minute to waste. It's in the house
next to the lighthouse at Skeleton Point by Half Moon
Bay. A squadron of cavalry from Fort Braxton could
be there in an hour."

Years of political debate and bureaucratic maneu-
vering had honed Mayor Nelson's ability to recover
fast from any setback. He half rose in amazement.
"Jack, that's marvelous news! Really incredible! The
whole ten tons?"

"Better make a telephone call and put a guard on
it," Jack said tersely, "before anyone else learns of it."

The mayor pulled forward the telephone, his astonishment still apparent. He gave orders to be connected at once to the commandant at Fort Braxton

and sat staring at the instrument, deep in thought. When the bell clanged, he picked up the earpiece, confirmed his identity and gave brief but imperative orders.

He had had time to compose himself when he hung up.

"Jack, I didn't lie to you. It's true that I didn't tell you everything. I couldn't. The men up on Telegraph Hill wouldn't let me tell anyone."

He meant the Big Three but Jack was not to be appeased.

"You told me you were concerned about dance hall girls being murdered," he said hotly. "All you were really worried about was the gold."

"I was concerned about the girls too," the mayor insisted. "Many of the saloon owners were worried—"

"Only about contracts and losing money," Jack snapped.

"Certainly, but some of them had feelings for the girls. I did too and I have no money in saloons."

Jack turned to a different approach. "It must have been consternation here when *The Jewel of the North* was unloaded and the wagon had no gold."

The mayor grimaced. "It was one of the blackest days since I took office."

"You must have had some suspicions," Jack persisted.

"I did not . . ." They argued. The telephone rang. The mayor picked it up. "I have an emergency situation," he said sharply into it. "It affects the future of our city. Tell the delegation to come back tomorrow." He slammed the receiver back on the hook.

"Now tell me the whole story," he instructed.

Jack did so—up to the point of shooting Captain Cutlass. The mayor listened spellbound. "Good Heavens!" he said finally. "That is devotion to duty of a kind I see rarely! They are dead? Both of them?"

Jack nodded.

"And the bodies?"

Jack told him.

The mayor drummed fingers on his desk. Then he said, "Jack, the least I can do after all you've been through is to tell you what I know. Fred Crocker's bank in Alaska buys all the gold the miners up there dig. They melt them into bricks and ship them here to their vaults in the city. This was an exceptionally large amount—ten tons at one time. Because of that episode at Humboldt Wells where a large gang robbed all four banks in one raid, it was decided to take special precautions with this shipment."

Jack waited.

The mayor continued, "It was my deputy, Carl Heindell, who came up with the suggestion of hiring General Walter Williams to handle the transfer. He's a brilliant man, he—"

"I know his background," Jack interrupted. "You're referring to his past. What about his future?"

The mayor drummed fingers again. "Ted Townrow told me you are a friend of Bierce. I suppose Bierce told you about the general and his ambitions?"

"They were more than ambitions," said Jack in carefully measured tones, and making no reference to Kipling. "General Walter Williams said he was going to be president again. He obviously meant president of Nicaragua. The ten tons of gold was to finance the revolution that would put him in that position."

The fingers stopped drumming. Mayor Nelson stared frozen at Jack for a long moment. "I didn't realize . . ." he murmured, half to himself. "This means that . . ." Again, thoughts were whirling in his brain.

He sat up straight in his chair. "I haven't told you everything—and I've admitted that. I am the mayor, after all, and I do receive confidences from the Big Three and others, and I would be violating my office if I divulged them. Several things have been bothering me but they are becoming clear now." He was looking

Jack directly in the eye and Jack had the feeling that this might be as much truth as His Honor wanted to tell.

"Do you have any proof that Williams had these girls killed?"

"I don't need any," said Jack. "Williams admitted it to me."

"He did?"

"Yes. Just before I killed him."

Jack added the rest of the story from the shooting of Captain Cutlass on to pushing General Walter Williams off the lighthouse platform. The mayor did not say a word until Jack had finished. He just listened.

He shook his head. "Incredible! Really incredible!" He tapped a newspaper on his desk. "The Congress commission on a canal is meeting again today."

"I haven't seen many newspapers lately," said Jack.

The mayor permitted himself a tiny smile. "I can understand that. A French company, the New Panama Canal Company, has offered to sell all its rights and acquired property to this country. The company's representative, Philippe Bunau-Varilla, I think his name is, made a presentation to Congress with maps and charts showing the location of Nicaragua's volcanoes. He says they could cause earthquakes. That makes a strong case for choosing Panama over Nicaragua."

He looked up at the ceiling. "However, with a lot of money to spend, that could be overturned—"

"You mean," Jack said brutally, "all this gold could buy a lot of congressman's votes."

"Well," the mayor temporized, "money is influential and, er, could be used to hire experts on volcanoes and earthquakes."

"But not now," Jack said.

"One other worrisome point," the mayor said slowly. "The murder of that Wells Fargo investigator—Wesley Montague. The means of murder was the same as the one used on those girls. That thin-bladed knife."

"That was Captain Cutlass, obeying Williams's orders," said Jack. "The slashing was his own idea."

"Montague must have been close to the truth, that's why they killed him."

"He was. I believe he had learned the identity of the man in your office who fed information to the Big Three."

Chapter 29

"Do you know who this man is?" the mayor asked.

Jack looked back at the mayor. "I thought you might."

Jack was trying to recall a scene from the recent past. His hectic activities had blurred some of those scenes together and several close escapes from death had pushed other memories into deeper recesses of his mind.

There was a knock at the door. Carl Heindell, the deputy mayor, came in with some papers in his hand. "Excuse me, Mr. Mayor, I wondered if you—" He saw Jack. "Hello, Jack," he said in surprise. "I didn't know you were here." He shook his hand. "How is the investigation going?"

"Come in, Carl," the mayor invited. "I have a remarkable story to tell you." A thought struck him. "Is Ted out there, do you know?"

"Yes, he is," said Heindell.

"Ask him to come in, would you? I think you should both hear this."

With the three of them sitting around the mayor's desk, the mayor gave a brief summary of Jack's tale. The two listened with mounting excitement as he did so. At the conclusion, Ted Townrow said, "Well, we certainly picked the right man for this job." His expression suggested that he meant *he* had picked the right man.

"So we have the gold back," said Heindell, still shaking his head in wonder.

"One point we have not cleared up yet," said Jack, "concerns Wes Montague, the Wells Fargo investigator."

"You knew him?" asked Carl Heindell.

"Not until these crimes began," Jack answered carefully. "Did he report to this office?"

"No," said Mayor Nelson. "The Crocker Bank hired Wells Fargo. Montague was assigned as their investigator."

"Crocker is one of the Big Three," Jack pointed out, "and they hired Williams to hijack the gold."

Heindell looked outraged. "Mr. Mayor, such monstrous accusations against our most prominent citizens cannot be permitted in this office!"

He was about to bluster on but the mayor stopped him with a wave of his hand. "I have already told Jack that it was your suggestion to hire Williams," he said quietly. "Jack understands the situation."

Ted Townrow was shaking his head. "Jack, really! You have been reading Bierce's column too much. He blames the Big Three for everything bad that happens in San Francisco. If a cable car goes off the track, he blames them. You sound just like him. Besides, why would Crocker hijack his own gold?"

Jack noted that this probably meant the mayor's involvement was deeper than he wanted to admit, especially after his earlier statement about "the men on Telegraph Hill. . . ." He thought of pointing out that Montague had unearthed a copy of an insurance certificate that probably answered Townrow's question. Bierce would be the first to point out that it would be a typical Big Three ploy to have Williams hijack the gold he was guarding, let him use it to finance the revolution while Crocker recovered the value on the insurance.

"But Williams's reputation as a mercenary is really

extraordinary," the mayor went on, "and he has never been known to act as a bandit."

"Montague found a witness who saw Williams at the Humboldt Wells robbery," Jack said. "That alone may have been enough for Williams to order Montague killed."

"That's ironic," said Heindell, "if it's true. It's saying that Williams was hired to transport the gold because it was vital to prevent a repeat of the Humboldt Wells robbery—which Williams had also been responsible for!"

"It wasn't a risk to hire Williams," Townrow pointed out. "According to what Jack is telling us, the reward on this occasion was too immense—Williams was being offered the presidency of Nicaragua!"

"From what we know of his character," said the mayor, "the stimulation of running a revolution with almost unlimited funds may have been just as enticing. He might not have stopped at the Canal Zone limits— he might have gone on to take the whole country."

Jack was surprised that His Honor knew about limits already being proposed for the Nicaragua Canal Zone. It confirmed his increasing suspicions but he went on from his previous comment. "That means that the Big Three knew of Montague's progress every step of the way. They tolerated his investigation at first, then when he got too close to the truth, they had Williams order his man, Captain Cutlass, to kill him."

Ted Townrow looked ready to contest Jack's depiction of the Big Three but calmed quickly. "I think you ran into Montague, Jack. You were both looking into the same crimes, after all. True, you were focusing on the deaths of the girls as we had asked you to do, whereas Montague was working on the disappearance of the gold. Now tell us, what did you learn from him?"

"I'll ask you a question, Ted," Jack countered. "What do you have to hide?"

Townrow frowned. "That's an insulting question!"

"Ted, you've had experience at hiding things," Jack chided. "You must have been in on the cover-up when *The Jewel of the North* was unloaded and the gold was gone."

The mayor stepped in to answer that. "We all were, Jack. It was a petrifying moment when the news came in."

Jack noted that the mayor did not refer to it as a surprise. He was becoming more and more disillusioned by the minute with the politics of San Francisco. He even felt a transient urge to run for office himself. Mayor of Oakland! Why not? He returned to the matter in hand.

"It was an outstanding cover-up," Jack commented. "You kept the news of the theft completely quiet."

There were no comments from the mayoral trio.

"I want to be honest with you," Jack said. "I don't really care about your gold that much—or your canal. You brought me into this because of the murders of the dance hall girls—so you said. I felt strongly about those murders and I wanted to help bring their murderers to book." He grinned wryly. "I guess I've done that. But now another matter has arisen and I can't let go until this is finished."

Townrow and Heindell were regarding him curiously.

Jack went on. "During Walter Williams's last moments, he told me that he had an accomplice in the mayor's office who was passing information. Some of this information related to Wes Montague's progress in his investigation and probably other information too. If this involved only the gold, I wouldn't care, but it probably caused the deaths of those girls as well. So I'm making it my business to find out which of you three is that traitor."

None of the three looked at the others. All looked at Jack with a blend of skepticism and amusement. The mayor was the first to speak.

"This is a grave accusation to make against my two colleagues," he said solemnly.

"I said three," Jack repeated. "Now, for a start—" He reached to the table and picked up the papers in front of Carl Heindell. He held them up and fluttered them, showing both sides.

"Blank paper." He turned to Heindell. "You didn't come in to speak to Mayor Nelson. You came in because you knew I was here and you wanted to know what I was saying."

"That's ridiculous, I—" The deputy mayor caught the looks of the others. "All right," he said defiantly, "I did want to know what was being said. I am very concerned. Why shouldn't I want to know?"

"I've been trying to recall something," Jack said. "It's been bothering me because it seemed it should be important."

"Something Williams told you?" asked Ted Townrow, his voice tight.

Jack stood up, took a few paces. He stopped, trying to make up his mind. "Does C5 mean anything?" he asked abruptly.

There was a silence.

"C5?" the mayor said. "What is that?" Townrow and Heindell looked equally puzzled.

"Does it have any connection with city hall?" the mayor wanted to know.

"Possibly," Jack said and nodded.

"The floors here in city hall are lettered. 'A' is the ground floor, 'B' the next and so on. Six stories. Rooms on each floor are numbered."

"So this floor is—?" Jack asked.

"This is 'D.' "

Jack felt his pulse quicken. His hunch had been right. The last note in Wes Montague's book must have meant that he had found Hannah Green and sent a report "through D4." Montague's continuing note had stated that Hannah Green was killed as a result.

The implication was clear. The person in room D4 was passing on information that had gone to Williams. Jack was glad he had covered up the true number.

"So how do the numbers go on this floor?" he asked, keeping his tone neutral.

"My office is D1 and my secretary is D2."

Jack looked at Ted Townrow and Carl Heindell. "So you two are D3 and D4?"

"Yes," said Heindell, puzzled. "What does this all mean?"

"I guess it doesn't mean anything," said Jack, trying to look defeated. "Mr. Mayor, can I have a few words with you before I go?"

"I need to get back to work." Townrow smiled, offering his hand to Jack. "Magnificent work, old chum."

"Very well done indeed," said Heindell, also shaking his hand. "I must get back too."

When both had gone, Mayor Nelson looked strangely at Jack. "You were about to reveal something there. You didn't. Why not?"

Jack explained about Wes Montague's notebook. He told him all except the room number. The mayor waited, then he shook his head.

"One of my most trusted aides has been passing privileged information outside this office. What is the room number?"

"D4," said Jack, and found he was holding his breath.

The mayor slumped in his chair. "Carl Heindell."

Chapter 30

When Jack walked into Luna's, he was still pondering over exactly how he should tell his story to Ambrose Bierce. He realized that he was overmatched—the feisty editor of the *San Francisco Examiner* had ways of wheedling and prying bits of information from his informers that they sometimes did not know themselves that they had.

Jack certainly wanted to see that as much of the truth as possible went into the newspaper account that would be read with astonishment the next day. He did not want to hold back on what he told Bierce on his own account, but he intended to omit the circumstances surrounding the mission assigned to him by the mayor. Corruption in the mayor's office and Heindell's role in it would be exposed as it should be, and Jack felt a further satisfaction in knowing that Bierce would not be sparing his condemnation of the Big Three and their manipulation of the Nicaragua Canal deal.

He maneuvered around the potted palms and saw Bierce at his customary spot at the brass-railed bar. "Well, young fellow!" Bierce greeted him. "Word around town is that you've been upsetting a lot of people!"

Jack put a foot on the rail. "That's right, Ambrose. That's why I'm here—so you print the truth about it."

Bierce's bushy eyebrows went up. " 'The truth,' you

say. Now there's a word you don't run across very often in the newspaper business." He looked at Jack's face carefully and his shrewd mind saw there the tensions and terrors of the past days that had not yet been erased. His tone eased marginally as he said, "Let me get you a drink. Better tell me all about it."

Jack did so. Bierce listened attentively, almost forgetting his Sazerac. As Jack concluded his story, Bierce picked up his glass and drained it.

"So the general has gone from the scene, has he?"

"His body hasn't been recovered but there can be no doubt that he is dead," Jack said.

"And good riddance to him," Bierce said vehemently.

"One of the most dangerous men in California—isn't that what you called him?"

"I have a way with words," agreed Bierce with a nod.

"But then Kipling said even more condemning things about the Big Three."

"Yes, well, their machinations are far more widespread—at least you've helped to foil them in this attempt. I'm sure Ruddy told you about his study of their evil intentions? Yes, by the way, I had a wire from him yesterday asking me to be sure to keep him up-to-date on your activities. He was no doubt allowing for the possibility that you might be dead and couldn't do that for yourself."

"I nearly was," acknowledged Jack with his boyish grin. "More than once. But do me a favor, Ambrose, don't make me out to be too much of a hero. I want to be known as a writer, not as a police agent."

"Don't worry," Bierce said tartly. "I won't even give the police the credit for enlisting your help."

Jack nodded. That was one hurdle overcome.

"But Ruddy will be delighted to hear this story. When he gets back from his reporting job in Africa, he'll be hot on the heels of those three rascals again,

I'll wager. Now—there are just one or two points I want to clear up. . . ."

Like the great newspaperman he was, Bierce picked up on point after point until he had the whole story in his mind, ready for printing. Jack answered his questions honestly, relieved that Bierce did not touch on any more tender spots. Then Jack finished his drink and said, "I have to go. I can just catch a couple of shows."

"Is this something I would want to print?" asked Bierce anxiously. "Let's be sure the account is complete so if there's something else—"

"I've given you enough for those bloodthirsty readers of yours," Jack said and smiled. "This is strictly personal."

The show at the Midway Plaisance was just starting when Jack arrived and ordered a schooner of beer and a whisky. Andy, the barkeep, raised an eyebrow at this unusual extravagance.

"Come into money, have you, Jack?" he chirped. "I'll bet you brought a sack full of nuggets back from the Klondyke and hid it away, didn't tell anybody. Now, you're digging into it—"

Jack raised a mock fist.

"All right! All right!" Andy covered his face with his hands. "Schooner and a shot, coming up—and I'll send word to Flo that you're here."

The dancers, in their already abbreviated travesties of Roman costumes, were getting more revealing by the minute. They were soon reduced to bodily exposure that would have been thoroughly impractical in the Colosseum. A couple of drunken miners had to be pulled off the stage when their impatience with the speed of discarding garments got the better of them.

The orchestra reached a volume peak that made them almost audible over the noise of the crowd, and the high notes of the violin fought their way through the thick pall of cigarette and cigar smoke.

Jack felt a tap on the shoulder. He turned—it was Flo. She wore a light blue dress of a silky material. It came down to her ankles, but over her shoulders it hung from two flimsy straps that revealed her creamy skin.

He put his arms around her and kissed her fervently.

"Well," she said, "you are glad to see me! You must have been in a fight again. You're always more passionate after a near brush with death."

"You could call it a fight," Jack murmured.

"You look five years older than you did last week," she said, shaking her head.

"I hope I haven't aged that much. I feel I've certainly matured though."

"I suppose you think that will improve your writing," said Flo with a reproving shake of her head.

"Well, I've certainly found out one thing these last few days," Jack said. "I need to unlearn everything the teachers and professors in high school and the university taught me."

"Why is that?"

"Oh, they know all about books written hundreds of years ago but nothing about life today. I feel I could write a dozen books, drawing from the experience of the terror and the pain of this past week. How many teachers of writing can say that?"

He winced at the touch of her hand on his back. She pulled away and looked at him reprovingly. "You haven't been careful like I told you, have you?"

"It's just a small cut," Jack said.

"Shaving?"

"No," said Jack with his boyish grin. "It was the sharp end of a cutlass, as a matter of fact." He saw her face cloud and embraced her again. "It's all right, though, Flo. It's all over."

Her eyes searched his face. "Is it, Jack? Is it really over?"

"Yes, Flo. The killer of the girls is dead and so is the man who gave him his orders."

"That's wonderful!" She stood on tiptoe to kiss him again. "My hero! Come and tell me all about it. I'll get us a table."

That sounded like an impossible feat in the crowded auditorium but a table magically appeared and somehow was squeezed into a corner. They sat close, side by side. In the brief intervals when the clamor of the crowd, the entertainment and the orchestra dropped below the thunderous level, Jack told Flo his story.

Her eyes grew rounder and rounder. She called for a glass of wine—a rare event for her. When Jack finished his tale, she was flushed with excitement and her full lips parted.

"You poor dear! You must have a lot more injuries that you haven't told me about."

"Maybe a few," Jack admitted, pulling a face that suggested excruciating pain.

"Are you going to make me find them for myself?" she asked, taking a delicate sip of wine.

"Before you do," Jack said, "I have something else to tell you. I was able to persuade the mayor to set up a fund for dance hall girls and waiter girls. I made him feel guilty about the four girls who were killed. A committee will be set up and compensation paid to any girls who get injured in any way. There are lots of details to be worked out but it's a start."

"Jack, that's marvelous news! You'll be the hero of all the girls when I tell them." Her eyes glowed then her face took on a serious aspect. "I have something to tell you too." She took another sip of wine. "The Palace Theater in Chicago wants me to recruit, organize and train a dance troupe. They want top quality, a team that will be as good as any in New York. When the girls are ready, we'll put on a series of shows in Chicago then go on tour all over the country."

Jack took a large swallow of beer and waited for a particularly noisy response of the crowd to die down into a hush of expectancy.

"Are you going to do it?"

Flo looked into her wineglass. "No, Jack, I'm not."

"It sounds like a great opportunity for you, Flo. I'd miss you, but maybe you should reconsider?"

"I don't suppose I could persuade you to come to Chicago too?" Flo asked. "You could write there as well as here."

"I can't see myself in a big city like that," Jack said. "I'm a San Franciscan—always will be."

Flo shrugged. "I thought you'd say that. I'm not a San Franciscan—but I love it here. I think I'll give it a while longer." She turned to look at the stage. "This is a smash finish—these girls are really good."

"They should be, Flo," Jack said softly. "You trained them."

Two hours later, the last show at the Duke of York was approaching its first climax. The trumpet blared out the melody of "Two Little Girls in Blue" slightly ahead of the piano and the violin. The drums were losing the race by a neck.

The girls in their prim, frilly blue gowns were earning some subdued boos and shouts of disapproval, for the last show attracted a rougher crowd than the earlier shows. Boots began to stamp on the wood floor, battling against the beat of the orchestra.

At a table near the stage, Jack smiled at the end dancer. She was very attractive, dark-haired and shapely. She gave Jack a smile in return and aimed an extra kick in his direction.

After the number had ended sensationally with the high-kicking "Ta-rara-boom-de-ay" and the stage was